PAPER LIVES

A Novel by
Compton Mackenzie

D1492739

1966
CHATTO & WINDUS
LONDON

Published by
Chatto & Windus Ltd
42 William IV Street
London, W.C.2

*

Clarke, Irwin & Co. Ltd
Toronto

© Compton Mackenzie 1966

Printed in Great Britain by
T. and A. Constable Ltd
Edinburgh

To
A. A. BRADSHAW
with much gratitude for all
the paper he has expended
on my life

Contents

CHAPTER	PAGE
1	9
2	24
3	42
4	53
5	69
6	81
7	94
8	107
9	125
10	139
11	151
12	162
13	175
14	183
15	197
16	216

Chapter 1

ALTHOUGH Sir Oliver Huffam, K.C.B., the Permanent Secretary of the Ministry of Sanitation, was getting near to sixty and retirement was in sight, nobody who saw that tall, slim figure emerge from Gloucester Road Station and step smartly out in the direction of Chillingham Gardens would have given him a day more than fifty-five.

The prospect of soon being back in his own house always had a rejuvenating effect on Sir Oliver Huffam. When South Kensington arose from the strawberry gardens and old farmland of West Brompton in the last quarter of the nineteenth century the Royal Borough of Kensington had disapproved of the neighbourhood's calling itself South Kensington; it was in fact, they maintained, still Brompton. The Royal Borough of Kensington had had the same trouble with West Kensington which was really Fulham, and with North Kensington which was really Notting Hill. In due course South Kensington had its own battles with that part of Earls Court which pretended it was South Kensington.

Sir Oliver smiled to himself at the memory of those battles long ago. What would the warriors of the nineteenth century say if they could see contemporary South Kensington? In Chillingham Gardens only Number Nine remained as itself; all the other houses were carved up into flats, and where leases had expired even such houses were being pulled down to erect concrete ant-hills of more convenient flats. As he walked along past the houses before Number Nine and saw the rows of bells beside each front door Sir Oliver took the latchkey from his pocket with satisfaction. Whatever inadequately considered schemes the Ministry of Accommodation might embark on, he would still have a house of his own.

Sir Oliver turned the key of the Yale lock and pushed

open his front door to stand in the hall and . . . perhaps yodel is not absolutely correct but to make a noise more like yodelling than anything else. At that moment, except that his red hair was now grizzled, Sir Oliver looked not much older than when he was Principal Private Secretary to Apsley Howe, the Minister of Waste, over twenty years ago.

"Is that you, Olly dear?" It was the voice of Lady Huffam in welcoming response as she came out from the dining-room to the head of the stairs.

"Have you had a tiring day?"

"Not more than usual, dear."

This question and this answer had not varied throughout their respectably married life except during the nightmare week after that disastrous broadcast by the Minister of Waste when Gertrude had suspected her husband of keeping another woman. However, their reconciliation had been complete; a year or two later Jeremy had arrived as the outward visible sign of it.

"Where's Jeremy?" his father asked on this fine October evening.

"He's not back from school yet, Olly."

Sir Oliver frowned.

"But it's well after six. I was kept late at the Ministry. You know, Gertrude, that young son of ours is becoming rather a problem."

In the drawing-room Sir Oliver returned to the problem of his younger son.

"I don't believe Nigel ever once got home from school after six o'clock. He and Joan were always at their homework by six o'clock, and look where Nigel is to-day. Already an Assistant Secretary at the Treasury."

"But, Olly dear, Nigel is older than Jeremy."

"Certainly. He's sixteen years older. I was talking of Nigel when he was Jeremy's age. Jeremy is now in his last year at St James's. I'm beginning to worry whether he'll get into Oxbridge at all, let alone gain a scholarship. I must have another serious talk with him. I shall not

have it to-night because I don't want to give him any
excuse for messing up his homework. I shall wait until
the week-end."

"And don't forget Nigel and Rosemary are dining with
us to-night. Poor Rosemary rang me up this afternoon to
say her baby-sitter had disappointed her, but she rang up
again not long before you came in to say that it's all right,
she's found another baby-sitter for little Noll."

Lady Huffam sighed.

"Oh, dear, fancy me a grandmother!"

In fact with her grey hair, her rather watery pale-blue
eyes, and that stoop which tall, thin women nearly all
develop with age Lady Huffam looked every inch a
grandmother; she was not altogether pleased when Sir
Oliver said,

"I think you make a splendid granny, Gertrude."

"I'm so glad Nigel and Rosemary call little Oliver
Noll. I have told you, haven't I, Olly, why I called you
Olly when we were first engaged?"

"Yes, yes, you have, Gertrude."

But Lady Huffam was not to be baulked of her
reminiscence.

"I can see the expression now on my dear old mother's
face when I told her that Noll Huffam had proposed to
me. 'Well, I'm not going to call him Noll,' she said, 'for
if there's one man I abominate it's that so called Pro-
tector, Oliver Cromwell, and he used to be called Noll.'
So that's why I always called you Olly. But I always regretted not calling you Noll like your men friends at
Oxbridge and I'm so glad little Oliver the Second will be
called Noll."

Sir Oliver relapsed into silence and presently buried
himself in the last White Paper issued by the Government.

"I must go and look up something," he said at last,
and strode out of the drawing-room to go upstairs to the
top of the tall South Kensington house where he had his
study.

Lady Huffam had long ago given up suggesting that he should move his study downstairs to the room behind the dining-room where Nigel and Joan used to do their prep and Jeremy did his prep now. Olly used to take such pleasure in looking through Nigel's Greek and Latin compositions and Joan's French syntax. She sighed. Nowadays Olly always emerged obviously distressed by Jeremy's homework.

"My dear Gertrude, you know I like the little exercise I get by walking upstairs," he had invariably replied. "After all, except for walking twice a day between Piccadilly and Cork Street, once a day to lunch at the Heraeum, and every morning and evening to and from Gloucester Road tube-station and Piccadilly tube-station it is the only exercise I get except for an occasional round of golf at the week-end when things at the Ministry are fairly quiet."

Sir Oliver came down to the drawing-room at seven o'clock.

"Jeremy's not back yet?" he ejaculated in a tone in which annoyance was almost hidden by astonishment.

"I do hope he's not had an accident," Lady Huffam murmured tremulously.

The front-door bell rang at a quarter-past seven.

"Ah, there he is," Sir Oliver muttered, and stalked out of the drawing-room to find what explanation his younger son would offer for his lateness.

But it was not Jeremy. It was Nigel and Rosemary.

"Apologies, Dad," said the former. "We're a quarter of an hour early, I'm afraid."

"It's my fault, Dad," Rosemary Huffam put in quickly, "but little Noll was so beautifully asleep I thought we'd go before he woke up. That might have made us late."

Nigel Huffam was as tall and thin as his father with red hair and the dead white complexion of many red-haired people who lead sedentary lives indoors. His wife was dark, pretty and *petite*. One might be forgiven for wondering what on earth had made her fall in love with Nigel Huffam and marry him.

"Where's young Jeremy, Mum?" Nigel asked after he had greeted his mother in the drawing-room.

"He's not back from school yet. Dad and I are beginning to get quite worried."

At this moment the front-door bell rang and Jeremy Huffam's arrival relieved his mother's anxiety. A superstitious observer might justifiably have imagined that Sir Oliver's younger son was a changeling. That two tall thin fair-haired parents should have produced this short dark thick-set son was extraordinary. True, he was not yet seventeen and a half and might perhaps add an inch to his 5 feet 7 inches, but even that would still make him look the improbable son of his parents, especially when he was standing beside his elder brother.

"What on earth's been keeping you?" Sir Oliver asked. "Do you realise it's nearly half-past seven?"

"Is it?" said Jeremy without displaying the slightest interest in the time. "Well, I had to see a chap about something."

"What about?" his father pressed.

"Well, about something."

"It must have been more than something," said Sir Oliver, "to occupy over two hours of your time after leaving school."

"Was it a *chap* you had to see?" Nigel Huffam asked, with what he hoped his wife would think was a roguish twinkle.

The Permanent Secretary of the Ministry of Sanitation was fond of his daughter-in-law, but when he noticed Nigel's glance in her direction he hoped she was not going to encourage her husband to be flippant. The last thing an Assistant Secretary at the Treasury should indulge in was flippancy.

"You'd better go and get yourself brushed up for dinner," he said quickly to Jeremy, and when the boy went off to brush himself up he turned to Nigel.

"I know you just meant it in joke, Nigel, but do remember Jeremy is only seventeen and it might put ideas into his head. These next three terms may be vital for his future."

"Sorry, Dad," Nigel said. "But of course it was a joke."

And imperceptibly to her father-in-law or husband Rosemary with the ghost of a smile shook her head. Lady Huffam also shook her head, but gravely, because she was afraid that what Nigel had meant as a joke must really have been the true explanation of Jeremy's late arrival from school.

"The *Times* crossword was rather a teazer this morning. How did you get on with it, Dad?" Nigel asked.

"I finished it all but two before we got to Piccadilly and the other two came to me when I was waiting to cross over from Regent Street to Vigo Street."

"That was pretty good. I was half a dozen down but of course I always go by bus and it's more difficult to concentrate on a bus than it is in the tube."

There ensued a discussion whether the clues that Nigel had failed to pick up were in fact as fair as one had a right to expect from the *Times* crossword.

"Is young Jeremy any good at crosswords, Dad?" Nigel asked.

Sir Oliver sighed.

"No, I'm afraid he's inherited his mother's lack of interest in them."

It was Lady Huffam's turn to sigh. She feared Olly was going to make one more attempt to explain to her the mystery of crossword puzzles.

"*I* never can understand crosswords," Rosemary declared.

Lady Huffam smiled gratefully at her daughter-in-law.

"Rosemary's hopeless," Nigel commented. "I asked her the other day what was feminine pleasure in the post. Word of seven letters, beginning with A and last letter but one S."

"Address," said Sir Oliver at once.

"Of course."

"But 'address' is where somebody lives." Rosemary protested. "What has that got to do with feminine pleasure?"

"Address. A dress. Aren't women supposed to be interested in dress?" Sir Oliver asked.

"But I don't spell 'a dress' with two d's," Rosemary pointed out. "I may not be good at crosswords but I do know how to spell."

Her father-in-law was on the verge of trying to explain why address was feminine pleasure in the post when the gong sounded for dinner.

"I always enjoy that sound," said Nigel. "One hardly ever hears a gong nowadays."

"No, and gongs will get rarer and rarer now that the Indian Civil is no more," his father prophesied. "So many of them went in our great drive for waste metal when I was still at the Ministry, but we didn't worry because we knew that the Indian Civil people on leave would always be bringing back gongs with them, and then the Indian Civil Service vanished."

They were all in the dining-room by now.

"Do you remember, Dad," Nigel asked over a suspended spoon of very hot soup, "when I first started late dinner and was a minute late and you asked me if I hadn't heard the gong and I said I was just finishing my hexameters and you said, 'I'm shaking my dactyl at you, Nigel, and warning you that when the gong sounds, even a spondee must wait'? I thought it was awfully good."

"What is a dactyl, Nigel?" his wife asked.

He hurriedly swallowed the soup in his pendant spoon which was still so hot that his tongue had to settle down before he could answer her.

"Dactyl is the Greek for finger," he managed to reply at last. "One long foot and too short feet like the joints of a finger."

"Well, if it's on your foot why isn't it called a toe?" Rosemary asked.

Nigel was saved from having to make any more attempts to explain to Rosemary what a dactyl was by Jeremy's taking his seat at the table.

"Didn't you hear the gong, Jeremy?" his father asked severely.

"Yes, of course I heard it."

"Didn't the sound suggest anything?"

It was then that Rosemary who was sitting next to Jeremy came to his rescue as he scowled silently at his soup.

"Dad, if the Ministry of Waste was looking for waste metal how did you manage to keep your gong?"

The Adam's apple in Sir Oliver's long thin throat bobbed up and down like an angler's float disturbed by a carp. His daughter-in-law had roused a guilty feeling which had been dormant for over twenty years.

"I really don't remember now," he said.

"I'm shaking my dactyl at you, Dad."

Luckily for Sir Oliver the spoonful of soup he swallowed was now not so hot. It only made him cough.

Nigel looked across the table at his wife in sudden apprehension. Had motherhood gone to her head? No, no, he reassured himself, it's just that she didn't understand Dad's joke. It's the same as her inability to understand crosswords.

Lady Huffam feeling that something was wrong murmured in a low voice to Jeremy.

"You know, dear, how Dad likes everybody to be punctual. Say you're sorry you were late coming in to dinner."

"Well, I'm not," Jeremy muttered to her.

At this moment, mercifully for Lady Huffam's anxiety about that rebellious reply by her younger son, her attention was directed to the turbot which Ethel the elderly parlour-maid was bringing in.

As soon as dinner was over Jeremy retired to what his father and elder brother still called the Den but which Jeremy himself called the Swotroom. Instead of getting

down to the Latin prose which should have been finished
by now if he had started his prep as he was expected to
start it at six o'clock, Jeremy unlocked a drawer in a
small cabinet and took out a passport, which he brooded
over, his eyebrows meeting. Last winter a master at St
James's had escorted a party of about half a dozen boys
to winter sports in Switzerland. Sir Oliver had thought
that such an adventure might stimulate his younger son
to work harder when he returned to school. Jeremy was
grateful now to that fortnight, not because of its stimulation to swot but because it had provided him with a passport. He looked at the sixteen-year-old face in the photograph. "I'll be twenty-one when this passport has to be
renewed. Phew! what a relief!" He put the passport into
his breast-pocket and sitting down at his table, took a
sheet of paper and began to write. But it was not Latin;
it was a letter in English. He had not written more than
'Dear Mum and Dad' in spite of a pent up expression
upon his face that suggested the construction of an
elaborate sentence, of which Cicero himself might have
been proud, when the front-door bell rang, and he heard
in the hall the voices of his sister Joan and his brother-
in-law, George Micklewright.

"Is Master Jeremy in the Den?" he heard his sister ask.

"Master Jeremy," the youngest Huffam growled as he
quickly pushed away under the blotter the letter he had
begun.

Joan Micklewright came in. Fifteen years older than
Jeremy she was tall, thin, red-haired and now heavily
freckled by the Costa Brava sun. Carrots was an old-
fashioned endearing name for red-heads; Carrot would
have been a suitable if not endearing name for Joan
Micklewright. After sturdy hard work at Somerton she
was now an Assistant Principal in the Children's Department of the Home Office, but without as yet any children
of her own. George Micklewright, an Assistant Secretary
at the Ministry of Movement, would presently be a
Principal Assistant Secretary. He was quite two inches

B

shorter than his wife but made up for it by having a very long chin. It was a puzzle to guess why Rosemary Huffam had married Nigel; it was as much a puzzle to guess why either Joan or George Micklewright had married the other.

"Hard at it, young Jeremy?" his sister asked, an eager almost an envious glister in her pale-blue eyes, as if she were back at St James's School for girls, mugging away in the Den at her French syntax for to-morrow.

"You're in your last year now at James's, by Jove," said George Micklewright to his young brother-in-law in that tone of synthetic heartiness which Jeremy thought was as slimy as margarine. The heartiness was succeeded by synthetic sentimentality which Jeremy found even slimier. "Yes, by Jove, one's last year at the old school. Mind you, it's not so bad at a day school, but of course I was at Reppingham."

"I know you were at Reppingham," said Jeremy coldly. "They play soccer there, don't they?"

"What's the matter with soccer?"

"It's just a bit more of a bore than rugger, that's all," Jeremy snapped.

"When you're my age, Jeremy, you'll wish you could still be playing either rugger or soccer. Golf's a great game but it's not footer."

"No, footer would be even more boring if it was played with a golf ball," Jeremy agreed.

"Come along, George, you two sportsmen must stop arguing," Joan put in. "Jeremy wants to get on with his prep and Dad will be wondering what we're doing."

When he was left alone Jeremy decided to take that unfinished letter up to his bedroom. He looked round the Den as if he were looking for anything that he might have forgotten. When he shut the door of the Den behind him he muttered to himself "Good riddance". On his way past the drawing-room he stopped to listen for a moment.

"Reppingham," he muttered contemptuously, and passed on upstairs.

George Micklewright was explaining about some business at the Ministry of Movement which had made him afraid that he and Joan would be too late for dinner, and Nigel Huffam was listening with the expression of pained disapproval which Treasury officials automatically assume when they are listening to tales from the officials of other Government departments, in case such tales might be a prelude to an increase of expenditure. Is the country sufficiently grateful to the No Men of the Treasury?

"By the way, Dad, are you having bother at your Ministry over that girl being sacked for spending half an hour in the lavatory?" his son-in-law asked.

"No, we considered it very carefully," said Sir Oliver, "but when fifty other girls came out on strike, we felt it would be overlapping with the Ministry of Work. Of course we sent an Inspector, or it may have been an Assistant Inspector, to ascertain if the girl's excuse that the lavatory lock was out of order was or was not justified. After all, our job is to see that the country's lavatories are in order, public *and* private."

Presently, when the ladies of the party were in the corner of the drawing-room, Sir Oliver told his son and son-in-law that the girl in the lavatory's excuse for staying in it for half an hour was not in fact what he had told them it was.

"Her excuse was that it was half an hour before she was able to—er—pull the plug, but even in these days when women don't seem to mind talking about anything . . . I suppose I'm a little bit old-fashioned but *autres temps autres moeurs* as our friends say across the Channel. I'm afraid to-day *outrés temps outrés moeurs* is nearer the truth."

"Oh, jolly good, Dad," George Micklewright exclaimed with a boisterous laugh. "I must remember that one. Our chaps at Movement House will appreciate it. Quite a few of them speak French well. Talking of Movement House, did you see that silly letter in *The Times* this morning from a fellow complaining of the noise made by planes over some suburb or other? These fellows with mediaeval ideas are a public nuisance."

"I don't entirely agree with you, George," said Nigel. "This craze for speed is costing the country too many tens of millions every year. This hope of getting to the moon is mere lunacy. Hullo, Dad, *I've* made a joke now. Quite unintentional, I assure you."

Sir Oliver smiled his encouragement, and then became grave.

"I had to do so much flying all over the place when I was at the Ministry of Waste that I never fly nowadays. Mum is apt to be airsick, too. You know, George, it's all very well for you to talk about people with mediaeval ideas, but many of the lavatories on your planes were mediaeval until we took it up at the Ministry with your people at Movement House."

"You've no complaints now?" his son-in-law asked quickly.

"George, George, you've been too long in the Civil Service to ask a question like that. So far as I am aware there is no positive complaint that we are considering at the moment, but there are always contingent problems which we have to bear in mind."

"And which all too often," Nigel added, "the Treasury is called upon to solve."

Sir Oliver looked proudly at his elder son.

"How right you are, Nigel," he said, "and how clearly we envisage those problems at the Ministry of Sanitation. I sometimes wish other Ministries would envisage them as clearly as we do."

"Yes, indeed," Nigel agreed. "I wish you people at Movement House could realise that all these millions you are spending on getting business men to Australia five hours sooner and hoping to land British astronauts in some extinct crater on the moon before American or Russian astronauts get there. . . ."

"You forget the employment the aviation industry provides," George Micklewright interrupted. "We've

been having enough difficulty with the Ministry of Work
over the rationalisation of railways. . . ."

"They were nationalised long ago," Nigel cut in.

"Rationalised not nationalised," George snapped.

At this point the argument was cut short abruptly by
Rosemary.

"It's high time we were off home, Nigel. Don't forget
you're a father now," she reminded him.

However long Nigel Huffam might have been willing
to argue with George Micklewright, he was not prepared
to argue with the mother of little Noll. Instead of the
familiar shake of the Treasury head, he nodded with what
might almost be called docility.

"And we must be going too," said Joan.

Dad and Mum were presently by themselves in the
drawing-room.

"Perhaps it is too late to talk to Jeremy about his extraordinary behaviour," said Sir Oliver.

"Oh, I think so, Olly," Lady Huffam quickly responded. "I'm sure he won't be late back from school
to-morrow and you'll be able to talk to him then."

"I certainly shall," her husband said.

"You won't be too hard on him?"

"I shall not be hard, Gertrude, but I shall be very firm.
Jeremy has got to realise that his whole future may de-
pend on the way he conducts himself during this last
year of school."

"Yes, of course, Olly," Lady Huffam agreed. "Of
course, of course," she murmured as she braced herself
to administer what she knew would be a severe shock to
the Permanent Secretary of the Ministry of Sanitation.

"And unless Jeremy puts his shoulder to the wheel,"
Sir Oliver went on, "he may not get into Oxbridge at all.
I've given up hope of his gaining a scholarship or even an
exhibition, but if he is going to have a good start in the
Civil Service it's essential for him to have a university
degree."

"Olly," Gertrude Huffam gulped, "I think I ought to

tell you something that may upset you." She gulped again. "Jeremy doesn't want to go into the Civil Service."

"Doesn't want to go into the Civil Service?" Sir Oliver repeated in amazement. "What, may I ask, is he expecting to do?"

"I don't think he has any clear idea yet of what he wants to be, but I do know that he doesn't want to enter the Civil Service."

"How long have you known this, Gertrude?"

"Jeremy confided it to me after he came back from that lovely holiday you gave him doing winter sports last January."

"But why wasn't I told?"

"I hoped it was only a passing fancy, and I didn't want to upset you unnecessarily."

"But now it's October and apparently he is still at the mercy of this insane notion. Yes, I must certainly have a *very* serious talk with Jeremy to-morrow."

The tall, thin figure of Sir Oliver Huffam paced the drawing-room for a minute or two in anxious silence while Lady Huffam's fingers fidgeted upon her lap.

"I hope Nigel and Joan are not aware of this fantastic notion of their young brother?" Sir Oliver asked presently.

"No, Olly dear, of course not."

"Or Rosemary?" he asked sharply.

"If Nigel doesn't know, how would Rosemary be knowing?"

The thin red line of Sir Oliver's eyebrows contracted to repel the threat of an unwelcome recollection.

"I thought she seemed a little inclined to encourage Jeremy at dinner. That remark she made about gongs was rather out of place. I hope she's not going to spoil our little grandson."

Lady Huffam was too much worried about her own younger son to speculate about the upbringing of her grandson.

"Olly, I know you're upset by what I've just told you

about Jeremy, but when you talk to him to-morrow about his future you won't be too severe with him, will you? You will remember, won't you, that he's at a difficult age? I do understand what a shock it has been for you to hear that he doesn't want to go into the Civil Service, but I'm sure that if only you'll be sympathetic and talk about other careers he'll come back to the Civil Service as the best of all careers."

"I think you must leave me to handle Jeremy in my own way, Gertrude. And now let us drop the subject. I have a busy day before me at the Ministry. You go on up. I have to read through something, but I shall not be more than half an hour."

Lady Huffam sighed and left the Permanent Secretary of the Ministry of Sanitation perusing a small pamphlet bound in green paper issued by the Ministry of Cultivation.

Chapter 2

"LATE for breakfast now," Sir Oliver observed as he and Lady Huffam took their seats at table next morning.

"It's only two minutes past a quarter-past," she said. "He may have forgotten to wind his watch. I'll ask Ethel to go up and tell him we'll be in the dining-room."

Presently the elderly parlour-maid came back.

"Master Jeremy's not in his room, my lady. I think he went out early this morning."

"Went out early?" Sir Oliver repeated.

"Yes, Sir Oliver. The front door wasn't bolted this morning and the chain was off. I thought you must have forgotten to see it was bolted last night."

"I never forget to bolt it."

"No, sir, that's what Cook and me said. So it must have been Master Jeremy."

"Thank you, Ethel," Lady Huffam put in quickly. She was afraid Olly might say something about Jeremy while Ethel was still in the dining-room.

"What on earth is the boy thinking about?" Sir Oliver exclaimed when they were alone. "Arrives back from school more than two hours after school is over and goes off to school two hours before it starts. The world is turning upside down."

The Permanent Secretary was so much puzzled by the way the world was being rocked by his younger son that in the tube on his way to the Ministry he was in greater danger of being completely defeated by the *Times* cross-word puzzle than he had ever been since that deplorable broadcast by the Minister of Waste nearly twenty years ago. As he walked along Piccadilly to the Ministry in Cork Street, instead of letting his mind dwell on the clues he had failed to solve, his mind was preoccupied with

Jeremy's future, so deeply preoccupied indeed that the Permanent Secretary almost failed to acknowledge the salute of the janitor, Sergeant-major Hadnutt, as at exactly five-and-twenty minutes past nine he entered the Ministry.

When the Ministry of Sanitation was established to exercise in England and Wales functions with respect to sanitation which in the main had previously been exercised by the Ministry of Hygiene and the Ministry of Accommodation, it had been felt advisable to establish it as near as possible to the Ministry of Hygiene in Clifford Street. An attempt had been tried to make the new Ministry responsible for Sanitation in Scotland as well as England and Wales, but this had been met with as dour a resistance as the English knights at Bannockburn and when the Scottish Office established a Department of Sanitation the drain pipes of Scotland were in kilts not trousers.

By the time the Permanent Secretary reached his own room he had resolutely turned his mind away from domestic worry to the problems of sanitation.

"Good morning, Humphrey."

In spite of Sir Oliver's mental effort Humphrey Mowart, who had been his Private Secretary for the last five years, realised that his Chief's normally cool equanimity was disturbed. However, he was too tactful to let Sir Oliver be aware that he had noticed anything unusual in his manner.

"Will it be all right, sir, if Dr Scratchbury comes to see you at eleven?"

"Scratchbury?"

"He's the Chairman of this new company which will shortly be producing Dandimilk and he is anxious to have the approval of the Ministry."

Sir Oliver frowned.

"I don't think he's asking us to approve it openly," said Humphrey Mowart.

"I hope not."

"I think he's merely anxious to know that we shall not actively disapprove."

"But why doesn't he get the approval of the Ministry of Hygiene? Why does he come to us?"

"I think that is what he wishes to explain to you, sir, in a personal interview."

"Very well. I'll see him at eleven o'clock," the Permanent Secretary decided.

At eleven o'clock precisely Sergeant-major Hadnutt directed a page to conduct Dr Emilius Scratchbury to the Permanent Secretary's room. The new arrival was as tall as Sir Oliver himself, but his dark complexion was as dark as Sir Oliver's was fair, his hair jet black against Sir Oliver's grizzled red.

"I felt it was my duty to acquaint you with the properties of Dandimilk, Sir Oliver. It is made from various vegetables and is a perfect substitute for cows' milk. We do not deny that cows' milk has a certain nutritional value, but we have to recognise that it was never intended by nature for human consumption. Again, while it leads perhaps not definitely to actual cruelty to cows, it does entail unhappiness for them by depriving them prematurely of their young. We must also remember that the drinking of cows' milk was one if not the main cause of tuberculosis and also an encouragement to typhoid and paratyphoid. I do admit that since milk was pasteurised a few years ago it is now much less dangerous."

"But much less like the milk we used to enjoy," Sir Oliver observed.

"Nevertheless, fifty million pints of milk are now being drunk every day in Britain, and we who believe that the consumption of cows' milk is one of the main causes of hardening of the arteries feel bound to protest against the advice given by television advertisement to drink a pint of milk a day. The Ministry of Hygiene has been responsible for securing the abolition of cigarette advertising on television...."

"But if you and your ... you and those who agree with

you, Dr Scratchbury, are seeking to obtain the abolition of milk advertising on television, surely you should approach the Ministry of Hygiene."

"With all respect, Sir Oliver, my company and I were not expecting, at any rate at present, the abolition of milk advertising. What we desire is an assurance by the Ministry of Sanitation that Dandimilk will not be opposed by the Ministry of Sanitation for reasons which I will explain. Dandimilk is a liquid food produced from various vegetables of which the dandelion is one. It has twice the nutritional value of cows' milk and can be kept in a cool place for as long as a week without impairing its taste or strength. It is a new flavour, an entirely new flavour, and may be an acquired taste for some. But is not cows' milk an acquired taste for many people? Has not it always been a problem when a child is weaned? How else can we account for the various baby foods which aim at making the transition from their mother's milk to the milk of the cow an easier process? Dandimilk looks exactly like ordinary milk, but as I say the flavour is different."

"I still fail to understand what bearing your new product has upon the activities of the Ministry of Sanitation," the Permanent Secretary observed, looking round at his Private Secretary.

"Nor I, sir," Humphrey Mowart agreed.

"Well, in addition to its other valuable qualities Dandimilk is a mild laxative, and when we remember what a price the country pays for constipation in loss of working hours and dilatory labour when workmen are not working as hard as they might, I am sure you will appreciate how much a pint of Dandimilk a day might help our exports. Moreover, and this, too, is important, Dandimilk has a beneficial effect on the kidneys. You may remember the French name for dandelion. I am sure you now understand, Sir Oliver, why we in our company were anxious to be assured that our new product would not be frowned upon by the Ministry of Sanitation. We do not seek even the mildest encouragement; we merely seek to know if there is any probability of active discouragement."

Dr Emilius Scratchbury sat back in his chair, momentarily exhausted by the passion with which he had pleaded for the virtues of Dandimilk.

"You will not expect me to answer your question immediately, Dr Scratchbury. All I can say at the moment is that the Ministry will give the matter its careful consideration."

"Oh, there is one more great advantage in Dandimilk, Sir Oliver. I have mentioned that the dandelion is one of its components. Knowing as I do how much the Government relies on official secrets being kept you will appreciate my inability to reveal the full composition of Dandimilk, but I do feel justified in adding that thistles and nettles are also included among the components of Dandimilk. These are all noxious weeds in the eyes of farmers and we are not likely to come up against any opposition to the gathering of them. In fact, if Dandimilk makes the appeal we expect, dandelions, thistles and nettles might become almost extinct."

"But you wouldn't be able to make any more Dandimilk if that happened," Humphrey Mowart put in with a smile.

"If that were threatened I know that I . . . that our chemists would be able to produce synthetically the qualities of all these weeds, as they are unjustly called. They form only *some* of the components of Dandimilk. There are others."

"We shall bear in mind what you have told us about the weeds," said Sir Oliver. "But I must point out that this aspect of Dandimilk is essentially one for the consideration of the Ministry of Cultivation." Sir Oliver looked at the clock as he said this, and Dr Scratchbury rose.

"I must thank you warmly on behalf of my company for the most encouraging way you have listened. . . ."

The Permanent Secretary broke in hastily.

"I must ask you, Dr Scratchbury, to avoid suggesting any encouragement by the Ministry of Sanitation. You have stated your case; I have listened to it. The matter will now be carefully considered, but please bear in mind that it is *under consideration*."

"I shall pay the strictest attention to what you say, Sir Oliver."

"Will you show Dr Scratchbury to the lift, Humphrey."

As the doctor and Humphrey Mowart were going out, the former stopped for a moment.

"Could I tempt you to try the taste of Dandimilk, Sir Oliver?" he asked, his dark eyes glowing into the pale blue eyes of the Permanent Secretary.

It might not be fair to say that Sir Oliver winced at this suggestion, but his thin figure did quiver for a moment.

"The Ministry of Hygiene is in Clifford Street," was all he said.

When his Private Secretary came back Sir Oliver asked if he had heard the advice he had given to Dr Scratchbury.

"I did, indeed, sir, but it would appear that Dr Scratchbury had already approached the Ministry of Hygiene and that they had advised him to approach us. So I took it upon myself to suggest that Dr Scratchbury should approach the Home Office."

"The Home Office?"

"Yes, sir. You will remember that the Home Office deals with explosives, dangerous drugs, poisons and intoxicating liquor."

"But have we any reason to suppose that this Dandimilk is dangerous, or even mildly intoxicating?"

"No, sir, but I thought it would avoid overlapping if the Home Office sent a specimen of Dandimilk to the Government chemist. You will remember, sir, that besides having statutory functions under the Food and Drug Act and the Fertilizer and Feeding Stuffs Act the

Department known as the Government Laboratory carries out advisory and investigatory chemical work for most other Government Departments."

"Yes, perhaps you were right to send Dr Scratchbury to the Home Office," Sir Oliver decided after meditating for a minute or two over crossed fingers on what he had feared at first might have been an impulsive suggestion by his Private Secretary but of which on consideration he approved. "And now I have to see this deputation from the County Council of Oatshire."

"That's not until noon, sir."

"I am not inclined to accept their objections to this new main drain with which we are proposing to link Oatcester with Hardingham. It verges on perversity the way every Rural District Council wants every main drain we propose to lay to be laid somewhere else. It's high time that Rural District Councils were all absorbed in County Councils."

"And these objections are escalating all the time," said Humphrey Mowart.

Sir Oliver frowned.

"I don't care for these American neologisms," he said. " 'Escalator' was a new word for a new invention, but it's an unwarrantable intrusion upon the English language to import a word like 'escalate' to take the place of grow or spread or rise or increase or intensify. I was shocked the other day to find it being used in a *Times* leader. Before we know where we are we shall find it in the crossword."

"I apologise, sir," said Humphrey Mowart, with what Dean Farrar might have described as a winning smile upon his frank and open countenance but is expressed more simply by the monosyllable "grin". "It's terribly easy to find oneself falling in with the latest word or pronunciation. Do you know I actually caught myself out saying contróversy the other day?"

"I hope you won't catch yourself out again, Humphrey," Sir Oliver told him. "However, we are all apt to trip. I caught myself tripping just now when I said 'Oatcester'."

"What's wrong with that, sir?"

"It always used to be pronounced 'Oster' to rhyme with 'coaster'. If my Scout Master had heard me call it 'Oatcester' I should have been for it. The B.B.C. has carried out its duties almost as efficiently as the Civil Service but strongly as I advocate centralisation, I make one exception; I do not want to centralise words. It all started with Daintry."

Humphrey Mowart looked puzzled.

"It was always Daintry before the B.B.C. started broadcasting from Daventry. But you took my mind off this main drain for Oatshire; we must get back to it. Let me look at that plan again. Obviously Mr Butterwick is right." Mr Butterwick was the Senior Quantity Surveyor. "The drain takes the shortest distance between Oatcester and Hardingham. But this farmer—what's his name—oh yes, Narbrow objects to its passing under his land. After all, it is *under* his land. It's not as if we were proposing to lay it across his land."

"He objects to the disturbance entailed for his cattle while the work is in progress. He evidently has influence. Otherwise we shouldn't be seeing this County Council deputation at noon. Mr Narbrow maintains that the drain could pass under Hardingham Heath without interfering with agricultural amenities."

"I'm not prepared to commit the Ministry to a heavy increase of expense merely for the sake of agricultural amenities," said Sir Oliver. "Production yes ; amenities no. If we interfere too much with production we may have trouble with the people at Harvest Home."

Humphrey Mowart was faintly surprised to hear the Permanent Secretary allude to the Ministry of Cultivation as flippantly as a young Assistant Principal.

"Apparently, sir, Oatcester and Hardingham are much visited by American tourists as two of the most representative towns of what England was like when the

Mayflower sailed. The Hardingham morris-dancers are famous."

"But surely they won't be dancing about over the six miles between Oatcester and Hardingham."

"No, sir, quite. But the main—the chief objection raised to our main drain is that apparently a Harvest Festival is held every year at Farmer Narbrow's farm, which tries to recapture the spirit of old harvest festivals. Farmer Narbrow maintains that the Americans who enjoy this occasion will be deterred by the sight of the work necessary for our drain and that the flow of visitors may diminish the following year in consequence."

"That is a point, of course. Ring Mr Butterwick and ask him to come to my room."

With the arrival of the Senior Quantity Surveyor, a small shrivelled man who suggested by his appearance the second half of his name more than the first, the reply of the Ministry to the Oatshire deputation was discussed again.

"Suppose we divert the main drain from Ye Olde Farme which is apparently what Mr Narbrow calls what the Ordnance Survey calls Bill's Bottom and carry it under Hardingham Heath. How would that affect the cost?"

"At a rough guess, Sir Oliver, another £50,000 at least. Probably more," said the Senior Quantity Surveyor.

Sir Oliver turned to his Private Secretary.

"Write to this new Ministry which has just been created."

"The Ministry of Immigration, sir?" the Private Secretary asked.

"Yes. Ask them to give you an estimate of the number of American tourists and of course Commonwealth tourists who visit Oatcester and Hardingham annually."

"Excuse me, sir, but I think that tourism is one of the functions carried out by the Ministry of Leisure. No, on second thoughts, sir, I believe the actual statistics of

tourists visiting Great Britain are compiled by the
Ministry of Movement, though probably the Ministry of
Leisure would be able to give us an approximate figure
for those who visit Oatcester and Hardingham."

Sir Oliver frowned.

"I'd rather we didn't get involved any further with
either of those Ministries, Humphrey. They are both of
them involved in this argument about which of them is
responsible for campers and hikers, and to-morrow the
Minister and I shall have to make it clear that whichever
is responsible for campers and hikers the responsibility
for the sanitary arrangements of both rests entirely with
us. And I don't think I am being too optimistic if I feel
confident that we shall be supported by the Ministry of
Hygiene. But these County Councillors will be here in a
few minutes. £50,000 is your estimate for the diversion,
Mr Butterwick?"

"At least," said the Senior Quantity Surveyor firmly.

"If only two thousand American tourists visit Oatcester
that will mean at least £50,000 apart from what they
spend on tips which cannot be less than another £10,000
and probably a great deal more," said Sir Oliver.

"I do agree with you, sir. Americans *are* very generous.
Last year an American who was visiting Little Hangover,
the village where my mother lives, found his own name
on a tombstone in the churchyard in seventeen something or other and was so pleased that he gave the vicar
a thousand dollars."

"I hope he included it in his income-tax returns."

"Oh, it did not come into the same category as his
Easter collection. It was given to him for the parish. It
was not a case of evasion."

"Well, we shall hear presently what the Oatshire
County Council says. But on the information at present
available it is possible that we may decide we shall be
justified in sanctioning the extra cost involved by laying
the main drain under Hardingham Heath."

"We may have a bit of trouble with the Oatshire

C

Hunt, Sir Oliver," said the Senior Quantity Surveyor.
"If a fox went to earth in our drain we can't have them
messing about in it with a lot of dogs."

"We must notify the Hunt that while work is in progress on the main drain linking Oatcester with Hardingham fox-hounds must be kept off Hardingham Heath,"
said Sir Oliver.

"And then there are the snipers," the Surveyor added.

"The officer commanding the local Territorials must
be asked to refrain from military exercises while our
main drain is being laid."

"No, Sir Oliver, not the military. Snipe-shooters."

"They must either abstain from snipe-shooting or
shoot their snipe somewhere else. I do not hesitate to call
this a frivolous objection, and I am sure the Oatshire
County Council will endorse our attitude."

"Then you've decided on the diversion, Sir Oliver?"
the Surveyor asked.

"I am going to give the diversion most careful consideration, after which the Ministry's decision will be
taken in due course."

And this was what the Permanent Secretary had just
told the deputation from the Oatshire County Council
when his Private Secretary came in to ask him if he could
speak for a moment on the telephone to one of the Senior
Commissioners of the Board of Control.

"Controlling what?" Sir Oliver asked as he passed into
his Private Secretary's room.

"Lunacy and Mental Deficiency," said the Private
Secretary. "I think the Home Office must have referred
him to the Ministry of Hygiene."

"Referred whom?"

"Dr Scratchbury, sir."

Sir Oliver picked up the receiver.

"The Permanent Secretary of the Ministry of Sanitation speaking. . . . You have a man sent to you from the
Home Office . . . oh yes, Dr Emilius Scratchbury . . . but
it was made perfectly clear to him that this substitute for

cows' milk was outside any of the functions carried out by
this Ministry. . . . He was recommended here to approach
the Home Office? . . . He must be under a misapprehen-
sion. . . . I think, Mr . . . oh, Mr Smith. I think, Mr Smith,
that you should take the matter up with the Home Office
. . . but I repeat, Mr Smith, it was made perfectly clear
to Dr Scratchbury that this substitute for cows' milk is
quite outside any of our functions. . . . I beg your pardon.
. . . Certainly not, orders will be given to the janitor that
on no account is Dr Scratchbury to be received here. . . .
I'm sorry to hear it, but if you cannot control lunatics at
the Board of Control you can hardly expect us to control
them at the Ministry of Sanitation. . . . I'm sorry but I'm
afraid I must leave the control of Dr Scratchbury to the
Board of Control. I have been interrupted in an important interview with a deputation from the Oatshire
County Council."

Sir Oliver hung up.

"I was afraid you *were* being a little impulsive, Humphrey, when you sent Dr Scratchbury to the Home
Office. Really, you know, what are we coming to when
the people responsible for lunatics try to foist them upon
us?"

Back with the County Councillors Sir Oliver addressed
them again.

"I apologise, gentlemen, for that interruption. As I
was saying, we shall consider the possibility of diverting
the main drain from the vicinity of Mr Narbrow's farm
and we shall bear in mind the interference it might cause
with the Harvest Festival celebrations at . . ." Sir Oliver
hesitated for a moment, "at Ye Olde Farme which I find
noted on the Ordnance Survey map as Bill's Bottom."

"That's right," one of the Councillors exclaimed in a
rich Oatshire accent which would have been envied by
any of the professional bucolics nurtured by the B.B.C.
"It was Bill Narbrow himself started calling it by that
unnatural name."

"Mr Narbrow's objections will be borne in mind,"

Sir Oliver said. "You will realise that the diversion of the main drain will involve the Ministry in considerable expenditure, but we are anxious to do all we can to preserve the amenities of our countryside and, I repeat, your suggestion will be carefully considered."

The deputation withdrew.

"You made it clear to the janitor that on no account was he to admit Dr Scratchbury, Humphrey?"

"Absolutely, sir."

"But you'd better find out if he did come back."

The Private Secretary returned with the news that Dr Scratchbury had come back and that after being refused admittance was now hanging about outside in Cork Street.

"I can't be buttonholed by him in public. I'll have to take a taxi to the Heraeum and miss some of the little exercise I ever get."

"I'll see there's a taxi waiting for you."

"You'd better come with me, Humphrey. I don't want to be buttonholed as I'm getting into the taxi. You'll be lunching at your club? I'll drop you there on the way. And you might draft a letter to this Board of Control confirming my telephone conversation with this Mr Smith."

"Yes, sir. I've looked up the Commissioners. Leonard Smith, O.B.E. I propose to communicate directly with him and when you return from lunch if you approve my letter I'll have it sent round by hand to Clifford Street."

"If I see Sir Henry Rowe at the Heraeum I'll ask him if as Permanent Secretary of the Ministry of Hygiene he has any control over this Board of Control, and, if he has, to notify them that Dr Scratchbury is quite outside our functional responsibilities."

Beyond bumping his head as he dived into the taxi to avoid being buttonholed by Dr Scratchbury Sir Oliver Huffam reached the Heraeum without mishap, where he welcomed Mr Henry Upjohn, the rosy-cheeked Minister of Sanitation who had smiled his way to the top of the poll to represent North Wessex for over twenty years.

"Will you take a glass of something before lunch, Minister?" Sir Oliver enquired almost awkwardly. This habit of having something to drink before lunch was still regarded by him as regrettable.

"Don't be too formal, Huffam," the Minister bubbled. "I'll have a vodka with a spot of ice."

In the sanctified calm of the Heraeum Mr Upjohn's voice whose resonance had served him so well at open air meetings in his constituency had to his host's embarrassment too much resonance when he asked for vodka. The aprons of two bishops sitting at an adjoining table flapped perceptibly. Two wealthy men who were helping to finance Moral Rearmament as a protection against Communism scowled. The elderly waitress standing by to take Sir Oliver's order looked as if an important part of her underclothing had suddenly become loose. Sir Oliver himself, sharply aware of the suspicion in the public mind at this time that Whitehall was becoming Redhall, felt that his Minister must already have had more than one glass before lunch.

"Vodka," he repeated. "I don't think we have vodka at the Heraeum."

"Extraordinary," Mr Upjohn bubbled. "Oh well, I'll have a pink gin. And will you tell the barman to make it a bit pinker than usual," he said to the waitress.

"And yours, sir?" she asked Sir Oliver.

"An Italian vermouth," he told her.

"My dear Huffam, do at least make it a gin and It. You'll be asking for Mother Siegel's Soothing Syrup next. I remember being given it when I was a kid and went bawling about the house, as my old nurse used to say."

"I never touch gin, Minister, though I do allow myself a small whisky every evening."

When the drinks were brought Mr Upjohn raised his glass.

"You've got to drink my health with a vengeance to-day, Huffam, even in that vermouth of yours. It's my birthday, and do you know how old I am? Fifty! But I don't feel it, by Jove. I said to my wife this morning 'Do I look any more like Methuselah than I did yesterday?' Still, fifty's fifty, Huffam. But I'll try to forget it to-night. We're having a little birthday dinner at Bambino's."

"You've not forgotten that we're having a conference to-morrow with the Minister of Movement and the Minister of Leisure?" Sir Oliver asked a little anxiously.

"No, no, Huffam. I may not look like an elephant, but I never forget."

Sir Oliver managed to steer his Minister away from talking loudly during lunch about the sanitary arrangements of campers and hikers, and when it was over led him away to the most remote corner he could find in a club mercifully full of remote corners.

"Our line must be to support Jane Fossey against Jack Wilbraham, Huffam, and if we do that the least she can do is to accept our regulations about campers and hikers. Of course, Jane and I aren't in the Cabinet and Jack is, but I think the two of us ought to be a match for him."

Sir Oliver did not approve of the way Ministers flung Christian names about, but he bowed to it as he had to bow to so many other regrettable habits of modernity.

"I am in agreement with you, Minister. I think that Dame Jane is fully entitled to claim entire responsibility for the movements of campers and hikers about the countryside ... but no, perhaps in the circumstances we should avoid calling them movements. One of the points made by the Ministry of Movement was that they were responsible for movements of any kind. I have it. We will insist that the movements of campers and hikers are in fact more strictly perambulations."

"So long as we can guarantee that some confounded Opposition back-bencher doesn't put down a question about babies' nappies for the Minister of Sanitation."

Mr Upjohn laughed so boisterously at his own joke

that his Permanent Secretary was more grateful than
ever for this remote spot in the Heraeum.

"If Dame Jane is given our full support, Minister,"
Sir Oliver continued when Mr Upjohn's laughter had
died down to a gurgle, "we shall be justified in expecting
her full cooperation in our efforts to make the—er—
perambulations. . . ."

Mr Upjohn began to laugh again.

"Perhaps 'wanderings' might be substituted for 'perambulations',," Sir Oliver suggested in the hope of
damping down Mr Upjohn's mirth. "Knowing Sir
Wilfred Clarkson, the Permanent Secretary of the
Ministry of Movement, I do know that if we call them
movements he will make the very most of it. He put every
difficulty he could in the way of our ensuring that the
lavatories on aeroplanes conformed with the require-
ments which we had laid down for lavatories. But he did
give way finally. Indeed, Minister, if I may make the
suggestion, you should stress that willingness, though
willingness is no kind of word to use for the amount of
correspondence and the number of conferences that were
held before the Ministry of Movement did accept our
proposals . . . but let willingness pass. You might impress
upon Dame Jane Fossey that the Ministry of Movement
did accept our proposals, in which case I feel reasonably
confident that Sir Wilfred Clarkson will support the
claim for our inspectors to control as far as possible the
sanitary arrangements of campers and hikers. I feel
the more confident because Sir Roger Buncombe, the
Permanent Secretary of the Ministry of Leisure, is
fundamentally. . . ."

"Fundamentally on our side, eh?" Mr Upjohn laughed
merrily. "That's the very adverb for it."

Sir Oliver ignored what he felt was a joke in the worst
of taste for a Minister of the Crown.

"Sir Roger Buncombe in my experience has always
been able to appreciate the danger of overlapping and I
do not anticipate that he will want to assume the responsi-

bility for the sanitary arrangements of campers and hikers. He will be sufficiently engaged in deciding where they are to camp and to hike, because inevitably he will find the Ministry of Leisure occasionally involved with the Ministry of Cultivation, should the Ministry of Cultivation try to restrict the move—the wanderings of campers and hikers over farm lands."

"Well, that's that, Huffam, but don't forget we still have Jane Fossey to deal with to-morrow morning, and, believe you me, she's a formidable woman. By the way, what happened about that deputation from Oatcester this morning?"

The Permanent Secretary gave the Minister an account of the meeting.

"I take it we'll agree to divert this main drain. After all £50,000 isn't worth arguing about in these days. I always make a point of paying attention to local opinion. Jock Ackroyd is a good friend of mine and our constituencies adjoin. I'll get him to speak to the Master of the Oatshire Hunt so that hounds are kept out of our main drain while they're laying it under Hardingham Heath. I've heard of this chap Narbrow and I wouldn't like him to have a grievance. It might get about in North Wessex. Well, I've enjoyed our lunch, Huffam. But do get these old fossils in your Club to realise that vodka is not the same as red biddy."

Sir Oliver decided to risk being buttonholed by Dr Scratchbury in Cork Street and to walk back to the Ministry from the Heraeum. As he was getting his hat and umbrella he heard one elderly member say to another.

"Did you hear that fellow asking for vodka before lunch?"

"Vodka? Well, I was saying only the other day, these Communists are infiltrating everywhere."

Sir Oliver hurried away as quickly as possible. To his relief there was no sign of Dr Scratchbury in Cork Street.

It was only half-past five when he reached Chilling-ham Gardens. As Lady Huffam appeared at the head of the stairs to answer his approximation to a yodel he asked if Jeremy was back yet from school.

Her answer was a flood of tears.

Chapter 3

"WHAT are you crying about, Gertrude?" Sir Oliver asked when he reached the drawing-room. A sudden thought struck him. "You haven't had a man called Scratchbury pestering you to drink a new production called Dandimilk?"

Sir Oliver was relieved to hear that nobody called Scratchbury had been pestering his wife to drink Dandimilk; his relief did not last.

"Read this letter from Jeremy," she said miserably.

Sir Oliver took the sheet of that paper on which he had been accustomed to read through, with ever increasing gloom about his son's academic future, the Latin prose or the Greek prose he was intending to hand in to his form-master next morning.

Instead of deteriorating Latin prose he read:

Dear Mum and Dad,

By the time you read this letter Dick Horner and I will be on our way to France because we have decided to hitch-hike our way all over Europe. I am sorry I could not let you know in advance about what I was intending to do but I did not think you would agree about what I was going to do. I was late back from school this evening because Dick Horner and I were making our final arrangements. You may wonder where I have found the money to go to France. Well, Dick Horner had a wonderful win in the football pools of £77 two weeks ago and he asked if I would come with him to Europe because he is bored with school like me, and when he left his father who is a solicitor wanted him to be a solicitor which he does not want to be. I know that you want me to go into the civil service and I don't want to go into the civil service. I do not want to spend my life seeing if people have filled up forms properly and I do not want to be arranging other people's lives on paper any more than I want other people to arrange my life.

Nigel and Joan love the civil service as much as Dad loves it but they are both much older than me. I belong to a different generation. I suppose I'm what the papers call an angry young man. Well, if I am, I'm doing something not to go on being angry instead of looking at television and getting more angry.

I know that what I'm doing will rather upset you and I'm sorry for that but you may have noticed that I was getting more and more gloomy lately and Dad was always worrying about my not making the most of this last year at school. But you can't make the most of something you loathe and I loathed school, more than ever after going abroad for the first time last January. Dick Horner was in that party which went to Switzerland and when we were there we realised more than ever what a bore school was. Perhaps I had better tell you the name and address of Dick's father. He is Augustus Horner and he lives at 22 Wingfield Mansions W.14. I will write about where we have been from time to time but not from where we are because I know that Dad would feel he must start making enquiries and that would be desastrous.

Jeremy

P.S. A chap at school is going to leave this letter on his way home to-morrow, but it took me till two o'clock this morning to write.

"Seventeen and a half and spells disastrous with an 'e'," Sir Oliver groaned.

"The poor boy must have been tired when he finished that letter," Lady Huffam pleaded, "But what *are* we going to do, Olly?"

"I must get in touch with this Mr Augustus Horner," Sir Oliver said.

"It was thoughtful of poor Jeremy to let you know where Mr Horner lived."

"Not thoughtful enough to compensate for the utter and incredible thoughtlessness which has led him into this preposterous adventure. I thought I was going to stimulate him to work harder when I gave him that winter-sports holiday. And the only stimulation it has been is to embark on this insane escapade. Another warning against impulsiveness. I didn't consider the plan sufficiently carefully when I let him have that holiday in Switzerland."

"But, Olly dear, you could not have expected he would do what he has done, however carefully you had considered the plan."

"Hitch-hiking," Sir Oliver muttered to himself. "And to-morrow I have to . . ." he pulled himself up. Throughout his married life with Gertrude he had never let her know anything about the work in the Ministry. It showed how much he had been shocked by Jeremy's letter that he had been on the verge of telling her about that conference to-morrow to decide about the sanitary arrangements of campers and hitch-hikers. He went quickly downstairs to find the telephone number of Mr Augustus Horner.

Before he rang up Mr Horner Sir Oliver carefully considered whether he should propose an immediate visit to 22 Wingfield Mansions or whether it would not be more suitable to invite Mr Horner to call at 9 Chillingham Gardens. He weighed the question meticulously for two minutes and finally decided that his position as Permanent Secretary of the Ministry of Sanitation would be appropriately emphasised by asking Mr Horner to call at 9 Chillingham Gardens. There was yet another question to be carefully considered. Should he ask Mr Horner to call on him before dinner or after dinner? 'The sooner the better' had never been a policy he had encouraged during his career in the Civil Service. Nevertheless, perhaps this was an occasion when the precipitate action he always deplored was justifiable.

The telephone was answered by a feminine voice.

"This is Sir Oliver Huffam speaking. I wish to speak to Mr Augustis Horner."

He heard the feminine voice shouting "Dad!" and presently a rich bass announced,

"Mr Horner speaking. Who is it?"

"This is Sir Oliver Huffam. I have just received a letter from my younger son to say that he has gone to France with another Jacobean who I understand is a son of yours."

"Yes, I found a letter from my boy Dick when I got back from my office."

Sir Oliver failed to note in the rich bass of this reply the least suggestion of anxiety, alarm, or even surprise, and thought it would be more dignified if he attributed his own anxiety to his wife.

"Lady Huffam is naturally a little worried by her younger son's letter and I was wondering if you could make it convenient to call at 9 Chillingham Gardens, South Kensington, so that we could decide on a course of action that would not involve any danger of overlapping."

"I'll come along right away, Sir Oliver. As a matter of fact by a coincidence I sent a letter off to your Ministry only this morning. A client of mine wants a Commit No Nuisance sign freshened up because it's become a regular place for committing a nuisance when a pub round the corner closes."

"Yes, well, I've no doubt one of our inspectors will be reporting on the matter in due course. Gloucester Road is our nearest station."

"That's all right, Sir Oliver. I'll be rolling along in my car as soon as I've had a cup of tea. Cheerioh."

Sir Oliver went upstairs to the drawing-room.

"This Mr Horner seems less concerned about this fantastic escapade than one would expect. I think it will be better for me to see him in the Den, Gertrude. Will you ask Ethel to put the decanter of sherry and two glasses there and show Mr Horner in when he arrives."

About half an hour later Ethel came up to say that Mr Horner was in the Den. Sir Oliver went downstairs to greet a plump genial man of about fifty.

"Don't worry, Sir Oliver," he said as they shook hands. "Boys will be boys as we used to say. I've brought along my own boy's letter. I thought you might like to read it. No thanks, I won't have any sherry. I'm trying to keep my weight down. You're lucky, Sir Oliver," he added with an admiring twinkle in his merry blue eyes. "Here's young Dick's letter." Sir Oliver read:

Dear Dad,

I won £77 in the pools and so I've decided to chuck school and hitch-hike all over Europe. After that I'll know whether I can be articled to Greaves and Horner. The trouble with school is that it goes on too long. I'll be eighteen next month and I don't want to waste being 18 at school. You only learn a lot of stuff you forget but if I learn something about life I won't forget it and if I do become a solicitor I'll be more use to the firm. Huffy is coming with me. He's fed up with swotting to get into Oxbridge. His father is something important in the Civil Service. He's Sir Oliver Huffam and he wants Huffy to go into the Civil Service but Huffy says nothing will make him become a native of what he calls Bumphland. By the time you get this we shall be in France or very nearly there. Don't let Mum worry if you don't hear from me for a week or two. I shall write about where we were not about where we are because Huffy thinks his father would be getting in touch with Consuls etc to control his movements and he is determined to find about Europe for himself. He doesn't say so but I'm pretty sure he intends to be a writer. Well, if it's ever going to be Greaves, Horner and Horner, this is the only way it will happen, but I don't think Huffy will ever be Sir Jeremy Huffam. Give my love to Mum and my two kid sisters.

Your loving

Dick

Sir Oliver handed back the letter to Dick's father.

"We never had a chance of winning seventy-seven quid in the pools," said Mr Horner, with half a sigh.

"Fortunately for us."

"Oh, don't say that, Sir Oliver."

"You surely don't approve of this behaviour, Mr Horner?"

"I never had a chance of finding out. Augustus was a

chubby lad, fat rosy cheeks Augustus had, and he still has them. Dick takes after his mother, and when she read that letter of his she just said 'Good for Dick' and that was good enough for me, too."

"Am I to presume then, Mr Horner, that you do not see your way to cooperate with me in securing the return of these two misguided boys to their homes?"

"Speaking as a lawyer, Sir Oliver, I certainly do not intend to take any kind of legal action. The boys have enough money not to be stranded. If they are unable to earn their way about the Continent and their money is exhausted it will be time to get in touch with some consul or other and pay their fares home. May I speak frankly, Sir Oliver?"

The Permanent Secretary's expression of cautious non-commital was one he had always assumed when somebody asked him that question at the Ministry. He waited in silence for Mr Horner's frankness.

"So far as Dick is concerned I shall do nothing, but if you are determined to get your boy back it is entirely a matter for you to decide on the ways and means. May I venture to say a word for . . ."

"Jeremy," Sir Oliver put in quickly.

He was afraid Mr Horner was going to call him 'Huffy'.

"For young Jeremy. He has always made on me the impression of knowing his own mind. That's the best thing a boy of seventeen can know. We middle-aged folk are inclined to wonder what on earth young people will be saying and doing next. But from what I can make out middle-aged folk have always been wondering that. I am only too glad that Dick has Huff—has Jeremy as his companion in this adventure, and if you deprive Dick of Jeremy's companionship I shall be deeply disappointed, Sir Oliver. I shall say no more. Perhaps I've already said too much. Oh, yes, there is one more thing. Have you considered the possibility, if you set on foot enquiries, that it might get into the papers?"

"Into the papers?" Sir Oliver echoed in a tone that verged on consternation.

The solicitor in Mr Horner at once took advantage of that tone.

"It's just the kind of story that would take the fancy of the popular Press. 'Is son of prominent Government official in Moscow?' "

"I shall bear in mind the contingency you have indicated, Mr Horner, and for the present I shall not consider any further action."

Mr Horner was on the point of taking advantage of the Permanent Secretary's acceptance of his argument to put in a word for his client about that faded warning to commit no nuisance, but on reflection decided he might be committing a verbal nuisance and said instead,

"I'm glad you find that the least said about this boyish prank the soonest mended, Sir Oliver. I'll let you know as soon as I have word from Dick, and now I must trot back to Wingfield Mansions."

After rejoining his wife in the drawing-room Sir Oliver told her that Mr Horner had agreed with him in thinking the wisest thing to do was to let matters take their course until the two boys had had their lesson.

"But, Olly dear, what will the Headmaster say?" she asked.

"I don't think the Headmaster will want it to get about all over the School that two of the senior boys have been behaving like two fourth-form boys. I shall write and let him know that Jeremy is abroad for his health. If, as I expect, Jeremy and young Horner find it not quite so easy to go hitch-hiking all over the Continent when this money of young Horner's is finished, I shall ask the nearest consul to provide them with the means of return to England. In that case Jeremy will go back to St James's at the beginning of next term."

Gertrude Huffam began to look a little more cheerful. What a help Olly must be to his Minister, she reflected proudly. He was the very personification of calm dignity. Then her brow wrinkled again.

"But what *will* Nigel say? We can't tell *him* that Jeremy has gone abroad for his health."

"Nigel will understand why I am taking no steps to repatriate Jeremy. And now, Gertrude, shall we drop the subject? I have an important conference to-morrow, and I must not allow Jeremy's reckless escapade to interrupt my train of thought."

Upstairs in his study after dinner Sir Oliver sat down at his desk to make some notes about to-morrow's conference. He wrote *Campers and Hikers* at the top of a sheet of paper and paused. He had certainly been right in agreeing with Mr Augustus Horner that it would be wiser to keep silence about the truants' behaviour. What chance would they have at the Ministry of persuading Dame Jane Fossey and Sir John Wilbraham to admit their claim to control the sanitary arrangements of campers and hikers if it got into the papers that the son of the Permanent Secretary was at this moment hiking about the Continent, where the sanitary arrangements were by British standards so notably lax?

Sir Oliver had not had time to indicate the third point of consideration for to-morrow when Ethel came in to tell him that a Doctor Scratchbody wished to see him and that she had shown him into Master Jeremy's room.

"I thought as Master Jeremy wasn't back yet it would be quite all right, Sir Oliver."

Sir Oliver decided to put a stop to any speculation that might be going on downstairs about Jeremy's whereabouts.

"Master Jeremy has gone abroad, Ethel."

"Gone abroad, sir? But his Sunday clothes are still in his bedroom. Oh, but I was forgetting. Of course, they don't keep Sunday on the continong, do they?"

And now it was Ethel's turn to seize an opportunity.

"Cook and me and Dorothy was wondering, Sir Oliver, if you'd erbject to us having the telly in our room.

D

Cook *was* going to this Coster Bravar on her holiday next year but both her married sisters have the telly and said what was the use of going to this place Coster Bravar when she could see it on the telly without being sick in the bus as so many of them are. My brother-in-law says he can get us a telly very reasonable."

Sir Oliver without even a moment of his usual consideration said he should be glad to present his cook, his parlour-maid and his housemaid with a television set. He hoped that this would stop any further speculation downstairs, either about Jeremy's Sunday clothes, the continental Sabbath, or the date of Jeremy's return.

"Oh, Sir Oliver, a telly! Oh, thank you ever so, Sir Oliver. Will I tell Doctor Scratchbody you'll be coming down? Cook'll be in a proper rapcher and Dorothy too."

"Yes, I'll be coming down, but, if Dr Scratchbury, not body, Ethel, if Dr Scratchbury calls again, neither I nor her ladyship are at home."

"Very good, Sir Oliver, and thank you again for the telly and I do hope Master Jeremy will enjoy his abroad."

When Sir Oliver entered the Den he saw upon the table where all his children had done their homework a large tin.

"I have ventured to bring you this gallon tin of Dandimilk, Sir Oliver, in the hope that you and your household will test its qualities."

"I made it perfectly clear to you when I gave you that interview at the Ministry that I was not prepared to express any opinion upon the merits or demerits of Dandimilk. The Ministry of Hygiene. . . ."

"But your secretary advised me to go to the Home Oflce. And when I got to the Home Office they advised me to go the the Board of Control in the Ministry of Hygiene where a Mr Smith advised me to go to the Ministry of Sanitation. But the janitor would not let me in and I waited for quite a while in Cork Street, but you were evidently in a hurry and I wasn't able to speak to you. So I thought the best thing to do would be to bring a gallon can of Dandimilk to your house. I think you'll be impressed by the patent opener and you'll find that Dandimilk will be as fresh in a week's time as it is now. If you keep it in a cool place, that is, just an ordinary cool place not necessarily a frigidaire. Of course our quart bottles will go into any frigidaire but these gallon tins are rather more bulky. . . ."

"I cannot allow you to leave this tin in my house, Dr Scratchbury. Surely I made it clear to you this morning that we cannot accept the responsibility at the Ministry of Sanitation of expressing . . ."

"I am not asking for an expression of opinion, Sir Oliver. I merely want you to satisfy yourself as Permanent Secretary of the Ministry of Sanitation that the mild laxative effect of Dandimilk is no more powerful than the well known milk of magnesia, but let me make it clear that we do not claim any comparably digestive effect for Dandimilk. It is not a medicine, it is a perfect substitute for cows' milk. And let me add that it can be warmed like cows' milk but *not* boiled. Gently warmed. That is all. And of course there is no need to boil Dandimilk, which for hygienic reasons is often a wise precaution with cows' milk. Might I suggest that before you retire to rest to-night, Sir Oliver, you shall drink a warm glass of Dandimilk? Please do not think I am suggesting that you suffer from night starvation."

As he said this the dark eyes of Dr Scratchbury seemed to be boring right into Sir Oliver Huffam's tall thin frame.

"I'm afraid I must ask you to let me bring this interview to a conclusion, Dr Scratchbury. I have had an extremely busy day at the Ministry. . . ."

"That's exactly why I've brought you this gallon tin of Dandimilk, Sir Oliver. You will find a warm glass of Dandimilk exactly what you need before you seek a well earned rest from your labours and responsibilities in sleep. What is it that Macbeth says 'Sleep that knits up. . . .' "

"What Macbeth says has nothing to do with this synthetic milk of yours. I must ask you to. . . ."

"In other words, buzz off as George Robey used to say," Dr Scratchbury put in with a hollow chuckle. "Well, I will be going but you won't mind if I leave the gallon tin of Dandimilk with you. It's quite a heavy encumbrance and makes people in the tube nervous. They stare at me as if I were an active anarchist."

With another hollow chuckle Dr Emilius Scratchbury was out of the room and Sir Oliver Huffam was left with the gallon tin of Dandimilk. He looked at it as twenty years earlier he had looked at that bath outside the house of the Minister of Waste in Eaton Square.

Chapter 4

SIR OLIVER slept less tranquilly than usual that night. Indeed, once he woke up to hear his wife asking anxiously.

"What's the matter, Olly? Are you in pain? You were groaning in your sleep."

"No, no, it was some kind of nightmare," he told her. "I was appearing on the television."

He shuddered at the recollection.

"Shall I give you one of my aspirins?"

"No, no."

"It might have been that television set you are presenting them with downstairs. Oh dear, you've no idea what pleasure it has given. It *was* so sweet of you, Olly."

"Yes, well, we mustn't start talking about television. I have an important conference to-morrow."

Sir Oliver turned over to seek sleep. He was spared any more nightmares but his night remained restless, and in the tube next morning the *Times* crossword puzzle was a mere skeleton of what it usually was by the time he reached Piccadilly. As he was walking along Regent Street to the Ministry the solution of one clue suddenly occurred to him. Cockney complains of irritation. Hitch! Of course, whenever Cockney appeared in a *Times* crossword clue it meant the lack of an "h" or the intrusion of one. He hoped that "hitch" was not an omen of any breach of compromise in the conference over the sanitary arrangements of hitch-hikers and campers. "Breach of compromise," he murmured to himself. "That's rather good. I must remember that phrase."

Sir Oliver tried it out on his Private Secretary when he reached the Ministry.

"I hope the conference won't end in a breach of compromise case."

For a moment there was a question in Humphrey Mowart's eyebrows before he realised what Sir Oliver meant, but only for a moment.

"That's awfully good, sir." He laughed with as much apparent relish as if he really did think it was awfully good. "Oh, I'm sure we shall reach a compromise with which everybody will be satisfied."

"I've been turning it over in my mind, Humphrey, and if Dame Jane Fossey is difficult I shall suggest to the Minister that we give up any responsibility for the sanitary arrangements of hikers and concentrate upon the sanitary arrangements of campers. That seems to be an equitable compromise."

"Absolutely, sir."

"I think the Minister was right to suggest that the conference should be held in the Ministry of Leisure."

"Absolutely, sir."

"I have only met Dame Jane Fossey on formal occasions, but I have read her book *The Leisure State* and agreed with much of it, though I think she sometimes goes too far, as for instance when she pleads for the modernisation of Shakespeare in order to make him intelligible to young people. I may be old-fashioned but I cannot think that *Romeo and Juliet* is made more accessible to the imagination of young people by making the Capulets what I believe are called Mods and the Montagues what I believe are called Rockers. Some dramatic critic was writing about this with apparent approbation in *The New World* last week. I remember my father used to talk of the pleasure he used to get from *Faust Up to Date* at the old Gaiety Theatre but that was in the nature of a deliberate parody. It was not intended to be taken seriously. Dear me, I'm letting my tongue run away with me. I spent a restless night, which is a rare occurrence for me. Dr Scratchbury arrived after dinner at Chillingham Gardens with a large tin of Dandimilk."

"And persuaded you to try it, sir?" the Private Secretary exclaimed in astonishment.

"Certainly not, though he did manage to slip away and leave the tin in Jeremy's room—the Den as we call it."

"And Jeremy drank some of it?" the Private Secretary asked.

Sir Oliver paused for a moment or two before replying.

"No. Jeremy has gone abroad." He paused again. "Humphrey, what I am about to tell you is in the strictest confidence."

"Absolutely, sir."

"When I got home yesterday evening I found a letter from Jeremy waiting for me. In it he announced that he had gone to France with the intention of hitch-hiking all over Europe. A fellow Jacobean called Horner had won £77 in what are called the Pools and this sum was being used as the financial *vade mecum* for their escapade. My first impulse was to get into touch immediately with our consular representatives in France, but you know how much I dislike impulse, Humphrey. You'll remember your sudden impulse yesterday to advise Dr Scratchbury to take his Dandimilk to the Home Office?"

"Yes, sir. I am sorry for that impulse," said the Private Secretary. "But you did agree with it yourself at the time."

"Yes, I'm afraid I, too, surrendered to impulse. Don't worry any more about it, Humphrey. I had my lesson, and after due consideration I decided not to take any action but to wait until Jeremy and his friend Horner had exhausted the funds at their disposal and could be repatriated. I have written to tell the Headmaster at St James's that on medical advice I have sent him abroad for his health and that is what I shall tell everybody. So you will realise why the explanation of Jeremy's escapade must remain a secret. It might invalidate our position with the Ministry of Leisure and the Ministry of Move-

ment if in putting forward our claim to be responsible
for the sanitary arrangements of campers and hikers it
leaked out—it became known that the son of the Permanent Secretary of the Ministry of Sanitation was hitch-
hiking all over Europe where sanitary control is so
frequently lax—er—inadequate. I am sure you agree
with me, Humphrey."

"Absolutely, sir."

"Moreover, at a time when the popular Press loses no
opportunity of suggesting that many Civil Servants are
in sympathy with Communism it would be nothing less
than disastrous if some irresponsible journalist pandered
to the public appetite for scandalous sensation by hinting
that the son of a prominent official was in Moscow."

"Of which the Press is quite capable," the Private
Secretary agreed. "And now, sir, I think it is time for us
to be on our way to the Ministry of Leisure."

"*Tempora mutantur*, but you know, Humphrey, one of
the saddest effects of the Great War was to make it impossible for Whitehall to remain self-sufficient. Imagine
what my father would have said if he had been told that
the *New Ministries and Secretaries Act* of 1916 would end up
with a Ministry in Cheyne Walk. I was only a small boy at
the time but I recall his disapproval when one of the new
Ministries housed itself in a Northumberland Avenue
hotel. 'It's the thin edge of the wedge,' he told my mother
when she said that Northumberland Avenue was almost
Whitehall. But Cheyne Walk! Yes, well, we must be
getting along, Humphrey."

On their way in the taxi the Private Secretary said to
his Chief,

"May I ask you rather a rude question, sir?"

"Ask away, Humphrey."

"I've sometimes wondered, sir, why you don't have a
car. Oh, I know you welcome the brief exercise you derive from walking from Chillingham Gardens to the
Gloucester Road tube-station and from the Piccadilly
tube-station to Cork Street and from Cork Street to the

Heraeum and back, but at the week-end for your round of golf?"

"Not every week-end."

"But wouldn't Lady Huffam find a car a great convenience?"

"I have from time to time carefully considered the question of acquiring a motor-car and I have decided against it—in case I should be tempted to drive a motor-car myself. You must have noticed, Humphrey, that I am often oblivious of everything when I am engaged in considering some problem major *or* minor connected with my work. In exploring every avenue I do *not* want to steer my motor-car into a cul-de-sac, or what would be even more serious steer my motor-car into another motor-car."

"In a fit of absent-mindedness?"

"Not absent-mindedness, Humphrey. Deep consideration cannot be called absent-mindedness. But apart from the temptation a motor-car might offer to myself it might tempt Lady Huffam into learning to drive which *would* be a mistake."

"But you could have a chauffeur, sir."

"When we are on vacation we can always hire a motor-car and when I am on vacation I never talk about official matters. So I am not worried by the presence of somebody who might overhear what I am saying."

The Private Secretary may have been tempted to raise the question of a car for his Chief by the difficulty of always getting a taxi as soon as it was wanted; in spite of Sir Oliver's discouragement he made another suggestion.

"I could always bring my car up to town when you had an appointment beyond walking distance."

At this moment the taxi swerved violently to avoid two beatniks who had started to stroll across a Chelsea road the moment the amber light went green.

"There you are, Humphrey," Sir Oliver said. "It would have been unpleasant if our taxi had knocked down those two young people. Think how much more unpleasant it would have been if you had knocked them down in your motor-car. You know how the Press delights in making the most of any opportunity to criticise the Civil Service."

The Private Secretary gave up; soon the taxi drew up before one of those great squares of glass and concrete which property developers put up for offices in the confident expectation that, even if they are unable to let a single office, a Government Office would rent the lot, and foot the bill for whatever alterations were needed.

Looking out as it did across the road to Battersea Park with its memories of the First Fun Fair, no site could have been found more suitable for the new Ministry of Leisure.

When Dame Jane Fossey became Minister of Leisure in the new Ministry created by the new Government the appointment was generally approved by all shades of public opinion, from vivid red to true blue. At St James's Girls' School she had been considered the best goalkeeper at hockey the school ever had and when she went on from St James's to Somerton College with a brilliant scholarship she became not only the best goal-keeper at hockey that the University of Camford ever had but the best goal-keeper that the women of England ever had. Moreover, she went down from Camford with a First and came up again with a Fellowship. She had written several historical works before she entered politics and had held two Parliamentary Under-Secretaryships. It was her great work *The Leisure State* which had made her the obvious choice as Minister of Leisure.

Dame Jane Fossey's work among young people had been widely acclaimed, and as she had never married she was able to believe that mothers who worried about the behaviour of their children were always in the wrong. "I'm keeping goal for youth nowadays," she used to say proudly.

An extract from *The Leisure State* may be quoted:
"We have now reached a stage in evolution when the

skill of mankind is turning machines into human beings. This will mean that not so far hence the slavery that turned men into machines will be a thing of the myopic past and that the work which mankind had to perform by the sweat of his brow will be done for him by a well-oiled machine and that the clerical work which involved so much wearisome calculation in dim and dusty offices will be done by a computer. Computers will multiply: commuters will diminish. Already in Great Britain we are on the way to being able to boast that less hard work is being done in our country than anywhere else.

"In what other European country are the hours of labour showing such a steady decrease? In what other country are the working men and women able to sustain themselves with as many cups of tea in working hours? And what is true of the working men and women is not less true of the managerial class. In what other country can the managerial class afford to make Saturday as sacred a day for leisure as Sunday? I venture to say without profanity that this is making the best of both the Old and the New Testament.

"And it is not only the slavery of men by work that we are conquering; we are beginning to lighten the slavery of women. It will not be too long before the primitive washing-machines of to-day will become as intelligently human as computers. Now that men are at last beginning to help in the washing up, the brain of man will devote itself to inventing all kinds of domestic machines as efficient as computers.

"But, paradoxically if you will, we must work harder than ever to make the most of our leisure. We must direct the leisure of the young toward enjoying the leisure of their old age. We may confidently expect that the prolongation of human life will slowly but surely increase with every decade of the future. It is our duty to prepare for this now so that the centenarians of the future will be able to enjoy the extra years that the achievements of technology will grant them. Am I being bolder than Jules

Verne or H. G. Wells if I prophesy that the centenarians of to-morrow will be able to enjoy a week-end on the moon as much as the septuagenarians of to-day enjoy a week-end in one of the home counties?

"My work as a historian has given me an insight into the past, but when I was a tutor at my college I realised how increasingly difficult it was to make my pupils take the slightest interest in the past. Those who were working hard for a good degree were able to absorb facts and dates, but they were most of them unable to realise that people in the past were human beings like themselves without any of the technological advantages that have made living conditions so much more comfortable, but nevertheless still human beings.

"I have recently been much struck by the way Topwiski and Vermicello and other great continental directors of drama have brought back Shakespeare from a museum piece to a vital influence by modernising some of his dramas. I hope that British directors will assist in this valuable restoration of Shakespeare to life in the present. I urge them to go further and try to modernise Aeschylus and Sophocles and Euripides. Would not Antigone be a more intelligible figure to young people if Creon were presented as a fascist? Are not Oedipus Colonus and Oedipus Rex nearer to the life of to-day when we see them through the eyes of Freud?"

Sir Oliver Huffam was hoping as he and his Private Secretary ascended in the lift to Dame Jane Fossey's room that she would not allude in the course of the conference to modernising Antigone. With a lifelong respect for compromise he could not compromise over that.

The walls of Dame Jane's room were hung with examples of pop art and abstract art, and Sir Oliver was glad when the rich voice of the Right Honourable Henry Upjohn greeted him and spared him from having to express an opinion about what he considered garish and incomprehensible ugliness.

"Ah, Huffam, there you are! I telephoned to say I

would bring you and Mowart along in my car but you'd
already left the Ministry. You know Dame Jane?"

"How d'ye do, Sir Oliver?" said the Minister of Leisure.

Sir Oliver shook the proferred hand of a monumental
woman in her late fifties with grizzled dark hair and a
nose that any actor playing Julius Caesar would have
envied. Luckily he was not given to imaginative evoca-
tions; otherwise he might have beheld her standing there
as formidable as once upon a time she had seemed standing with shinguards in the Camford goal to repel the
attacks of the Oxbridge forwards.

"I feel sure the Minister of Leisure will appreciate the
fundamental—the logical strength of our arguments,"
the Permanent Secretary murmured to the Minister of
Sanitation in a cautious aside.

"Yes, I hope so, but Jane can be a terror," Mr Upjohn
rumbled in what he supposed was an answering murmur.
"But I'm told she pays a good deal of attention to what
Buncombe says and you've always found him. . . ."

Sir Oliver intervened to introduce the Permanent
Secretary of the Ministry of Leisure to Mr Upjohn.

"I don't think you've met Sir Roger Buncombe,
Minister."

In spite of a long and often laborious career in the Civil
Service Sir Roger looked as jovial and rubicund as Mr
Upjohn himself.

"I was reading *The Times* this morning about that
deputation you had from the Oatshire County Council,
Minister. I'm glad you seemed to see your way to encourage this fellow Narbrow. We regard him as rather an
asset down in Wessex. Dame Jane is most anxious to
encourage a revival of rural sports and pastimes. By the
way, Oliver, do you know anything about smock-racing
at Ascension-tide?"

"About what?" Sir Oliver gasped.

"Apparently it was the custom once upon a time for
girls to race in their smocks for some prize or other."

"That sounds rather amusing," Mr Upjohn observed.

"In these days when young women are wearing less and less in public we thought it might be revived. It's on the agenda for this team and we're sending them round the country to enquire about rural sports and pastimes which have become obsolete. Not blood-sports, of course."

Further enquiries into smock-racing at Ascension-tide were cut short by the arrival of Sir John Wilbraham, the Minister of Movement, with his Permanent Secretary, Sir Wilfred Clarkson; presently the conference was in session.

"Our point is, Dame Jane, that we at the Ministry of Movement are responsible for all and every kind of movement," said Sir John Wilbraham firmly. "When the Cabinet decided it was advisable to amalgamate the Navy, Army and Air Force into a single Ministry of Protection it was felt that a comparable amalgamation of Civil Airlines, Railways, Omnibuses and all other road traffic, and indeed any form of movement in a single Ministry would go far to solve the problem of ever escalating traffic. When the scheme for making the railways pay by raising fares and freight charges drove more and more firms and private individuals to use the roads it became apparent that the problem of movement could only be solved by nationalisation and centralisation."

"Are you proposing to control boy scouts, Sir John?" the Minister of Leisure asked.

The dark eyebrows of Sir John Wilbraham met in a frown.

"We are not proposing to control boy scouts, Dame Jane, but if we found that the movements of boy scouts were a hindrance to traffic we should reserve the right to indicate certain areas where the circulation of boy scouts seemed to be escalating in such a way as to cause inconvenience. And that is why we feel we should reserve the right to indicate certain areas where the escalation of hikers and campers might obstruct the far-reaching plans of the Ministry of Movement, to establish an equitable compromise between the claims of the roads and the railways to transport people and goods. However, I shall make it clear to the Cabinet that the Ministry of Movement will do all in its power to assist the valuable work which is being done by your Ministry, Dame Jane, to direct the public towards making a fuller use of the continually escalating opportunities afforded by the steady escalation of automation."

"I accept that assurance, Sir John, and in return I will give you my assurance that the Ministry of Leisure will always pay the most earnest attention to any undue movement of campers and hikers that might interfere with future projects of the Ministry of Movement."

Sir John Wilbraham said something to his Permanent Secretary, who nodded vigorously.

"Sir Wilfred Clarkson and I are grateful for the willingness with which the Ministry of Leisure has agreed to cooperate with us, Dame Jane. And let me make it perfectly clear that the Ministry of Movement makes no claim to control the movements of campers and hikers...."

"Might I put in a suggestion, Sir John?" the rich voice of Mr Upjohn asked. "Sir Oliver suggested that a more suitable name for the movements of campers and hikers would be 'perambulations'."

This suggestion obviously pleased both the Minister of Movement and his Permanent Secretary. A polysyllable is always a temptation even to a simple soldier. Dame Jane Fossey was less pleased.

"I think 'treks' would be better," she said.

"Provided it didn't lead to a lot of young people demonstrating outside South Africa House. They feel very strongly about apartheid, and 'trek' is definitely an Africaans word," said the Minister of Movement, who was unwilling to relinquish "perambulation" in favour of a mere monosyllable.

"I think we shall soon find a better way for people to take advantage of their extra leisure than demonstrations," Dame Jane Fossey said. "But there is no urgent necessity to decide whether we call the movements of hikers and campers 'perambulations' or 'treks'. What is of immediate importance is to decide how far the Ministry of Sanitation is justified in claiming to interfere with their sanitary arrangements."

"I assure you, Dame Jane, that my Ministry has no desire, no desire whatever to interfere with their sanitary arrangements," said Mr Upjohn. "We do feel, however, that in view of the many regulations we are trying to enforce for domestic sanitation it would add greatly to the work of our Inspectors and Assistant-Inspectors not to mention our Quantity Surveyors if householders could point to the absence of all regulations for hikers and campers. We had the same difficulty over our regulations for railways when it was pointed out that no regulations had been framed to provide for the sanitary arrangements of aeroplanes. We took the matter up with the Ministry of Movement and I am glad to recall the helpful co-operation of Sir John Wilbraham."

"I can assure you, Mr Upjohn," said Dame Jane, "that the last thing my Ministry wants to do is to cause any obstruction in your sanitary arrangements, but I think in view of the important part that hiking already plays in our national life and the still more important part it will play in the life of the Leisure State nothing should be done to discourage hikers. I am glad to see that Sir Oliver Huffam agrees with me."

In fact, Sir Oliver's nod had not been inspired by agreement with the Minister of Leisure; his nod had been in gratitude to the caution which had prevented his impulse to make enquiries through consular channels into the whereabouts of his younger son, who at this moment might be hiking away anywhere in Europe. He jerked himself back into the conference.

"I was considering a compromise, Dame Jane," he said, "a compromise which Mr Upjohn and I have carefully considered, and which I understand he will put before you."

The word compromise sounded as sweet to that con-

ference as the song of the skylark to Shelley, as the melody
of the nightingale to Keats, as the call of the cuckoo to
Wordsworth. All waited in bright-eyed attention for the
Minister of Sanitation, who did not keep them waiting
for a moment.

"The last thing that I or my much esteemed Permanent Secretary wish is to put forward any proposal that
might discourage hiking, football, cricket and not least
hockey." To indicate how well aware he was of Dame
Jane's prowess at hockey Mr Upjohn smiled at her,
which she acknowledged with an answering smile.
"These games are all an essential British heritage, and
let me say that our success in teaching the natives of the
Continent to play football has probably been the major
influence in preventing the cold war from escalating into
a hot war. We must remember, however, that hiking
is as valuable a form of exercise as even golf, and not
merely an exercise for the body but also for the mind.
The hiker as he hikes over hill, over dale across our beloved countryside is hiking his way back into history.
When he hikes up to the top of Skiddaw he recalls the red
flame on Skiddaw that roused the burghers of Carlisle.
When he hikes even as far as Barnet he has hiked back
into the Wars of the Roses. When he hikes along
Hadrian's wall he is hiking not with a knapsack but with
the shield of a Roman legionary."

Sir Oliver felt that his Minister was in danger of finding himself upon a platform in his North Wessex constituency and whispered "compromise".

"I have said so much about hiking," Mr Upjohn continued, "because I am anxious that Dame Jane should
know what importance we attach to her encouragement
of it by her Ministry. If she feels that our suggestion to
occupy ourselves with the sanitary arrangements of
hikers will militate against hiking we are prepared to
abandon our proposal and leave their sanitary arrangements to hikers themselves. The sanitary arrangements
of campers come into a different category. The hiker is

E

here to-day and gone to-morrow. The camper may be here for a week. The Ministry of Sanitation has already undertaken the task of supervising the sanitary arrangements of caravans and has made certain regulations which our Inspectors and Assistant-Inspectors are called upon to strictly enforce, to enforce strictly that is." Mr Upjohn was under the impression that his Permanent Secretary had winced as sharply at the split infinitive as if he had split one of his own nails.

"To enforce most strictly," the Minister of Sanitation went on. "That being the case we feel that people camping without caravans should conform with our regulations. We must all have remarked how much 'No Camping' signs have been escalating all over the countryside. I suggest that the objection of farmers and landed proprietors to camping is the laxity—the looseness—er—the disregard of all sanitary arrangements. So if the Minister of Leisure can see her way to accepting our supervision of the sanitary arrangements of campers we for our part are willing to abandon any effort to supervise the sanitary arrangements of hikers."

Mr Upjohn sat back in his chair with an expression on his face that was probably seen on the face of the village blacksmith when he felt his work had earned a night's repose. That expression was justified when Dame Jane Fossey replied gravely.

"I'm sure that Sir Roger Buncombe will agree with me when I say that the Ministry of Leisure greatly appreciates the compromise offered by the Ministry of Sanitation."

"Yes, indeed," her Permanent Secretary agreed.

"We have never contested the right—indeed the duty of the Ministry of Sanitation to make the strictest regulations for the sanitary arrangements of caravans. People who own caravans or even hire them can well afford to bring their sanitary arrangements into line with the regulations laid down for domestic sanitation. Campers without caravans are often forced to make a more economical use of their leisure and carry with them their own tents, but, as the Minister of Sanitation reminded us, whereas hikers are here to-day and gone to-morrow the camper is inclined to remain for a week or even longer where he has pitched his tent. That being so, Sir Roger Buncombe and I feel that we are justified in withdrawing our objection to the supervision of the sanitary arrangements of campers and we accept the compromise offered to us by the Minister of Sanitation."

It was now the turn of Dame Jane Fossey to sit back in her chair, not perhaps with the satisfied expression on the face of the village blacksmith but with the expression of Jane Fossey of Somerton when she had just sent the ball spinning away from the hungry Oxbridge forwards. She looked across to her Private Secretary, Miss Susan Greathead, M.B.E., who presently returned with a tray on which was a decanter of dark sweet sherry and nine glasses.

"Jane's still at Somerton, Henry," Sir John Wilbraham murmured to Mr Upjohn.

"Thank god it's not cocoa," said Mr Upjohn. "But, Jack, you should have seen them at the Heraeum yesterday when I was lunching with Huffam and asked for a vodka before lunch. It was like a Bateman drawing. You'd have thought Trotsky had come down the chimney."

Sir Oliver joined them at this moment.

"Are you pleased, Minister, with the compromise we have agreed upon?" he asked anxiously.

"I'm quite happy, Huffam. I was grateful to you also, Jack. If you'd stuck out over directing the movements of hikers, Jane would have protected the sanitary arrangements of campers like a hen with her chickens. I think she's making a mistake over calling them 'treks'. If she insists on a monosyllable why not 'hikes'?"

Mr Upjohn declined a glass of Dame Jane's sherry and presently offered to drive the Permanent Secretary and Humphrey Mowart back to Cork Street.

"Now that we've settled things with the Leisure people Huffam, we can get down to this main drain between Oatcester and Hardingham. I'll be going to my constituency at the week-end, and I thought that, if you and Lady Huffam could come and spend it at our place, you and I might drive over to Oatcester and talk to this chap Narbrow. I know it would make a good impression if we fell in with the ideas of these Oatshire people, especially as it's the next constituency to mine."

"We should enjoy a week-end at Shrimpton Magna, Minister."

"I suggest we call for you at Chillingham Gardens on Friday afternoon about three, that'll get us down comfortably in time for dinner at the Grange."

"That's rather a long week-end for me, Minister," Sir Oliver demurred.

"Well, you know, Huffam, I agree with Jane Fossey. I think all Ministries should be closed by one o'clock on Friday. In fact all offices of any kind. The week-end is a sacred British institution. In my opinion it was the week-end which enabled us to pull through two great wars. Why did Hitler always plan his major offensives at the week-end? Because he knew we should be keeping our week-end. And what good did it do him? In my opinion Hitler's disregard of the week-end lost him the war. The Germans were worn out before we were."

"I don't entirely agree with you, Minister, but exceptions prove the rule and next week-end shall be a long week-end for me."

To compensate for what he thought a reckless agreement to leave the Ministry at lunch time next Friday Sir Oliver made up his mind not to leave it till six o'clock on the preceding days.

Chapter 5

WHEN Sir Oliver emerged from the Gloucester Road tube-station it was close on half-past six that evening. The achievement of that compromise at the Ministry of Leisure, the extra hour's work at the Ministry of Sanitation, the rout of the *Times* crossword puzzle, whose defences had held out on the way to Piccadilly this morning, and the pleasure Gertrude would derive from the news of the forthcoming long week-end at Shrimpton Grange, a pleasure unmarred by having to worry about Jeremy's dinner, all these reflections gave a buoyancy to his gait which suggested that of an Olympic champion who had lowered the record for the 100 metres by a tenth of a second rather than the day's end of an overworked Civil Servant. His greeting to Lady Huffam was the nearest he had reached to an authentic Tyrolean yodel for a long time.

"Olly dear, have you had news of Jeremy?" she asked eagerly.

"No, no, but no news is good news," Sir Oliver assured her. "The boys are evidently perambulating about the Continent without causing concern to the local authorities by any breach of regulations."

He put away his coat and hat and joined Lady Huffam in the drawing-room where to her surprise he said he had told Ethel to bring up the sherry.

"Skol," he proclaimed, raising his glass.

"Yes, I do realise how worried you are about Jeremy's missing school, Olly, but it won't be for more than a term, I'm sure."

"Skol is the Scandinavian toast."

"Do you really think we ought to have this rye bread, Olly? Neither of us is putting on weight. Rye bread is so dry. They say it's slimming but I'm sure people who take

rye bread for slimming have to use so much more butter
that they might just as well eat ordinary bread, though
I'm bound to say that although bread gets whiter and
whiter all the time it does taste less and less like the bread
we used to get."

"Skol means 'good health', Gertrude. It has nothing
to do either with school or any kind of bread. I am drinking your good health because we have been invited to
stay with Mr and Mrs Upjohn for a long week-end. They
are calling for us about three o'clock on Friday to drive
us down to Shrimpton Grange. I am an hour later than
usual in getting back from the Ministry, and I may be
even later to-morrow because I shall not be there next
Friday afternoon. Skol." Sir Oliver repeated gravely
before he sipped his glass of sherry.

"What do I say, Olly?" his wife asked.

"You say 'skol' too."

So Lady Huffam said 'skol' and took a sip from her
glass.

"I shall have to get a new frock for our week-end,
Olly," she said with what was almost a glint of Spring in
her pale autumnal eyes.

"You'd better get yourself two," Sir Oliver told her.
When he said this Lady Huffam was so much overcome
that she swallowed the sip of sherry the wrong way and
could only cough an astonished acknowledgment of her
husband's prodigality. For her it was as surprising as the
eruption of an immemorially quiescent volcano.

Whe Lady Huffam's cough had died away Sir Oliver
asked her if she had played hockey at school.

"Not skol," he added, surrendering to a little joke in
the remembrance of that successfully achieved compromise at the Ministry of Leisure. "We did not play it at
St James's."

"Yes, I did play hockey. They made us. But I wasn't
very good at it, Olly; I was apt to trip up over my hockey-
stick and get my shins banged by the other girls. Why do
you want to know if I played hockey at school?"

His rule never to talk about his work at the Ministry prevented Sir Oliver from saying anything about the Minister of Leisure's former prowess at hockey.

"It just occurred to me to ask you, Gertrude," and to banish hockey from the conversation Sir Oliver went on to ask if Ethel had remembered to give that tin of Dandimilk to the dustman.

"Oh, yes, Ethel remembered. But the dustman wouldn't take it away. Ethel and Dorothy gave it to him but he shook it and said his job was to empty dustbins not to turn himself into a milkman. He was so unpleasant about it that Ethel and Dorothy brought the tin back in again."

At this moment Ethel came into the drawing-room to say that Mr Upjohn was on the 'phone and wanted to speak to Sir Oliver.

"Oh, is that you, Huffam? Sorry to bother you but do you know anything about a man who calls himself by the extraordinary name of Scratchbelly?"

"Bury, Minister. Dr Emilius Scratchbury," Sir Oliver corrected.

"Oh, you do know him."

"He was at the Ministry yesterday, asking for our approval of some kind of vegetable milk. I told him that the approval of any kind of milk, vegetable or otherwise, was a matter for the Ministry of Hygiene, not for the Ministry of Sanitation."

"Well, this fellow Scratchbury apparently arrived in Hertford Street with an enormous tin of this milk when my wife was playing bridge and I was at the club. He left it with a note, no address. I'll read it to you.

Dear Mr Minister of Sanitation, I feel that you will want to decide for yourself whether the favourable verdict which Sir Oliver Huffam will pass upon Dandimilk is justified. I am therefore taking the liberty of leaving with you a gallon tin. This if kept in a cool place will provide you with a supply of Dandimilk for a week, at the end of which time I will call on you again and

if as I confidently expect, you and Sir Oliver Huffam enthusiastic-
ally endorse all that we claim for the tonic and mildly laxative
qualities of Dandimilk, and most of all for its freedom from the
insanitary and unhygienic qualities of cows' milk, I venture to hope
that you will give Dandimilk the official recommendation of the
Ministry of Sanitation. Yours faithfully Emilius Scratchbury

"Yes, I see you're right as usual, Huffam. It *is* Scratchbury. Well, what do we do about this fellow? He's not
in my constituency, thank goodness. I'd be out at the
next election if it went round that I was encouraging a
fellow to make milk out of vegetables."

The voice of the Minister ceased to vibrate in the ears
of his Permanent Secretary.

"I hardly know what to advise, Minister, until I get
to Cork Street to-morrow morning and ascertain exactly
what are the duties of the London County Council."

"What on earth have the L.C.C. got to do with this
Scratchbury fellow?"

"I was coming to that, Minister. Yesterday evening
Dr Scratchbury brought a gallon tin of this Dandimilk to
my house, and before I could stop him he slipped away,
leaving the tin behind. I told our maids to give it to the
dustman when he called this morning, but I have just
been informed that after a certain amount of unpleasant-
ness the dustman refused to remove it. As soon as I ascertain which of the various committees of the London
County Council controls the removal and dumping of
waste material I shall communicate by letter with the
officer responsible for carrying out the Committee's
regulations and ascertain if the dustman was acting according to those regulations in refusing to remove this
tin. When we have received an answer, probably toward
the end of next week, we shall be able to know where we
stand as to the disposal of waste material in London."

"But what do we do meanwhile with these damned
tins?"

"I am instructing our maids to put the tin Dr Scratch-

bury left in Chillingham Gardens into our area dustbin.
May I suggest, Minister, that you give instructions to
your domestic staff along the same lines?"

"But this Scratchbury fellow says it must be kept in a
cool place. This October sunshine isn't summer sunshine but it may make the inside of a dustbin too warm."

"If I may say so, Minister, it seems to me immaterial
what happens to the contents of these tins."

"You don't think they might explode in a warm place?
Perhaps it would be wiser to open and empty them."

"I beg you not to empty the tin, Minister. Dr Scratchbury might claim that we had both of us drunk a gallon
of his Dandimilk. Imagine what the popular Press would
make of a story that the Minister of Sanitation and the
Permanent Secretary of his Ministry had been drinking
Dandimilk. Before we knew where we were they would
be hinting that we were financially interested in the
success of Dandimilk."

"Yes, I see your point, Huffam."

"Rely on me, Minister, to ascertain to-morrow morning the right procedure to obtain the removal of these
undesirable tins. And before you hang up the receiver
may I say how much Lady Huffam and I are looking
forward to next week-end?"

As he was walking back upstairs to rejoin his wife in
the drawing-room Sir Oliver was remembering those
telephone calls of over twenty years ago from the Minister of Waste when he was only a Principal Private Secretary and his prospect of getting the Bath in the New Year's
Honours was clouded by the difficulty of removing that
bath deposited outside Mr Apsley Howe's house in Eaton
Square. To-day the removal of that gallon tin of Dandimilk from Mr Henry Upjohn's house in Hertford Street
left him as a Permanent Secretary and a K.C.B. completely unperturbed.

In Cork Street next morning Sir Oliver asked Humphrey Mowart what was the quickest way to find out about
the constitution of the London County Council.

"Whitaker ought to tell us. What exactly were you wanting to know?"

"I want to ascertain the appropriate quarter in which to enquire what are the exact duties of a dustman. It was remiss of me not to ascertain this before, Humphrey. True, the Ministry of Waste is responsible for Waste Material throughout England, Wales *and* Scotland, though I remember we had our usual difficulties with the Scottish Office over this. At the same time, our Ministry is responsible for drawing the attention of the Ministry of Waste to any accumulation of waste material that seems to be affecting the sanitary conditions of the immediate vicinity. Let me look at Whitaker."

Sir Oliver, head bent over the column, read 'The method by which the Council discharges the multitudinous duties entrusted to it is a generous delegation of powers to committees under well-defined rules, subject to the reservation to the Council itself of decisions or questions of finance, matters of principle, and to periodical reports of action taken. In addition to members of the Council, co-opted members are included on the following committees: Children's, Education, Health, Housing and Welfare."

"The London County Council doesn't seem to have any committee to deal with the cleansing of streets," Sir Oliver observed.

"I fancy that's in the hands of the Borough Councils, sir."

"So that we would have to communicate with the Council of the Royal Borough of Kensington. I don't like the idea of asking a Borough Council about the duties of a dustman, Humphrey. It would be—well, to put it frankly, a little *infra dig.* for the Ministry of Sanitation to be unaware of what the duties of a dustman are."

"May I ask, sir, why you want to find out about the duties of a dustman?" the Private Secretary asked.

Sir Oliver told him about the two gallons of Dandimilk in Chillingham Gardens and Hertford Street.

"Well, sir, as I feel a little responsible for Dr Scratchbury's pestering you and the Minister. . . ."

"You *were* a bit impulsive, Humphrey, when you sent him to the Home Office but you are not in the least to blame for his leaving those two gallons of Dandimilk with the Minister and myself. But what were you going to suggest?"

"I was going to suggest, sir, that I would collect the two gallons and return them to Dandimilk."

"But do we know where this Dandimilk is made?"

"No, I've not yet found out that, but we do know that they have an office in the City in Gog and Magog Lane. I've got my car and I suggest calling at the Minister's house and yours and taking these gallon tins to Gog and Magog Lane. I'll go in the lunch interval."

"But what about your own lunch, Humphrey?"

"I'll get a snack somewhere, sir. Don't worry about that."

Humphrey Mowart's offer to relieve the Minister and the Permanent Secretary of those tins of Dandimilk may have struck him as an easier procedure from his point of view than drafting a series of letters to various bodies constituted by the *Local Government Act* 1888 to ascertain what were the duties of a dustman. Whatever may have been the underlying motive the offer was gratefully accepted by his Chief.

While the Permanent Secretary of the Ministry of Sanitation and the Permanent Secretary of the Ministry of Leisure were agreeing over a lunch table at the Heraeum about the success of the compromise achieved at yesterday morning's conference, Humphrey Mowart with two gallon-tins of Dandimilk was on his way to the City. It took him some time to find Gog and Magog Lane, an ancient cul-de-sac which had survived both the Fire of London and the German Blitz. It took him even longer to discover a parking place for his car, which the City police would not allow him to drive into Gog and Magog Lane.

"I want to leave these two tins at Number Thirteen. I can quite easily back out."

"I'm sorry, sir. But we have to forbid cars to drive into the Lane to avoid them parking there."

"But I shouldn't be a moment."

The City constable shook his head.

"Well, may I leave the car at the entrance while I take these two tins to Number Thirteen?"

"No, sir, I can't let you do that. The nearest parking place is where the old Smockmakers Hall used to be. You'll probably find a place all right as it's the lunch hour."

Humphrey Mowart did manage to park his car in an open space not yet covered by one of the glass and concrete ant-hills of financial industry and with a gallon tin of Dandimilk under each arm he made his embarrassed way to 13 Gog and Magog Lane. He read with relief "Dandimilk (Ltd)" on the third floor, but when he reached it and knocked on the door, there was no reply. Humphrey looked at his watch. It was close on two.

"They may not be back for another hour," he said to himself. "And Huffy will be back in Cork Street by half-past with that long week-end in view. I'll just have to leave these confounded tins outside the door."

Humphrey was on the point of descending from the third floor of 13 Gog and Magog Lane when Dr Emilius Scratchbury himself appeared.

"Ah, I'm glad you've come, Dr Scratchbury," said the Private Secretary. "The Minister of Sanitation and the Permanent Secretary desired me to return these two tins of your Dandimilk and to say that on no account are you to approach them again except through official channels. I am further instructed to enquire where this Dandimilk is manufactured."

Dr Scratchbury's dark eyes gleamed as triumphantly as those of a conspirator after a successful assassination.

"That is a secret," said Dr Scratchbury. "And not being an official secret it is likely to remain a secret."

"In that case I must notify you that strict instructions

will be given that should you enquire for any of the
officials at the Ministry of Sanitation you will not be admitted. I hope that is clear."

As Humphrey walked downstairs from the Dandimilk
office he wished he could feel as sure as he should like to
feel that it *was* clear.

After the job he had to extricate his car from what had
been the site of the Smockmakers Hall and with every
traffic light against him from the heart of the City to
Cork Street it was twenty minutes to three when Humphrey Mowart reached his Chief's room.

"I've been back twenty minutes," said Sir Oliver.

"Yes, sir. I'm sorry, but I had rather a job to find Gog
and Magog Lane, and the traffic was worse than usual.
However, I saw Dr Scratchbury, handed over the two
tins and made it clear to him that he would not be admitted to the Ministry with or without tins of Dandimilk.

"And also, I hope, that he was not to leave tins of this
stuff in Hertford Street or Chillingham Gardens?"

"I made it clear that he was only to approach us
through official channels and when he refused to tell me
where this stuff was made I impressed on him that
official channels were now definitely closed to him at the
Ministry of Sanitation. I don't think we shall have any
further trouble with Dr Scratchbury."

"I hope not," said Sir Oliver. "But one must always be
on one's guard against premature optimism."

"Oh, definitely, sir," Humphrey agreed, remembering
his lost lunch. It was just as well that one of the Ministry
messengers was able to secure him a sizeable bun for his
tea; Sir Oliver did not leave the Ministry until nearly
seven o'clock.

"I'm letting you get away like myself on Friday,
Humphrey, so you may be a bit later to-morrow and
Thursday."

On Friday morning Lady Huffam rang up Humphrey
Mowart at the Ministry and asked him to tell Sir Oliver
that a letter had arrived from Jeremy by the second post.

Humphrey was quick to let Sir Oliver hear this news; to his relief, his Chief was striding away toward the Piccadilly tube before noon.

"Neither Sir Oliver nor I will be back this afternoon," he told Sergeant-major Hadnutt.

For a moment Sir Oliver was taken aback to see a case going through the front door of 9 Chillingham Gardens. To his relief it was not another tin of Dandimilk but the television set for downstairs.

"They're going to fix it up for them after we leave. Something has to be done about something they call an aerial," said Lady Huffam. "And here is Jeremy's letter, Olly."

"Somewhere in France," Sir Oliver commented as he read the address. "That takes me back to the time when my father used to get letters in the Great War addressed 'Somewhere in France'."

Sir Oliver continued to read:

Dear Mum and Dad,

Dick Horner and I crossed over by Southampton and Havre because it was the cheapest crossing. The people in France are awfully decent and we are hitch-hiking on our way to Italy. We tossed up to see whether we should hitch-hike to Spain or Italy and it came down Italy. I was glad about this because Spain is absolutely overrun with English people, and although there wouldn't be quite so many as there were in August and September there would still be plenty.

I am writing this in a barn (grange in French) and we hope to get into Italy by the beginning of next week. You cannot imagine what a relief it is to be finished with school. . . .

"Finished with school?" Sir Oliver commented severely.

"Oh, I'm sure in two or three weeks he'll feel differently about school," said Jeremy's mother.

"I hope so, indeed," said Jeremy's father, as he read on.

... and to be writing this letter to you instead of a Latin prose or a boring English essay. I'm sure even Dad must get tired of paper at the Ministry. The moon is shining and I feel happier than I've ever felt, so I hope you are not worrying about me. It's a pity we are too late for the vendange (vintage). We might have earned some good wages but the farmer in whose grange we are staying is hanging up tobacco and we are going to work for him to-morrow. He gave us a jolly good supper. With love to you both

Jeremy

P.S. Will you tell Nigel I was a bit surprised to find the English pound is only worth thirteen francs and a bit. The Treasury will have to pull its socks up!

"Let me look at the postmark," said Sir Oliver. He looked and shook his head. "Post offices seem to be deteriorating everywhere. Illegible. But even if it was legible we shouldn't know the name of the farm."

"I wonder if Mr Horner had heard from his son. Would it be a good idea to ring him up, Olly?"

Sir Oliver thought it was a good idea. To the feminine voice that answered the telephone Sir Oliver announced that Sir Oliver Huffam was speaking.

"Mr Horner's at his office, but he'll be out at lunch now."

"Is that Miss Horner speaking?"

"It's Susan Horner, yes."

"I wonder if your father had a letter from his son in France this morning?"

"Yes, rather. My mother read it to him over the 'phone. It came by the second post."

"Will you tell your father and mother that we have had a letter from my son Jeremy."

"Good old Huffy! How is he? Dick says they're having a fabulous time."

"Did your brother put an address in his letter?"

"No, he just put 'Somewhere in France'. We tried to make out what the postmark was but it was all blurred. Dick said they were making for Italy."

"Thank you, Miss Horner."

Sir Oliver hung up and returned to the drawing-room.

"I was not able to communicate directly with Mr Horner, but it would seem that Mrs Horner read her son's letter to him over the telephone. It confirms their intention of hiking to Italy."

"I read Jeremy's letter to Rosemary, and she did laugh so over the postscript for Nigel."

"It hadn't occurred to me that it was particularly funny," said Sir Oliver.

It was ten minutes past three when Mr Upjohn's Rolls-Royce stopped outside 9 Chillingham Gardens. The long week-end had started.

Chapter 6

IT was just after five when the Rolls reached the ancient village of Shrimpton Magna, and at the other end of it turned into the avenue of limes that led to Shrimpton Grange.

"This is, of course, your first visit to the Moated Grange, Huffam," said the Minister. "I bought it when old Lord Shrimpton died five years ago and Molly has done marvels with it. About all that's left of the old place inside is the ghost."

"Ghost? Is there a ghost?" Lady Huffam asked nervously.

"We've never seen it," Mrs Upjohn laughed.

She was a merry blonde who looked five years younger than her forty years in spite of two boys at Eton and a daughter at Roedean.

"But of course we don't let them think in the village that the ghost has gone with all the other junk we had to get rid of," said the Member for North Wessex. "It would cost me a few votes if they thought we'd got rid of the ghost."

Tea was in the Old Hall and as they sat round a log fire under the beams of a vaulted ceiling Lady Huffam murmured,

" 'Mariana and the Moated Grange'. That takes me back to my schooldays. And the ghost? What is it the ghost of?"

"Oh, the usual thing," said the Minister. "Somebody stalking around with his head on a plate."

After tea the Minister took his Permanent Secretary to the library; Mrs Upjohn suggested that Lady Huffam might like a rest before dinner.

"Jock Ackroyd and his wife are staying with us for a

F

couple of nights," the Minister told his Permanent Secretary. "But they won't be here before seven. Ackroyd is very pleased to hear we're proposing to divert that main drain."

"The diversion is still being carefully considered, Minister."

"Yes, but I'm sure it's the right thing to do. I thought you and I would have a morning round of golf and then drive in to Oatcester where Ackroyd has arranged lunch at the Blue Bull at which we'll meet Colonel Halfhead—he pronounces it Halford. He's the big Territorial drum, and we shall want his O.K. when we start digging up Hardingham Heath. Brown-Brown, the M.F.H. of the Oatshire, will be there too. And also the two Mayors. But the important contact is this farmer, Narbrow. I've arranged with my wife that you and I and Ackroyd will have an early dinner and go along to Ye Olde Farme for a display by the Hardingham morris-dancers in his barn. Then I thought I'd make a little speech and say how sympathetic we were at the Ministry to rural sports and pastimes."

"Dame Jane won't think that is overlapping?" Sir Oliver queried doubtfully.

"No, no, but if you think it wiser, I'll say we are sympathetic with the Ministry of Leisure's interest in the revival and preservation of country sports and pastimes and that we have decided to divert the new main drain between Oatcester and Hardingham by taking it across Hardingham Heath instead of the more direct route by Mr Narbrow's farm. Molly is going to have a few people to dinner for bridge afterwards. Is Lady Huffam a great hand at bridge?"

"No, my wife doesn't play cards at all."

"Well, she'll have to entertain the dummies."

"I'm sure she'll be only too glad to visit the deaf and dumb school."

"You evidently don't play bridge either, Huffam."

"No, I never learnt. But to return to our main drain,

Minister. You have carefully considered the additional cost?"

"As long as it doesn't escalate beyond £75,000 I think it's justified."

"The Chief Quantity Surveyor estimated £50,000 but said it might be more. I think we can feel reasonably sure that it will not rise above £75,000."

Sir Oliver slightly emphasized "rise". He refused to encourage the escalation of escalation.

"By the way, you might thank that Private Secretary of yours for the way he got rid of that tin for us. Mowart, isn't that his name? My wife wants to ask him to dinner one night."

"I'm glad he was able to dispose of that tin satisfactorily. We had some difficulty at my house with the dustman and I had considered taking up the matter with the Borough Council, but I decided that immediate action was imperative and I empowered Humphrey Mowart to take such action."

When the Minister of Sanitation went up to dress for dinner, his wife with a merry laugh suddenly cried,

"Got it."

"Got what, Molly?"

"What that Permanent Secretary of yours reminds me of. A plug."

"A plug?"

"Yes, a long dangling plug. I suppose that's why he is Permanent Secretary of the Ministry of Sanitation. And that wife of his. Phew!"

"She's quite an agreeable woman," said Mr Upjohn.

"She's too agreeable. She agreed with everything. But you didn't have her for half an hour after tea. You were pulling the plug in the library."

"For goodness' sake, my dear, don't give Huffam the idea that you're bored by this week-end."

"I'm not such a bad hostess as that, Henry."

"No, of course you're a marvellous hostess, and don't think I don't realise what a part you've played in my political career when I say how much any Minister is dependent upon his permanent officials. Without them he'd be lost. What kind of a showing should I make at question time without the answers provided for me by the permanent officials at my Ministry? What do I know about sanitation?"

"You know how to pull the plug and that's what you do, Henry."

"Yes, but please don't make that crack to Betty Ackroyd. You know how indiscreet she is. Suppose Huffam heard you'd compared him to a plug? He might resent it. He might even give me the wrong answer for question time. After all he *is* human."

"Is he?"

Luckily for the Right Honourable Henry Upjohn there was no doubt about his wife's humanity.

"Don't worry, Henry. When the P.M. has his next shuffle, I'll do all I can to see that he deals you a good hand. Hurry up now and finish your dressing. I hear the Ackroyds arriving."

The member for Oatshire looked like what the member for Oatshire ought to look, a large and jovial man proud of his constituency, which had somehow escaped the inclusion of any industrial centre to disturb his comfortable majority.

"I always rely on Betty to keep me in touch with what's going on in town," he used to say.

And indeed Mrs Ackroyd with her dark bright eyes was never out of touch.

"I'm glad dear old Jock isn't in the Cabinet," she said to her hostess that night when Sir Oliver and Lady Huffam had retired.

"But Henry isn't in the Cabinet."

"Well, I mean in office or whatever it's called. You must admit, Molly, that the Huffams are on the heavy side."

The Minister of Sanitation looked apprehensive.

"Oh, well, you know, Henry depends a great deal on Sir Oliver's advice," said Mrs Upjohn.

The Minister gave his wife a grateful smile. She had resisted that quip she had made about Huffam before dinner.

"Yes, if Jock ever gets into office. . . ."

"Which he never will, thank god," said Mrs Ackroyd.

"If Jock had to be responsible for sanitation all over England and Wales he'd be very grateful to his Permanent Secretary," Henry Upjohn averred.

"If Jock was responsible for sanitation we should all have typhoid. Wouldn't we, Jock?" his wife laughed. "You've no idea what a job I had with him when we were bringing Tailbrush Manor out of the fifteenth century into the twentieth. 'You'll never be a *Privy* Councillor,' I used to tell him."

The Right Honourable Henry Upjohn thought for a moment about trying that joke at the next political meeting in his constituency but ruled it out at once. A North Wessex audience was not a North Kensington audience.

At breakfast next morning the member for Oatshire announced that he and his wife were going to drive into Oatcester.

"Betty has to visit a couple of girls' schools and my agent wants to have a pow-wow with me. She'll come back and I'll meet you and Sir Oliver at the Blue Bull at twelve-thirty when you've had your round."

Molly Upjohn's merry eyes were clouded. Should she suggest that Lady Huffam and she should go into Oatcester with the Ackroyds? No, that would mean she would have to maunder round the cathedral with Lady Huffam while Betty Ackroyd was at her girls' schools.

"You'll come back from Oatcester as soon as you can, Betty, won't you?" she pleaded in a voice which, if it had been heard in the week's good cause over the Radio, would have wrung cheques out of all the Scrooges in Great Britain. "You mustn't leave Lady Huffam and me *too* long?"

Betty Ackroyd recognised the appeal and winked at Molly Upjohn.

"I'll be back before you and Lady Huffam have finished looking at your fabulous chrysanthemums."

"Chrysanthemums, oh, I *am* so fond of chrysanthemums," Lady Huffam almost gushed. "I always say what would autumn be without chrysanthemums."

"That's splendid," Mrs Upjohn exclaimed. "Burrows will adore showing you his chrysanthemums. He's hoping for an A.M. at the Vincent Hall at the end of the month. I shall leave you and him together. He doesn't often have a chance to talk about his chrysanthemums with a connoisseur."

"I could hardly call myself that, Mrs Upjohn," Lady Huffam gently protested.

"But you will be when you've had an hour with Burrows," her hostess assured her.

At the golf-links the Minister of Sanitation enjoyed the satisfaction of defeating his Permanent Secretary.

"It was that bunker at the twelfth which cost you the game, Huffam."

"We have so many bunkers to negotiate in Cork Street, Minister, that I can't get in as much golf at the week-end as I should like."

"No, I appreciate that. You're certainly scratch for paper bunkers."

When they reached the club-house the secretary, who had the not inappropriate name of Greenman, asked if he might speak to the Minister.

"It's about this proposed main drain between Oatcester and Hardingham, Mr Upjohn. Word is going round that it is to be diverted to pass under Hardingham Heath."

"This is Sir Oliver Huffam, Mr Greenman, the Permanent Secretary of the Ministry of Sanitation."

"The proposal to divert the new main drain under Hardingham Heath is being carefully considered," said Sir Oliver.

"I think I ought to let you know, sir, that the North

Wessex Golf Club has been approached by the Oatshire
Golf Club with a view to joining with them in laying out
a nine-hole course on Hardingham Heath for beginners.
Our Club and the Oatshire Club are getting many complaints from members of the way beginners are apt to
obstruct the game. We have been in communication
with the Ministry of Leisure who are prepared to contri-
bute half the cost of the new links. Our committee has
gladly accepted this proposal and I have no doubt the
committee of the Oatshire Golf Club will be equally
glad to accept it."

"That sounds very satisfactory. I do agree that
novices are often just walking bunkers," said Mr Upjohn.
"When do you hope to begin laying out the new course?"

"That is the problem, Mr Upjohn. We are anxious to
know whether the proposed main drain will pass over the
area we have in mind for the new course. That is why I
ventured to bring the matter before you," said Mr Greenman.

"If a decision is finally made to take the main drain
under Hardingham Heath," Sir Oliver said, "the afore-
said main drain will not pass *over* Hardingham Heath."

"I appreciate that, Sir Oliver. It's the preliminary
excavation we are anxious about."

"You mean it might make too big a hole in one of your
greens even for a novice at putting to keep his ball out
of it?" Mr Upjohn chuckled.

Mr Greenman did not think this was a particularly
good joke but he thought it tactful to laugh at it.

"What we really want to know is when you intend to
start work on this main drain."

"You can hardly expect the Ministry of Sanitation to
give you even an approximate date," the Permanent Secretary observed reproachfully. "The proper proceeding
is to notify the Ministry of Sanitation of this scheme for
a new nine-hole course. At the same time to notify the
Ministry of Sanitation that the Ministry of Leisure has
approved the scheme. The Ministry of Sanitation will

then communicate with the Ministry of Leisure to ascertain if the Ministry of Leisure has approved it. Should the answer be in the affirmative the Ministry of Sanitation will require a detailed plan of the area envisaged for the new golf-course on Hardingham Heath. In due course a Quantity Surveyor from the Ministry of Sanitation will survey the area, after which he will in due course make his report. The report will be carefully studied in order to ascertain to what extent work on laying this projected main drain will affect the laying out of the projected golf-course. All this will take some time, and if I may offer you some advice *un*officially, Mr Greenman, I should advise you to do your best to deter your committee from taking anything in the nature of precipitate action."

By the time Sir Oliver had finished leading Mr Greenman up the appropriate steps to communicate with the Ministry of Sanitation the little secretary looked as exhausted as a mountaineer who had managed to scale the difficult face of an Alpine peak.

"Don't worry, Mr Greenman," the Minister told him with fruity geniality, "we will do our best at the Ministry to further your plans. I'll take the first opportunity I get of telling the Minister of Leisure how much her attitude towards the new golf-course is appreciated in North Wessex and Oatshire."

Sir Oliver sighed gently to himself, as Mr Greenman said gratefully,

"Thank you very much, Mr Upjohn. You won't mind if I tell my committee what you've just told me?"

"Not at all."

"It'll buck them up no end," the secretary of the North Wessex Golf Club assured him. Sir Oliver sighed again.

In the car on the way to Oatcester, he said,

"I hope Mr Greenman won't give his committee the impression that we consider this golf-course of as much importance as our main drain, Minister."

"No, no, no, you made that perfectly clear, Huffam.

But I didn't want it to go round the constituency that we were being obstructive. North Wessex is one of the safest seats in the country and I want to keep it safe. You permanent officials don't always realise how lucky you are in not having to think about votes."

There was silence for a while which was broken by the Minister's asking,

"Wasn't there a battle in the American War of Independence called Bunker's Hill?"

"I believe there was."

"And we were bunkered as I remember. It was lucky for the Yanks that they were up against the soldiers. If they'd been up against the Civil Service they might have been bunkered themselves. In fact I'm quite sure they would have been."

It was after half-past twelve when the car came over the edge of the Wessex Downs and the twin towers of Oatcester Cathedral were seen in the wide level landscape below under the blue and white of the October sky.

"Do you know our cathedral, Huffam?"

"I haven't been round it since I was here during the last war. It was when the Ministry of Waste was making that great drive for metal. I remember a difficult interview I had with the Dean and Chapter who were making objections to our proposal to remove the old wrought-iron railings at the entrance to the Close. The Dean himself was most co-operative but some of the Canons were definitely unpatriotic. I recall one of them who was more in touch with the present saying, jokingly of course, 'I hope the Ministry won't think some of my reverend brethren are old gun-metal'."

"I bet that was old Canon Bates."

"And we had trouble too with the City Council," Sir Oliver continued. "There was a handsomely chased Spanish Armada cannon in the Market Square, a valuable piece of scrap metal, but there was a meeting to protest against its removal at which a man called Narbrow. . . ."

Sir Oliver stopped and clicked his fingers.

"Of course. I knew that name was somehow familiar to me, and it's suddenly come back to me. Yes, this Narbrow man walked about beating what he called Drake's drum until the military authorities intervened on security grounds. They were afraid the Home Guard would think it was a signal that the Germans had landed in South Wessex."

"I was in Africa at the time," said the Minister, "and I remember my wife writing me an amusing letter about it, but that bit about the Home Guard must have been blotted out by the censor people. I hadn't heard that before. You must remind Narbrow of Drake's drum when we visit him this evening."

"If you'll forgive me, Minister. I feel that would be unwise. In the first place what happened on that occasion in Oatcester is technically an official secret. I was myself in a Civil Service battalion of the Home Guard. I don't suppose it would be treated officially as an official secret, but I think at a time like this when the papers are making so much about security in the Civil Service it would not do for a high permanent official like myself to talk about what is technically an official secret. There is, moreover, a really serious objection to my reminding Mr Narbrow about Drake's drum. We were unsuccessful at the Ministry of Waste in obtaining that cannon as a piece of scrap metal; remembering our lack of success which he may attribute to his beating of that drum, Mr Narbrow might feel he was in a poition to dictate to the Ministry of Sanitation about the direction of the main drain. We should remember, and I do hope you will make this clear to Mr Ackroyd and the other people we shall be meeting at lunch, that the direction of the main drain is still being carefully considered and that whatever decision is finally made that decision will be made by the Ministry of Sanitation."

What the Minister was inclined to think was a sermon by his Permanent Secretary was brought to an end by their arrival in the Market Square of Oatcester where the salvaged Armada cannon still presided over a large bed of Michaelmas daisies. They were warmly greeted by the Member for Oatshire when they alighted at the Blue Bull from the Rolls.

"Ah, here you are. Good! We've time for your vodka before lunch, Henry. It'll be the first bottle of vodka ever uncorked in Oatcester but I've promised the barman it won't explode."

They passed into the smoke-room where Sir Oliver sipped very slowly a glass of vermouth, hoping the while that his Minister's glass of vodka would not lead him into making rash promises or even worse into precipitate action.

"Now let me go over again who's coming," said their host. "First there are the two Mayors. John Gollop, the Mayor of Oatcester, has a big ironmonger's shop. He's given a lot to party funds and I'm hoping to get him a K in the Birthday Honours next year. I'm told there's no chance in the New Year's Honours. I do wish the P.M. would realise that, however safe these two seats are at the moment, there's always the risk of their becoming marginal when one of these confounded new towns is planted on us."

"I don't think Eddy Pinkney will do that," said Henry Upjohn.

"No, I hope not, but he's damned ambitious and he has got the P.M.'s ear. He's making a big splash as Minister of Accommodation. Pinkney's a good name for him. However, sufficient for the day . . . the other Mayor, William Chuff, is a builder and of course he's anxious to see Hardingham expand. I'm bound to say the new Council houses they've put up there are quite good. Well, those two are the most important people for you to get on your side over this main drain and I know you'll appreciate that, Henry. And of course Narbrow. I didn't ask him to this lunch because we'll be seeing him this evening and I didn't want him to take up the whole of the conversation. Colonel Halfhead . . . for god's sake remember he pronounces it Halford . . . is in such a rage at the moment about the Ministry of Protection's threat to the future of the Territorials that it would be tactful, Henry, if you said something about your admiration for the way the Territorials fought in Africa. That'll set him off laying into the Ministry of Protection, and he'll forget all about the main drain. The M.F.H., Rupert Brown-Brown, is the son of a fellow who made a fortune out of some patent food. He was up at Trinity the same time as I was, and is quite harmless when dismounted. All you've got to do with him is to say you'll notify him in good time when you are going to start work on the drain so that hounds meet in another part of the country."

"And now there's one more guest, whom I only invited this morning. That is Walter Lindfield, the Captain of the Oatshire Golf Club. Apparently there is a proposal to make a new nine-hole course. . . ."

"Yes, Sir Oliver and I have just been hearing about that from the secretary of the North Wessex. I think it's a jolly good idea, but we made it clear to Mr Greenman that we are not yet in a position at the Ministry to say definitely what direction the drain will take nor when work upon it will begin."

The Minister looked round for his reply to be approved by his Permanent Secretary. Sir Oliver gave his approval with a grave nod, and Mr Upjohn felt as pleased as a small boy who has been patted on the back by his headmaster for the success of his answers in a general knowledge paper.

"I'll tell Lindfield what you say. He's quite a good chap. He takes golf rather too seriously for me, but then most golfers do."

During lunch the Minister of Sanitation avoided committing himself to any positive answer to the various questions he was asked. He sat on the fence as easily as Blondin trod the tight-rope. What mattered was that when the lunch was over the guests all went away from the Blue Bull, convinced that the main drain between Oatcester and Hardingham would be of the greatest benefit to Oatshire and that in the construction of it the interests of everybody would be carefully borne in mind.

On the way back to Shrimpton Grange Sir Oliver Huffam reflected gratefully that at last he was piloting a Minister who believed discretion really was the better part of valour.

Chapter 7

THE golden hunters' moon was shining down when the Minister of Sanitation, the Permanent Secretary and the Member for Oatshire arrived at Ye Olde Farme to be greeted by Farmer William Narbrow in the rich dialect of Oatshire. No attempt will be made to reproduce it phonetically. The reader who is familiar with the professional bucolics of the B.B.C. will know how Farmer Narbrow said what he said.

"Come right in, gentlemen, come right in, and drink a glass of good old Saxon mead such as King Alfred himself would have relished."

One would have expected Farmer Narbrow to look as richly bucolic as his voice. In fact he looked much more like the member of a repertory company, with the blue chin of a well-shaved actor. One might then have suspected from his appearance that he was a better actor than farmer. In fact he was a thoroughly competent farmer and his herd of Oatshires held its own with the Friesian invaders as doughtily as King Alfred held his own with the Danish invaders.

When his guests were sitting in the farmhouse parlour with brimming glasses of mead in their hands, Sir Oliver in a Glastonbury chair looking like an early example of Gothic sculpture, Farmer Narbrow started to hold forth with a slow relentless garrulity that would have baffled even a B.B.C. question-master's powers of interruption.

"You'll admit, gentlemen, that a herd of Oatshires like mine oughtn't to be put off their milk by a drain right across their favourite bit of grazing. I hold with farming as farming was. I'm not cutting down all my hedges. I'm not poisoning good ground with these so-called pesticides. They may kill the blooming pests but they're killing the butterflies and the birds just as fast. I don't hold with tractors. I plough my land with decent shire horses. You can't get mushrooms with tractor-manure. You put this main drain right across my land and all I've done to keep Ye Olde Farme like what a farm used to be will go for nought.

"But there's another side to it. I'm holding on fast to old country sports and pastimes. It's tilting the quintain at Ye Olde Farme not darts. We had some young fellows here from this new Ministry of Leisure and we put 'em on to chasing a greasy pig and they were so taken with it I had a letter from the Ministry to say how much they were indebted (yes, those were the very words; I can show you their letter) how much they were indebted to me for bringing my quintain to their notice and that they were bearing in mind tilting the quintain as a valuable substitute in summer for darts.

"What I want you gentlemen to realise is that Ye Olde Farme is now a recognised attraction for tourists, particularly American tourists. My harvest home celebrations every September are famous and next year they will be on television. I'm going to show the reapers coming to the last bit of corn and all of them reaping it together so that Seers don't round on 'em. . . ."

"Seers?" Mr Upjohn put in.

"Seers, the Roman goddess of the harvest. They used to make an image of her out of the last bits of corn which they called the Nack. And I've one old reaper of over eighty who can still do it. If this main drain is being laid across my farm when the television people are here, well, it's not going to improve the picture of the waggon coming back from the cornfield with the gleaners singing folk songs and me holding up Seers to bring luck for next year's harvest."

"I could go on for ever about what I've tried to do all my life to keep up the Old England. Mr G. K. Chesterton came down once to Oatcester to give a talk to our debating society and he said I was going the right way and no mistake. Of course I didn't have Bill's Bottom in those days. I only wish he could have seen what I've done with Ye Olde Farme."

"But you didn't keep up its name," the Minister managed to get in when Mr Narbrow was just too slow in taking in fresh breath.

"Well, Mr Upjohn, my name being William and being known always as Bill Narbrow it was a bit awkward for me, and which was why I called it Ye Olde Farme. But to come back to this main drain. I can assure you that everybody in Oatshire was pleased when they heard you were hoping to take it by way of the Heath. The Oatcester and Hardingham folk have had their arguments from time to time. I'm not denying it, and when you find the Oatcester and the Hardingham folk agreeing about something it's a big argument for the Heath. Mr Ackroyd will tell you I've always been a great supporter of his and I wouldn't like something this Government did to make any of the Oatcester and Hardingham folk think it was time to give the other side a chance. Still, there it is, people being what they are. Oh yes, I know these golfers are grumbling a bit because they're afraid the drain may interfere with this new golf ground they're talking about. Now even if I wanted to, it wouldn't be any use for me to try and stop people from playing golf, but what I say is there's a place for everything and there's no place for golf on an old English farm, and if my best grazing is to be spoilt because the Government's afraid of a few golfers, all I can say is the Government isn't what we all hoped it was going to be. Golf? It isn't even a good old English game. Who gave us golf? The Scotch. And why did they give it us? The Scotch don't give away anything for nothing. We all know they gave us golf so as we'd waste time playing golf and let them get all the best jobs. Oh, they knew what they were doing all right, the Scotch did."

Whether it was that Sir Oliver could no longer bear to hear his only exercise thus maligned or that if Mr

Narbrow did not stop talking his occasional sip at the mead would end in his emptying the mug, or perhaps because he had already taken so many sips, Sir Oliver came as near to precipitate action as he had ever come in his life.

"You may take it, Mr Narbrow," he said, "that the main drain between Oatcester and Hardingham will not pass your farm but will be diverted by way of Hardingham Heath. I think that is your decision, Minister."

"It certainly is, Sir Oliver, and I hope, Mr Narbrow, that if you ever pass through Shrimpton Magna you will give me the pleasure of visiting the Grange. It is a fine old relic of our country's past. Incidentally, we have a ghost. Have you ever seen a ghost?"

The farmer smacked his thigh.

"Well, darn me if that beant a proper coincidence. That ghost of yours at Shrimpton Grange, don't it go mouching around carrying its head?"

"So they say," Mr Upjohn replied. "It's the ghost of a former Earl of Shrimpton whose head was cut off in the Wars of the Roses. Though, mind you, I haven't seen it myself."

"Listen to this for a coincidence. All my days I've been hoping to see a ghost, and darn me, this very evening just before the moon came up I saw a ghost, and he were carrying what must have been his head in his hands. I couldn't see his face because it were covered with a helmet. Well, I'm properly jiggered. I was so pleased when I thought what an attraction this ghost was going to be for the tourists that I couldn't think of nothing else for the moment. And when I looked again it was gone. Come along, gentlemen, let me fill up your mugs."

The two members declared that much as they had enjoyed the mead they would not drink any more. Sir Oliver said nothing. He merely put a hand over his mug.

"Well, the morris-dancers will be here by now. We'd better be going along to the barn," the farmer told his guests. "Of course ordinarily they dance in the streets of Hardingham not in a barn. Come May Day they'll dance from Hardingham to our Maypole at Ye Olde Farme. Then at Whitsuntide they dance from Hardingham to Oatcester and when the tourist season is in full swing they'll dance from Hardingham to Oatcester again. It was so blooming hot last August that the hobby-horse had a heat stroke two mile this side of Oatcester and had to be sent back home in a motor-car. Poor old Dick Hodgkin, he missed the spread the Mayor and Council give them in the Town Hall. Oh, but he'll hobby-horse about to-night as lively as ever.

By now they had reached the great barn and were introduced to Mr Jacox, the antiquarian, of whom Hardingham was much prouder than many other places are of their local antiquarian. Moreover, he looked like an antiquarian and when he was pointed out to visitors they eyed him with as much respect as the old market cross. It was Mr Jacox who had revived morris-dancing in Hardingham and personally directed its performance.

"You may be interested to hear, gentlemen," he said, "that in all England the morris-dance as it was familiar to Shakespeare, who makes one or two allusions to morris-dancers in his plays, is to be seen only in Hardingham. Only here will you see them in the green satin and spangled white fustian of their traditional costume. Only here will you see each of the dancers with six garters hung with bells on each leg. Only here will you see the five chief characters—Robin Hood, Maid Marian, the Hobby-Horse, the Fool and the Friar. Morris-dancing has been revived by local enthusiasts in various parts of England, but apart from a few bells and some ribbons the performers would hardly be recognised as morris-dancers by the folk of good King Charles's day. Yes, I have delved deeply into the past and we flatter ourselves in Hardingham that our morris-dancers are unique. You have explained to our visitors, Mr Narbrow, that for morris-dancing in its full glory they should see the Whitsuntide dance from Hardingham to Oatcester?"

"Oh, I made that clear, right enough, Mr Jacox."

"But Mr Narbrow, whose enthusiasm for the rural sports and pastimes of the past has been of such help to me, was anxious for you to realise that, if this projected main drain between Hardingham and Oatcester were to be laid across the meadow opposite his farm, all that he and I are doing to attract visitors to see the England that was once upon a time would suffer a serious set-back. And, when you have seen our morris-dancers even in the comparatively restricted space of a barn, I feel confident that you will do all in your power to divert the projected main drain from Mr Narbrow's farm to link Hardingham with Oatcester by way of Hardingham Heath."

The two M.P.'s and Sir Oliver were offered seats on what looked like three small haycocks. Mr Jacox clapped his hands and with a loud jingling of bells the morris-dancers came bounding into the barn, the time for the dance being kept by one of the dancers with a tabouret.

"You know how morris-dances got their name?" Mr Jacox asked just as Sir Oliver pulled in his long legs to avoid tripping up the hefty young woman who was plunging about as Maid Marian.

Sir Oliver felt that complete ignorance would not become his position. So he covered the negative with a little joke.

"Nothing to do with William Morris, eh?"

Mr Jacox unfortunately did not realise Sir Oliver was making a little joke.

"No, no, no," the antequarian said earnestly. "The original morris-dance was a variant of the fandango and reached France from Spain in the fourteenth or early fifteenth century where it was known as the Morisque or Moorish dance. From France it reached England where . . ."

But the antiquarian's earnest little lecture was cut short at this moment when the Hobby-Horse in a sudden swing round as the dance came to an end unseated the Member for Oatshire from his haycock, who in falling over managed to unseat the Minister of Sanitation as well. They both made light of the little incident.

"Though I hope that isn't an omen for the next General Election, Henry," said the Member for Oatshire.

"Don't you be afraid of that, Mr Ackroyd," his host assured them. "When I put it around the way you've persuaded the Government to take their main drain by Hardingham Heath you'll get more votes than ever you had."

Sir Oliver who was still seated as a permanent official should be, whatever the result of a general election, frowned. He did not like the idea of encouraging backbenchers to suppose they could influence the decisions of a Government office. In his opinion they already enjoyed too much licence at question-time in the House.

"Oh, well, well, Mr Narbrow," said the Member for Oatshire, "it's the Member for North Wessex you must thank."

"Yes, and I'll see to it as the folk in North Wessex don't forget what a grand Member they've got in Mr Upjohn."

After some singing of folk-songs and another jingling display by the morris-dancers ale was handed round to refresh the company, before drinking which they had to listen to a speech by their host.

"I ask you to raise your mugs to the health and long life of the Right Honourable Upjohn and our own well beloved member, Mr Ackroyd, who in this age of chop and change are keeping the flag flying for Old England. It is my proud task to tell you that the new main drain between Hardingham and Oatcester will pass across the Heath and not as was originally intended in front of Ye Olde Farme. Next year with the help of Mr Jacox we shall be reviving more old English sports and pastimes for the benefit of our visitors from overseas. The future is bright, folk, and provided we don't get too dripping a summer brought on by these jet planes we can hope to beat all records in the number of visitors coming to

Oatshire. Here's to the Right Honourable Upjohn and Mr Ackroyd."

The toast was drunk with acclamation and the host in a resonant bass sang "Like a fine old English gentleman" to much applause.

"Well, I must say I thoroughly enjoyed myself," the Minister of Sanitation declared. "You enjoyed yourself, didn't you, Huffam?"

"Oh, yes, it was quite an experience, Minister. But I hope there wasn't any reporter present."

"Even if there was it'll be too late for the Sunday papers," said Mr Upjohn. "Everybody's so worn out by reading the Sunday papers that nobody reads Monday's papers; and now we ought to be getting back."

"You'll come in to the parlour, gentlemen, and take one for the road?" Farmer Narbrow pressed. "That ale we just drank beant the old October ale of once upon a time. What you need is a good drop of punch. My housekeeper brews a rare good punch."

As neither of the two members was driving they felt they could savour the punch with impunity and Sir Oliver with a faint sigh followed them to the parlour where they were presented to a round and rosy woman of about fifty who was introduced by the inappropriate name of Miss Withers. She was slowly stirring a large bowl on the table from which was rising a richly fragrant steam.

When it came to Sir Oliver's turn to accept the proffered glass from his host he shook his head.

"Thank you, not any for me," he said. "That mug of mead was much more than I usually drink."

"Why, that's just fermented honey. This is good rum punch. Mind you, it *is* real honey, all from my own bees. It's not the stuff they sell nowadays for honey."

"I found your mead quite potent enough for me, Mr Narbrow."

"Darn it, you must take a drop of something from Ye Olde Farme."

"Might I perhaps have a glass of your milk?" Sir Oliver suggested.

"Ah, and it is milk too," Mr Narbrow said. "None of your thin Friesian stuff all quantity and no quality. Sure enough, you shall have a glass of real milk. Margery, go you and get Sir Oliver a glass of our milk."

Mr Ackroyd had just declared he had never drunk a better glass of punch in his life and was holding out that glass for another, when a loud scream was heard.

"I'll lay that's a bat in the dairy," Mr Narbrow averred. "Ever since a bat got caught in her hair when she was doing it up for the night Margery can't abide bats. She won't lift up her skirt for a mouse but put a bat in the room and you can't hold her."

At this moment Miss Withers herself appeared, looking pale and much shaken.

"You was right, Mr Narbrow, when you saw that ghost. When you told me you'd seen a ghost before supper I said 'That's one of Bill's—one of Mr Narbrow's ideas he gets.' But you was right. I just seen it myself."

"You'd better pull yourself together, Margery, with a glass of your own punch."

"Which is really most excellent," Mr Ackroyd put in.

Miss Withers took a couple of sips and told her tale.

"I went into the dairy to get a glass of milk for that gentleman, and the moon being so bright I didn't bother to take a lamp and when I turned round with the jug in my hand I saw a tall dark kind of a shape carrying his head in his hands as you said, Mr Narbrow, and I screamed for all I was worth and dropped the jug in my fright and whatever it was let something fall with a great clang and then I screamed again, and whatever it was faded away and my heart's still thumping."

"Didn't you see what the ghost dropped?" her employer asked.

"I didn't wait to see nothing. I was out of that dairy as quick as lightning before whatever it was came back."

"Perhaps it didn't drop anything solid," Mr Narbrow

suggested hopefully. He was naturally anxious that his housekeeper's experience should confirm his own ghost story. "I'll go along and see for myself." He took a lamp from the wall of the passage and set out.

"The sooner Mr Narbrow gives way and we get the electric light at Bill's Bottom," said Miss Withers, "the better I'll be pleased."

"He's against electric light, is he?" somebody asked.

"Well, it's all a part of this craze of his for keeping things as they were when he was a nipper. But anyone can carry anything too far and I think it's carrying things too far in these days to have all the bother of paraffin lamps. He won't even have a motor-car. Must drive all over the place in a horse and trap and then grumbles because he can't find a good livery stable. Still I suppose he's made that way, and there it is."

A minute or two later Mr Narbrow came back from the dairy with a large tin.

"It must have been a somebody, not a ghost at all," he commented in obvious disappointment. "And there's a note tied on to it addressed to Sir Oliver Huffam, K.C.B."

Sir Oliver shuddered. An actual ghost would have disturbed him much less than the sight of that envelope on which was printed 'Dandimilk for Health and Happiness'.

As he opened it his long fingers seemed to be touching something noxious.

Dandimilk (Ltd)
13 Gog and Magog Lane
E.C.1.

Sir,
    Hearing that you will be in conference with Mr William Narbrow of Ye Olde Farme nr. Hardingham, Oatshire I should be grateful if you would draw Mr Narbrow's attention to our product and invite him to co-operate with us in gathering the various vegetable products we require from his farm, our laboratory being only a few miles from his farm.

We are particularly anxious to obtain Mr Narbrow's co-operation because we have been informed of his refusal to employ any kind of insecticides or pesticides on his property. We are hoping to get in touch with all farmers who employ his methods, and I take this opportunity of establishing what I hope will be a happy co-operation between Mr Narbrow and Dandimilk.

You will no doubt be informing him that the Ministry of Sanitation welcomes Dandimilk as a great contribution to the welfare of our national health.

Yours very truly

Emilius Scratchbury

Sir Oliver Huffam K.C.B.

"Have nothing to do with this man, Mr Narbrow," Sir Oliver said quickly. "The Ministry of Sanitation has no administrative interest in patent medicines, patent foods or indeed any patents except those which affect sanitation. This man came to the Ministry, claiming that his company were proposing to make milk out of dandelions and various other weeds because cows' milk was a threat to the health of the nation. It was made clear to him that the Ministry of Sanitation had nothing to do with the health of the nation except in so far as such health may be adversely affected by faulty sanitation."

"Says good cows' milk be bad for old England's health, do he?" Mr Narbrow rolled out indignantly. "Well, if I find him picking our dandelions I'll have him put in Top Meadow with King Alfred."

"King Alfred?"

"Our prize Oatshire bull. After he's run round Top Meadow a bit with old Alf after him he won't come picking dandelions again on Ye Olde Farme."

"Yes, that'll give him a good lesson," Mr Upjohn laughed.

Sir Oliver hastily intervened.

"If this Dr Scratchbury commits an act of trespass, Mr Narbrow, the proper course would be to take proceedings against him for trespassing. It would be extremely

injudicious to run any risk of Dr Scratchbury's being
tossed or perhaps gored by a bull. I suggest that you
write to Dr Scratchbury at 13 Gog and Magog Lane and
notify him that any attempt by him personally or any of
the employees of Dandimilk to gather dandelions or any
other form of vegetation on the land farmed by you will
involve him in legal proceedings. I further suggest that
you should communicate with the Ministry of Cultivation, notifying them that there is a laboratory somewhere in this neighbourhood encouraging trespass. The
Ministry of Cultivation will probably communicate with
the Home Office, and the Chief Constable of Oatshire
will no doubt be advised by them to enquire into the
whereabouts of this laboratory. When the whereabouts
of this laboratory have been established the Chief Constable...."

"That's Major Botwood. He's a bit of a know-all. I
tried last year to get him to put back the Oatshire police
into the green uniforms they used to wear before the
Great War."

"I never knew the Oatshire police used to be in green
uniforms," said the Member for Oatshire.

"You didn't, Mr Ackroyd? Look at that now. Yes,
they were all Robin Hood and his merry men, the Oatshire police were in the good old days."

Sir Oliver coughed and continued his instructions.

"When, as I was saying, the whereabouts of this
laboratory have been established the Chief Constable
will communicate his information to the Home Office
where no doubt in due course such information will be
passed on to the Ministry of Cultivation where no doubt
it will be carefully considered and in due course the
Ministry of Cultivation will no doubt take whatever
action is decided upon as appropriate."

The grandfather-clock in the parlour struck the hour
as Sir Oliver concluded his advice to their host.

"We must be getting back to Shrimpton, Mr Narbrow," said the Minister. "Thank you for such a memor-

able evening. I have seldom enjoyed myself as much. And thank you, Miss Withers, for your remarkable punch. I hope you won't be disturbed by any more tins to-night."

As they were walking along to the Rolls Mr Narbrow asked what he ought to do with the tin of Dandimilk. He was advised to open it and empty the contents.

"Unless you sample a glass of it," the Minister suggested. "If this stuff gets on the market you'd be in a stronger position to speak up against it if you knew what it tasted like."

On the way back to Shrimpton Grange the Permanent Secretary said to his Minister.

"I was a little afraid, Minister, that if Mr Narbrow thought he was being encouraged by you to put Dr Scratchbury in a field with his bull and the bull tossed him, one of the Sunday papers might suggest he was acting on your advice, and I'm sure you'll agree with me that it was wise to avoid giving some Opposition back-bencher an opportunity to put down a question in the House."

"I was only joking, Huffam."

"I fully realised that, Minister. But I'm sure you'll agree with me that if in replying to a question in the House you said you were only joking the Opposition back-benchers might make political capital out of your reply."

"Sir Oliver's right, Henry," said Jock Ackroyd.

The Right Honourable Henry Upjohn did not argue the point. Every Minister, whatever party he belongs to knows that his Permanent Secretary is always right.

Chapter 8

ABOUT three weeks after that long week-end his parents received a letter from Jeremy which gave Sir Oliver a good deal of pleasure. He was in a relaxed mood. A definite decision had been taken about the main drain between Oatcester and Hardingham. The cost of laying it under Hardingham Heath had been estimated not to exceed £78,000; it was hoped to start work on it in the early spring. Nothing had been heard or seen of Dr Emilius Scratchbury. The preliminary report on the suggested measures to be taken to ensure that the sanitary arrangements of campers were brought into line with those laid down by the Ministry of Sanitation for England and Wales had been drafted. When this report had been carefully considered it would be embodied in a leaflet which the Ministry would be issuing. It had been agreed with the Ministry of Leisure that the distinction between hikers and campers should be whether a tent was carried personally, in which case the carrier would rank as a hiker. All other people with tents or caravans would be considered campers.

"I think, Gertrude, that it would be a happy idea to have a little dinner-party next Saturday when I will read Jeremy's letter to Nigel, Joan, Rosemary and George."

"Would you mind very much if we had our party on Sunday, Olly?"

"Why is Sunday better than Saturday?"

"Apparently there's something they call a serial on the television every Saturday evening. That's why Ethel forgot to put the ladle in the soup last Saturday. She was very apologetic and explained that something was happening to somebody on the television just as she was bringing up the soup."

"I fear I made a mistake when I offered to install the television downstairs."

"Oh no, Olly, they *are* so happy with it. But I wouldn't like Ethel to be thinking about what's happening in this television serial when the children are dining with us."

Sir Oliver frowned.

"There's a time for everything," he observed severely. "And if the television is going to be allowed to disorganise our domestic arrangements I shall have to consider whether we shall not have to allow it only at certain fixed hours."

"Oh, I do hope you won't do that, Olly. Even if it sometimes does upset domestic arrangements it does solve so many domestic problems."

"It's against my principles but I happen to be in an indulgent mood. So be it. Our little dinner-party shall be on Sunday instead of Saturday."

"Rosemary will find it easier to get a baby-sitter for dear little Noll on Sunday. So many people want to go out on Saturday evenings."

"As far as I can see they want to go out every evening of the week."

"But it's natural, isn't it, after being cooped up in an office all day?"

"I suppose I am what you call cooped up in an office all day. Yet I am more than content to find myself at home."

Lady Huffam knew better than to plead with her husband for the cooped up.

"You're different, Olly," she said fondly.

The argument about the noise of jet-planes was renewed at dinner between Nigel Huffam and George Micklewright on that Sunday evening.

"People must realise that it's impossible to stop progress," said George Micklewright, whose promotion to be a Principal Assistant Secretary at the Ministry of Movement seemed to have added at least an inch to his already long sententious chin.

"I wish you people at Movement House would realise that progress is not just a matter of moving faster," Nigel responded severely. "You've made a complete mess of British Railways."

"You people at the Treasury were always moaning that the railways were losing money," said his brother-in-law. "We were proposing to make them pay."

"And in order to do that you are entirely disregarding the convenience of the general public," Nigel continued. "Don't you agree, Dad?"

But before Sir Oliver had had time to commit himself to a carefully considered opinion George Micklewright was off again,

"What the country must realise is that movement by railway is already obsolete, or at any rate obsolescent. But we are still handicapped by lack of suitable roads for motor traffic. When we have managed in spite of Treasury obstruction to make suitable roads, they in due course will become obsolescent because I have no doubt whatever that perhaps even by the end of this century everybody will be flying. And do remember, Nigel, that all this will give employment. You *must* get computer-minded and appreciate that with the development of automation more and more people will be out of employment."

The argument went on until Rosemary Huffam laughed.

"What are you laughing at, Rosemary?" her husband asked in surprise.

"I was thinking how funny you'd look, Nigel dear, flying off to the Treasury with a pair of wings I'd have to help you buckle on every morning."

"I'm not arguing that this will happen for many years yet," George Micklewright said seriously. "But it will happen. It must happen. Nobody thought motor-bicycles would happen when the first motor-cars had to be preceded by a red flag."

"Well, I'm longing to hear what Jeremy has been

doing," said Rosemary. "The horrible future hasn't arrived yet."

Her mother-in-law gave her a grateful smile.

Up in the drawing-room after dinner Sir Oliver took out the letter and cleared his throat.

"Poste Restante, Athens," he announced.

"He's in Greece, Nigel!" Rosemary exclaimed, "Fancy Jeremy getting to Greece before you!"

Nigel Huffam was taken aback. His First in Mods, his First in Greats, and his mention among those competing for the Chancellor's prize for a Greek essay had been snatched from him by that younger brother.

My dear Mum and Dad.

Dick Horner and I have been having a fabulous time. We got to Italy quite easily from France because a lorry-driver gave us a lift all the way. He had been in England with the Free French during the war and he wanted to talk about his time there because he had married an English girl and last year she died. She came from a place in Sussex near where the Horners always go for their summer holidays. Dick Horner didn't actually know any of the people he talked about but he did know one or two of the places, so this lorry-driver whose name is Gerard Delfont was awfully glad to talk about where his wife came from. We were awfully sorry for him because evidently he was still feeling very sad about losing his wife.

Gerard Delfont was driving to Genoa and he said that when we got there he would find a lorry-driver who was going to Rome and perhaps even as far as Naples. We stayed a night in Genoa and got a lift as far as Rome where we found a very cheap albergo and went all over Rome for two days. Will you tell George that if he wants to know what noise is he'd better come to Rome and that if the Ministry of Movement want to make London even noisier than Rome they'll have quite a job. All the same we liked Rome very much. The weather was glorious and we would have stayed longer but it happened that there was a lorry-driver in the albergo where we were staying and he is going on a job to England early next year and he was very anxious to practise his English with us. He was driving to Naples and he said he thought we might find a boat there on which we could get to Greece but that if we couldn't we should get to Brindisi somehow, where we could be sure of finding a boat for Greece on which we could travel cheaply.

And that's what we did, hiking some of the way to the Adriatic and getting an occasional lift. The Italians are awfully friendly and two of the contadini . . .

"What are contadini?" George Micklewright asked.

"Peasants," said Nigel Huffam who, although he had not been to Greece, was glad to remind his brother-in-law that unlike him he *had* been to Italy.

"I'm so glad Jeremy likes the Italians," said Rosemary. "I think they're pets."

Sir Oliver feeling this was a rather exaggerated epithet to describe Italians, read on quickly,

Two of the contadini gave us beds for the night and some bread and cheese called probalone, I think. It's made of buffalo milk. We were lucky to find a boat going to Patras in Greece and from there we hitch-hiked to Pylos. I wanted to go there because we were reading old Thicksides last term and I wanted to see what Sphacteria looked like. And then we found that this was where the Turks lost the whole of their fleet in the battle of Navarino. After Pylos we hiked across the Taygetus range to Sparta. A road has been made across it which is absolutely terrific. There's barely anything left of Sparta. I thought what an example it was for everybody to-day, all trying to do the same thing at the same moment.

"What on earth does he mean by that?" Nigel asked.

"I think I know," said Rosemary. "I don't know anything about Sparta but if there's hardly anything left of it, I'm not surprised."

Sir Oliver quickly read on:

We hiked all the way from Sparta to Athens, though we often had lifts for a bit of the way. I'm glad now I went on with Greek.

Quite often I would say a word in old Greek and pronounce it like modern Greek and they would understand what I was saying. And I've at last understood why they used accents. I used to get fed up with the way we had to get the accents right without apparently having anything to do with the pronunciation. If they're going on teaching Greek at school it's about time they learnt how to pronounce it. After all they learnt how to pronounce Latin. We saw over a baker's shop ἀρτοποιο. . . ."

"Jeremy has written it in Greek," Sir Oliver broke off to explain.

But when I asked for some ἀρτος the baker didn't know what I wanted. They only use artos when they're writing about it. They call bread ψωμι and as the baker couldn't read he didn't know that artopoyos meant bread-maker.

"Athens is absolutely fabulous, but I feel that if I tried to write about in a letter I should spoil it for myself because I would never be able to explain what it has made me feel like. We haven't decided yet whether we will hike about the north of Greece or whether we will try to get to Crete and perhaps to Cyprus. We want to go to Cyprus because we think that the English papers write a lot of prejudiced rot about Cyprus. You'd think that the Turks were Christian martyrs according to the English papers. I can't tell you how glad I am to be finding out what life is like for myself and not reading about what life is like on paper. I hope you are both very well.

Your loving
Jeremy"

"I hope young Jeremy isn't going to get mixed up in Greek politics," said George Micklewright. "We have enough on our hands at Movement House over Cyprus without having to arrange for those two kids to be flown home."

"I can't understand it," Joan sighed. "Jeremy never took the least interest in politics here."

"Oh dear," said Lady Huffam, "I do hope Jeremy won't get mixed up in Greek politics. I was so relieved when he and his friend went to Italy instead of Spain. It would have been terrible if he had been put in prison by Franco."

"I don't think we need worry, Mum," her elder son assured her. "I hardly see Jeremy as a second Byron."

"Nigel is right," said Sir Oliver, as he began to fold his younger son's letter. "I am pleased to think that what seemed at first a reckless escapade seems to have stirred his imagination. It's obvious that the money the two boys have will not last indefinitely and I have little doubt that in due course Mr Horner and I shall be called upon to provide what is necessary to bring them back to England. What has pleased me is that Jeremy when he returns to school will apply himself to Greek with much more attention. His adventure has obviously given him a genuine interest in the language. You won't accuse me of exaggeration, Nigel, if I say that Jeremy's first sight of the Parthenon has brought proparoxyton and properispomenon to life."

"Are they two Greek heroes?" Rosemary asked.

Sir Oliver and her husband smiled charitably at this ingenuous question.

"Proparaxyton, Rosemary dear, is an acute accent on the last syllable but two; properispomenon is a circumflex accent on the last syllable but one."

"And you think Jeremy's coming back to school to get excited over properomminons or whatever they're called? I don't. I think he's escaped."

"But he's not in prison, Rosemary," said Lady Huffam.

"No, but he felt he was in prison. Anyway, Jeremy's letter has made up my mind for next year. When you take your holiday, Nigel, we are going to Greece. Noll can go to my mother while we're away."

"Oh, but we'd like to have him here for part of the time wouldn't we, Granddad?"

Sir Oliver's face was puckered for a moment as by a clue in the *Times* crossword; it was the first time Gertrude had called him 'granddad'. The puckers vanished.

H

"Our little grandson will be very welcome in Chillingham Gardens," he said.

"Yes, as sure as eggs are eggs we'll go to Greece next year," Rosemary declared, "though I ought to say as sure as eggs *were* eggs because nowadays you can't be sure if they *are* eggs, even when somebody on television says they are in B.B.C. Mummerset."

"I didn't know you had the television in your flat, Nigel," Sir Oliver exclaimed to his elder son. "We have it here, but of course it's downstairs."

"Yes, Dad. Well, I thought I ought to listen to those quarters of an hour the B.B.C. and the I.T.V. allot to the political parties in turn. It's useful to know what fresh extravagances they're all proposing."

"Come off it, Nigel," his wife laughed. "You know you have been looking at all those cowboys and Indians."

"Cowboys and Indians, eh?" said Sir Oliver, with what in a less pale eye might almost have been called a gleam. "If I may come round on Thursday I think it would be as well if I heard what my Minister has to say."

Sir Oliver did not explain why he wanted to avoid listening to his Minister in his own house, or even less, as the Minister had suggested, at T.V. headquarters in Shepherd's Bush. He had read through and carefully considered the script of what Mr Upjohn was proposing to say and he had managed to get one or two remarks omitted, but Ministers being what they were no Permanent Secretary could feel at ease until the ordeal was over and he did not want to run the risk of suggesting in front of them downstairs or of viewers at the B.B.C. that something his Minister had said should better not have been said.

"Well, here's the final draft," Mr Upjohn told his Permanent Secretary on Monday morning. "Will you look it through and if there are any more alterations you think it wise to make will you let me know before I send it round to the T.V. people? I'll come along to your room for the verdict in half an hour's time if that's all right for you."

Sir Oliver took the script with him and read slowly through what Mr Upjohn had to say about the record of social service his party could proudly offer to the nation.

"Yes, yes, this seems quite harmless," he thought to himself. "The Minister is not going into details about the work of the Ministry," he added to his Private Secretary. "I'm glad he took my advice about that, Humphrey. In his first draft he was committing us to those new sewage farms in Northumberland, Montgomeryshire and Cornwall which are still under consideration. I urged him to stress what we *had* done, not what we were going to do. He also made what I thought was an unwise allusion to that Oatshire deputation; we do not want to have to deal with deputations from Northumberland, Montgomeryshire and Cornwall. However, that is no longer in. The other thing he omitted on my advice was any mention of the proposed regulations for the sanitary arrangements of campers. I pointed out that it would greatly impede our work at the Ministry if, before a leaflet setting out those regulations could be issued, we were inundated with suggestions from campers all over the country, and not only suggestions but premature agitation against what they would call interfering with the liberty of the individual. Moreover, that happy compromise we reached with the Ministry of Leisure might be adversely affected. Many years ago now when I was Private Secretary to the Minister of Waste—the present Lord Braintree—I had bitter experience of the harm that could be done by a sound broadcast, and from what I can gather about the television the harm done to-day could be even more disastrous."

When the Minister came in for the verdict of his Permanent Secretary he was gratified by the approval of his forthcoming quarter of an hour on television.

"I'm glad you think it's all right, Huffam. But you

know I'm a bit nervous about this damn business. On a platform when I'm speaking directly to an audience I'm never the slightest bit nervous. But this is something quite new to me. I was looking at Eddy Pinkney when he was bragging about these dam new towns with which the Accommodation people are infesting the countryside and creating marginal constituencies all over the place. And I suddenly realised he wasn't looking at the audience at all but reading it from some contraption they have for looking as if you weren't reading. They offered me this contraption, but I said 'nothing doing'. I shall have my speech by heart. And I have, Huffam. I've nearly driven poor Molly into a decline, hearing me say it over and over again."

After dinner on Thursday Sir Oliver walked along quickly to the flat in Queen's Gate. He arrived as Nigel was watching the last ten minutes of "Deadwood Gulch" and a screenful of Indians and United States cavalry.

"I wonder what's going to happen to Captain Quick. Well, we shan't know till next Thursday," Nigel said as the fifth instalment of "Deadwood Gulch" faded away for the Right Honourable Henry Upjohn, M.C., M.P., to interrupt the competition between chocolates and detergents on I.T.V. and leave the future of Captain Quick bound to the stake on B.B.C.1 in abeyance.

When the quarter of an hour came to an end Sir Oliver gave a deep sigh of relief.

"He said nothing that was not in the script, and I think he said it very well, didn't you, Nigel?"

"I'm not an authority on drains, Dad, but there is one thing that can be said for drains, they're not as expensive as new roads."

Rosemary came in at this moment.

"Is that dreary talk about politics over? How nice to see you, Granddad. Noll is sleeping like an angel. Do come along with me and look at him."

Sir Oliver followed his daughter-in-law and gazed at the infant Huffam in his cot with an expression on his

face of what he hoped would suitably convey his patri-
archal pride.

"He's not going to have the Huffam hair," he said to
his daughter-in-law when they returned to the sitting-
room. "But then after all Jeremy hasn't got the Huffam
hair."

"No, dear Old Jeremy is the dark horse in the Huffam
Stakes," Rosemary said with a smile.

"Well, I must be getting back to—er—Grandma,"
Sir Oliver said. "I must come along again soon. Will you
be at home next Thursday?"

"Why don't you and Mum come along and dine with
us?" Nigel suggested. "You won't mind looking at
'Deadwood Gulch'? It comes on at eight."

"Wasn't that what you were looking at before the
Minister came on?" Sir Oliver asked in as casual a voice
as he could contrive.

"Nigel, you really are the limit," Rosemary expostu-
lated. "Fancy asking Granddad and Grandma to have
their dinner interrupted by Indians and cowboys yelling
all over the place."

"They weren't cowboys. They were United States
cavalry," he corrected. "And its the end of this
serial."

"Thank goodness! But I suppose you'll start looking
at another one almost at once."

"Don't worry, Rosemary. Mum and I—Grandma
and I will be with you next Thursday at half-past
seven," her father-in-law promised.

Sir Oliver walked back buoyantly to Chillingham
Gardens. His Minister's television appearance had been
a model of evasive enthusiasm and he was looking forward
to congratulating him on it to-morrow morning. As he
walked along his mind, no longer preoccupied with
fears of a ministerial indiscretion, turned to the fate of
Captain Quick after being captured by the Carroway
Indians. He would no doubt be rescued but it *would* be
interesting to know *how* he was going to be rescued. Per-

haps after all it was his duty as a conscientious Civil Servant to know what was happening in the world. To be sure he always read the news in *The Times* on his way home from the Ministry, but he was sometimes tempted to return to the crossword puzzle if he had not been able to finish it between Gloucester Road and Piccadilly, and then he was apt to forget about the news. If he installed a television set in the drawing-room?

When Sir Oliver went up to his room at the Ministry next morning he said to his Private Secretary,

"I thought the Minister came through well on the television last night, Humphrey. In fact I'm considering whether it might not be a good idea if I were to have the television installed in Chillingham Gardens. My son at the Treasury has it and says there's something called Panorama which might be useful for me to look at. What's the matter, Humphrey? You're looking very worried. Don't you think it might be useful for me to have the television?"

"It's not that, sir. It's this."

Sir Oliver looked distastefully at one of the organs of the popular Press which Humphrey Mowart had put down on his desk. Under the heading THREAT OF COWS' MILK Sir Oliver read:

"In an interview with a representative of the *Daily Switch* Dr Emilius Scratchbury, the managing director of Dandimilk, declared emphatically that the nation's health is being undermined by cows' milk.

'I regard cows' milk as a more serious menace to health than cigarette-smoking,' said Dr Scratchbury. 'Owing to the recent advances in technology a substitute has been discovered for cows' milk made entirely from vegetable matter. It is called Dandimilk and will presently be available to the public at a penny less than at whatever price cows' milk is being offered to the public.'

'So you do not think that the advice to "drink a pinta milka day" is justified?' our representative asked.

'It is dangerous advice. What would the doctors say

if one of the tobacco firms advised the public to "smoka cigaretta day"?'

Dr Scratchbury went on to enumerate the many ills which flesh is heir to through drinking cows' milk.

" 'Fortunately thanks to the discovery of Dandimilk the nation need no longer be exposed to the perils of cows' milk. Dandimilk in addition to its pleasant taste and nutritional value has mildly laxative qualities, and in these days when the morning rush-hour imposes such a strain on those who have to catch trains and omnibuses I do not need to stress the importance of those qualities. Happily I am able to say that the Ministry of Sanitation is aware of the important contribution Dandimilk will make to their invaluable work, and I have little doubt that the Ministry will presently take appropriate action.'

"Viewers who heard last night Mr Upjohn's account of the work which his Ministry is performing for the sophistication of the country's sanitation will be interested to hear that Mr Upjohn has himself tried the new milk and expressed himself well satisfied with its effectiveness. The dairy-farmers who have recently been agitating for an escalation in the price of milk may have to reconsider their attitude if this new product wins the favour of the milk-drinking public."

Sir Oliver put the paper down on his desk with a groan.

"Mr Upjohn has himself tried the new milk and expressed himself well satisfied with its effectiveness," he repeated in tones in which dejection bordered upon despair.

"I think that's the reporter, sir, not Dr Scratchbury. All he apparently stated positively was that the Ministry is aware of Dandimilk," said Humphrey Mowart.

"Aware of the important contribution that Dandimilk will make to their invaluable work," Sir Oliver read. "That implies we think the stuff *is* important."

The telephone buzzed in the anteroom. Humphrey Mowart came back presently.

"It's the secretary of the National Association of

Dairymen. He has read in the *Daily Switch* of the interview with Dr Scratchbury and wants to know what time would be convenient for the Minister to see him."

"No time will be convenient," Sir Oliver snapped.

Humphrey Mowart hesitated.

"Don't you think, sir, if we say that it may give an impression that we are in fact prepared to recommend Dandimilk? I expect you'd rather see this man before he sees the Minister. You have no other appointment between 11.30 and 12; I'm sure you feel that the sooner this unfortunate business is clarified the better."

"You may be right, Humphrey. Very well. I will see him at 11.30."

No sooner was Humphrey Mowart back than the telephone buzzed again.

"It's the secretary of the Society for the Prevention of Cruelty to Cows. It's a woman, sir. She wants to know what time it would be convenient for the Minister to see her. From what I could gather she wants to thank him for his support of Dandimilk."

"Thank him?" Sir Oliver gasped.

"Yes, sir, she says that the demand for cows' milk is the cause of cruelty both to cows and calves and she wants to ask him to be the patron of her Society."

"Tell her to communicate with the Minister of Sanitation by letter. He is unable to grant interviews owing to the heavy demands made upon him by his official duties. What's this woman's name?"

"Veale," Humphrey Mowart chuckled. "She was rather excitable and I thought at first she was going on about this cruelty to calves. And suddenly she said, 'Miss Veale with an "e", not veal without an "e" for slaughter'."

"You'd better warn the janitor that if a Miss Veale comes to the Ministry she must be got rid of as soon as possible."

Once again no sooner was Humphrey Mowart back than the telephone buzzed again.

"It's the *Evening Post*, sir. Has the Ministry any comment to make upon the interview with Dr Scratchbury in this morning's *Daily Switch*?"

"None," Sir Oliver snapped.

The Private Secretary was worried. He had never known his Chief snap like a dog suddenly woken from sleep. He could hardly believe that it was himself who was suggesting prudence to one who had so often warned him against precipitate action.

"If I may say so, sir, from my slight knowledge of Fleet Street, they're inclined to feel that 'no comment' suggests embarrassment. There may be a paragraph in this afternoon's *Post* hinting that we have been embarrassed at the Ministry by this morning's *Switch*. May I say that a communiqué will be issued to the Press at the earliest possible moment and that pending the issue of such a communiqué the *Evening Post* will appreciate that any comment would be premature?"

When his Private Secretary came back he felt able to assure Sir Oliver that the *Evening Post* did appreciate that any comment would be premature.

"But I hope the Minister will soon be here, sir. We do want to get our communiqué to the Press as soon as possible."

"Yes, you are right, Humphrey. You'd better draft a communiqué and when the Minister comes in he and I can study it and delete or amplify where we think it advisable."

When the Minister arrived in Cork Street his Permanent Secretary hurried to his room.

"You've seen the *Daily Switch*, Minister?" he asked.

"No, I never look at the rag nowadays," said Mr Upjohn. "I used to take it in when Stallion was their racing correspondent but when he left them I gave it up. Why do you ask?"

Sir Oliver handed Mr Upjohn the *Daily Switch*.

"But, before you read an unpleasant piece of sensationalism, Minister, I should like to congratulate you on your television appearance last night."

"You heard it, did you?" Mr Upjohn exclaimed with obvious gratification. "But it's a tricky business, Huffam. Dear old Molly said I looked as self-conscious as our boy Simon, when she and I go down to Eton for the Fourth." He opened the *Daily Switch*, and his Permanent Secretary pointed a long thin finger at THREAT OF COWS' MILK. "But this is a lot of bloody lies," the Minister spluttered when he had read the account of the interview with Dr Scratchbury. "I never tasted a drop of the beastly stuff."

"Mowart is drafting a communiqué for the Press which when it has been approved will be sent immediately to all the London journals. I fear that some of the damage done by this piece of sensationalism has already been done. The Secretary of the National Association of Dairymen has been in communication with us and I have given him an appointment for 11.30 this morning when I think it would be advisable for you to see him personally, Minister. *Tempus fugit.* I shall come back with the draft for your approval as soon as possible."

"I hope this won't be a question in the House from one of those confounded Opposition back-benchers."

"We all hope that, Minister."

His Permanent Secretary left him to see how his own Private Secretary was getting on with the communiqué.

The final draft was approved as follows:

"In view of certain erroneous statements made in the Press the Ministry of Sanitation has issued the following official correction:

"An announcement that a synthetic substitute for cows' milk has been approved by the Ministry of Sanitation is devoid of any foundation. The fitness for consumption of any nutritional or allegedly nutritional substance is outside the scope of the Ministry's activity which is solely concerned with questions of sanitation. If any repetition or circulation of such erroneous statements is made either by individuals or by any organ of the Press the Ministry of Sanitation will be compelled to take appropriate action."

"What would be appropriate action?" the Minister asked.

"I believe in the case of the Press it would be to bring the matter before the Press Council. In the case of Dr Scratchbury himself I think we should have to consult Treasury Counsel to ascertain if he is liable to be charged with criminal libel," said Sir Oliver.

"Wouldn't it be as well to threaten him with that?" the Minister suggested.

"I think the threat is covered by appropriate action, Minister. It is always better to avoid being too specific without taking legal advice beforehand."

"Yes, but what I object to," said Mr Upjohn, "is the way that damned rag suggests I'd been mopping up this infernal Dandimilk before my television broadcast. Can't he say in our communiqué that the Minister of Sanitation has never tasted the beastly stuff?"

"I feel that might be undignified, Minister," said the Permanent Secretary. "A Ministry should never convey the impression that it is a human individual. That was the mistake old Lord Braintree made in his broadcast many years ago. Listeners got it into their heads that *he* was the Ministry of Waste. What I believe they now call viewers might be liable to react in the same way."

"But I didn't make that mistake, Huffam," the Minister protested. "Don't you remember how careful you were to cut out any suggestion that I was personally interested in sanitation, when you were going through the script of my speech? Yet here's this blasted newspaper suggesting that the laxative qualities of this stuff are occupying my attention as a Minister of the Crown."

"That is why I think it inadvisable to bring you into the communiqué personally. Before you knew where you were you might find yourself inundated with samples of all kinds of aperients. The more impersonal the disassociation of the Ministry from Dandimilk, the more effective it will be."

"I expect you're right, Huffam. You always are."

Sir Oliver acknowledged this little tribute with a grave nod.

"And may I suggest, Minister, that when you give an interview to the secretary of the National Association of Dairymen, while deploring the erroneous statements in the *Daily Switch*, you do not give him such an idea of your enthusiasm for cows' milk that they'll commit the Ministry to advising the public to drinka pinta milka day, one of these so-called slogans which are to be seen defacing advertisement hoardings."

Chapter 9

THE secretary of the National Association of Dairymen
had evidently been convinced in the course of his
interview with Mr Upjohn that the report of his attitude
to Dandimilk in the *Daily Switch* was a canard, the wings
of which would at once be clipped. After reading the
communiqué from the Ministry he at once assured Mr
Upjohn that the emergency meeting of the Association's
Council he had been on the point of calling would not
be called.

"I don't think we shall have any more trouble with
the milk people, Huffam. Next time I lunch with you at
the Heraeum I shall ask for a glass of milk instead of
vodka."

Sir Oliver took this seriously and frowned gently.

"I think it would be as well, Minister, not to be involv-
ing yourself with milk at this moment. Some member
might have a guest connected with Fleet Street; the
story might appear in one of these gossip columns."

"I didn't seriously mean I would ask for a glass of milk
before lunch at the Heraeum. I was joking, Huffam."

Sir Oliver felt that good manners demanded a smile
and he produced one.

"Your tooth hurting you?" Mr Upjohn asked
anxiously. "I expect you have your own dentist, but if
you're not satisfied with him I have a splendid fellow in
Wimpole Street, and I know you'd find him absolutely
first-rate."

Sir Oliver was assuring Mr Upjohn that he had not
had toothache for years without adding that he had no
teeth of his own left to ache when one of the Minister's
Assistant Private Secretaries came in to say that Mrs
Upjohn was on the telephone and anxious to speak to
him.

"One of these confounded reporters, I expect," said Mr Upjohn as he lifted the receiver.

"Hullo, Molly, my dear . . . a Miss Veale? Never heard of her. . . . Society for the Prevention of Cruelty to Cows? . . . Never heard of it. Tell her to buzz off . . . she won't go? . . . showering you with leaflets? . . . wants to see me personally? . . . but we've nothing to do with cows and calves at the Ministry . . . she's muddling up Sanitation with Cultivation. Cows and calves are their pidgin . . . she wants to thank me for telling the world about my horror of cows' milk. . . . No, of course you didn't know I had a horror of cows' milk . . . yes, of course, I always take it with tea and coffee . . . well, I'll ask Sir Oliver. . . ." The Minister turned to his Permanent Secretary. "Could you manage to spare Mowart for an hour, Huffam? I could let you have young Wood while he's away. My wife thinks he'll be able to get rid of this Miss Veale as he got rid of that tin of Dandimilk. Do you think this woman's an agent for that wretched stuff?"

Sir Oliver agreed to let his Private Secretary go like a knight-errant to the rescue of Mrs Upjohn in Hertford Street. He was the more willing to do this because Humphrey would know what Miss Veale looked like, and if by chance she should evade the vigilance of Sergeant-major Hadnutt he would be able to protect his own Chief.

"As a matter of fact, Minister, this Miss Veale rang up the Ministry earlier this morning to ask for an interview with you. She had read about Dandimilk in the *Daily Switch* and believing that you had given your approval to it she wanted to ask you to be the patron of this Society of hers. The janitor has been warned about her but we have no reason to believe that she has any connection with Dr Scratchbury."

When Humphrey Mowart reached the Minister's house in Hertford Street, Mrs Upjohn was waiting for him.

"How terribly kind of you to come along, Mr Mowart, but I'm afraid you're going to find Miss Veale more of a

problem than that tin. And before I forget, can you dine
with us next Monday? You can? Oh, that's marvellous.
Eight o'clock. Well, this woman is in the drawing-room.
Henry knows nothing about calves. I can't think why
she wants him to be patron of this Society."

Humphrey Mowart told Mrs Upjohn about the interview in the *Daily Switch*.

"And Henry's supposed to be an advocate of Dandimilk?" Mrs Upjohn laughed merrily. "My dear Mr
Mowart, you must get hold of some for me. I'd love to
see Henry's face when I put it in his coffee without his
knowing. But first of all you must get rid of Miss Veale.
I'll let you go up to the drawing-room without me. I
don't know how you're going to get rid of her, but I'm
sure you'll manage it."

"I'll do my best, Mrs Upjohn," he promised, and went
upstairs.

Humphrey was a little taken aback when he went into
the drawing-room to see a woman with what could be
called bright red hair sobbing to herself in an armchair
with a bundle of leaflets on her knee.

"Miss Veale?" he asked.

"Yes, young man?"

"You seem distressed about something."

She handed him a leaflet.

"Read that, young man. Then you'll understand why
I'm distressed. And I hope *you'll* be distressed when you've
read what they do to poor little calves."

Humphrey tactfully accepted the leaflet and read
about the way calves were now being deprived of fresh
air and sunlight in order that their flesh might provide
whiter meat when they were slaughtered. He was sincerely shocked by the leaflet.

"I agree with you, Miss Veale, that if this is true it *is*
a disgrace."

"True? It is too true, young man. And that is why when
I read in the *Daily Switch* this morning that the Right
Honourable Upjohn was behaving in a right honourable

way and encouraging people to drink this new milk and leaving their mothers' milk to be drunk by poor little calves, I felt I must go down on my knees and thank the Right Honourable Upjohn. I have not yet been able to procure any of this noble Dandimilk. I enquired at Woolworth's on my way to Hertford Street from Notting Hill but Woolworth's hadn't heard of Dandimilk. I was so looking forward to drinking milk again with a clear conscience, because when I gave up drinking milk with my tea it never tasted the same. Somebody advised me to try mint with it but when I think of the way they slaughter poor little lambs and cover them with mint-sauce I couldn't bring myself to put mint in my tea. So you can imagine my joy this morning when I read about Dandimilk. I have been trying to explain to Mrs Upjohn why our Society wants to have the Right Honourable Upjohn as our patron but she never seemed to listen properly to what I was saying, even when I explained why I had come to her home. I told her that I had rung up the Ministry of Sanitation but that somebody in that place had told me the only way for me to get into com-munication was in a letter. I thought to myself 'yes, you might just as well tell anybody to post themselves in a pillar box', and I thought the best thing for me to do would be to call at the Right Honourable Upjohn's house because when I went to the Ministry in Cork Street, W.1, the commissionaire told me nobody could go in. I said to him 'Yes, Cork Street is where you ought to be and what you need is a corkscrew', but he paid no attention and I found a telephone box and rang up the *Daily Switch* to ask what was the Right Honourable Upjohn's address at home and I'm bound to say they were most polite and told me his number in Hertford Street. So I found a taxi and drove there right away. Civil Service? Yes, I had a cousin, well, a cousin once removed actually, in the Civil Service and I said to him once because he was always a bit crabbed 'Uncivil service, that's what it ought to be called'."

Miss Veale paused just long enough for Humphrey Mowart to get a word in.

"I'm sorry you think that, Miss Veale. I'm afraid I'm in the Civil Service. But the Minister of Sanitation has asked me to let you know that he is unable to be the patron of your Society because a Minister of the Crown must avoid patronising anything. He has also asked me to say that an entirely unwarranted use has been made of his name by this new product which he knows nothing about."

"But I read it in the paper that he found it a splendid substitute for cows' milk."

"You know, Miss Veale, we can't always believe what we read in the papers."

"Well, that is so sometimes, I'm bound to admit. I remember reading once that a Mr Baillie whom we knew well and who spelt his name with an 'e' the same as I do had been run in for being drunk and incapable and all the time it was a Mr Bailey who spelt his name with a 'y'."

"There you are, Miss Veale. And now as Mr Upjohn isn't at home and as he is too much occupied with the work he is doing for the country's sanitation to spare time to see you, I'm going to suggest that you go back to Notting Hill. And to show you that the Civil Service isn't always uncivil I'm going to suggest that I should drive you back in my car."

"Well, that is very civil, I'm bound to admit."

Miss Veale gathered together her leaflets and followed Humphrey Mowart downstairs. She talked without stopping all the way to Gladstone Terrace but as Humphrey Mowart was preoccupied with the traffic he heard little of what she said. When he opened the door of the car for her to get out, Miss Veale wished him good-bye.

"And will you tell the Right Honourable Upjohn, young man, that a vote of thanks for his support of the cows and calves will undoubtedly be passed at the next meeting of our Society."

She hurried up the steps with her bundle of leaflets;

I

a moment later her bright red hair vanished behind the front-door.

Humphrey Mowart got back to Cork Street just as the Minister was coming out.

"You saved the situation, Mowart," he was told. "My wife is tremendously grateful to you."

"She was just a harmless eccentric, sir. I didn't have any difficulty in persuading her to let me drive her back to Notting Hill."

"Have you ever thought of chucking the Civil Service and going in for politics?"

"Well, sir, as a matter of fact I have."

"You're dining with us next Monday, my wife tells me. We'll have a talk about it."

The Private Secretary went up to his Chief's room with something like a feeling of gratitude towards Miss Veale.

"Ah, there you are, Humphrey. The Minister was very pleased with the way you managed to eliminate this Veale person from Hertford Street. Is she elderly?"

"It was rather difficult to tell her age. She had the brightest red hair I ever saw."

Sir Oliver frowned.

"It was probably dyed," he said severely.

"It certainly was very bright, sir. She was quite bright herself in an odd way. I suggested she should ask Dr Scratchbury to be the patron of her Society."

"I hope we've heard the last of Dr Scratchbury, Humphrey. The Ministry's communiqué will be in the *Evening Post* and the *Moon* this afternoon, and in all the papers to-morrow morning, and now I must be getting along to the Heraeum."

But just as Sir Oliver rose from his chair the telephone buzzed.

"It's Mr Narbrow, sir, ringing from Oatcester. He wishes to speak to you personally. Shall I say you won't be back at the Ministry till later?"

"No, I'll speak to him myself. He's probably just read about Dandimilk in that degraded newspaper."

Sir Oliver lifted the receiver.

"This is Sir Oliver Huffam speaking . . ." but it was some time before Sir Oliver Huffam could speak again, so rapid was the flow of bucolic eloquence at the other end. . . . "Yes, I can readily understand, Mr Narbrow, that you were surprised by what you read in the *Daily Switch* . . . yes, quite so, Mr Narbrow, but the *Daily Switch* was in error when it reported that the Minister of Sanitation has approved of this imitation milk . . . please tell any farmers in Oatcester who have been reading the *Daily Switch* that to-morrow morning they will see an official contradiction . . . yes, we shall be much obliged if you will assure any farmers with whom you come into contact that. . . . I didn't catch what you said . . . you have discovered where this stuff is being made . . . but we have already arranged to divert our main drain. A fresh diversion in another direction would mean many weeks, perhaps many months delay . . . no, no, what you suggest is not possible. However, I am glad to have been able to set your mind at rest about this imitation milk, but I was a little surprised to see in one of the illustrated weekly papers the picture of an Oatshire cow acting as foster-mother to a Friesian calf."

Sir Oliver quickly hung up.

"People who live in glass houses, Humphrey, should not throw stones. Mr Narbrow dislikes Friesian cattle as much as Dandimilk. Do you know what he was suggesting we should do? He wanted us to divert our main drain again so that it might go under this place where Dandimilk is being made."

"But that might involve us in a heavy claim for damages, sir."

"Exactly. And yet the public still fails to appreciate the time and care we devote to avoiding unnecessary expenditure. Ah well, Humphrey, when you've been as long as I have in the Service you'll realise what an example we set to the rest of the community."

These words of the Permanent Secretary would come

back to Humphrey Mowart when he was driving to Little
Hangover after dining at Hertford Street and as they
came back they were accompanied by that talk he had
had with Mr Upjohn at the end of which the Minister
had said,

"Well, if you do decide to go in for politics, I'm pretty
sure I can find you a constituency that will welcome you
as a candidate. Of course, it would be a hopeless majority
to tackle but if you could bring it down a bit you'd get a
chance of contesting a marginal seat and if you won that
you'd be on your way."

Like a signpost on the road ahead of him Humphrey
saw that tall desiccated figure and heard him once again,
". . . when you've been as long as I have in the Service".

"Shall I look like Huffy one day?" he asked himself.
"Shall I feel like Huffy one day?"

Mrs Mowart was still awake when her only son came
in and called him to her room.

"Did you have a jolly evening, darling boy?"

Humphrey told her about the dinner-party and then
fell suddenly silent.

"What is it?" his mother asked. "Is there something
on your mind?"

"Well, there is in a way."

Mrs Mowart braced herself to receive the news that
her son was engaged to be married. Ever since her husband died four years ago she had been preparing herself
for this moment. Now it had come.

"The Minister asked me if I had ever thought of
chucking the Civil Service and going in for politics. I was
rather shaken because as a matter of fact I have wondered
about that."

"You never talked to me about it, Humphrey."

"It was really too vague an idea to talk about, but this
evening the Minister said he was sure he could find me a
hopeless constituency but that if I could lower the majority
he had no doubt Party Headquarters would get me
adopted as candidate for some marginal seat at the next

election. So as I was driving back to-night what had been a sort of dream at the back of my mind became something I had to make up my mind about. What do you think, Mother?"

"All I think is that you must make up your own mind and whatever you decide you know that I shall always understand your decision."

Humphrey leaned over and kissed his mother.

"I know that only too well," he assured her. "Anyway, whatever I decide, I couldn't resign just now. Poor old Huffy has been having a hectic time lately with one thing and another."

Sir Oliver continued to have a hectic time that week. In spite of the communiqué dissociating the Ministry of Sanitation from any encouragement of Dandimilk indignant letters kept arriving; worse still there were grateful letters from vegetarians for the encouragement the Minister of Sanitation had given to those who believed that animal food in any form, liquid or solid, was largely responsible for everything wrong in the country from its financial position to the common cold.

The climax was reached when a paragraph in the *Daily Switch* appeared on Thursday morning.

"The new vegetable milk brought to the notice of the public last week in an interview Dr Emilius Scratchbury gave to a reporter of the *Daily Switch* is again in the news. Yesterday the old cathedral city of Oatcester was literally buzzing with excitement when a large open-air meeting was addressed by Mr William Narbrow, the well-known farmer whose Harvest Home every year at Ye Olde Farme brings many visitors from the United States and the Commonwealth.

"Mr Narbrow declared that if the new vegetable milk were encouraged by the Government the whole future of dairy-herds would be imperilled. He had been dismayed to learn that a centre for manufacturing this vegetable milk had been established at Beechwood Farm, within three miles of Oatcester. He had read to his amazement that a Dr Scratchbury claimed to have received encouragement for his product from the Ministry of Sanitation, but he had been glad to read a contradiction of this in the *Oatcester Courant* and other papers. Moreover, he had received a personal assurance from the Minister of Sanitation that nothing would be done by him to encourage this vegetable milk. The Rt. Hon. Henry Upjohn, the popular member for North Wessex, had recently honoured Ye Olde Farme by visiting it in company with Mr John Ackroyd, the popular member for Oatshire, and Sir Oliver Huffam, the Permanent Secretary of the Ministry of Sanitation, where they had been privileged to see a display by the world-famous Hardingham morris-dancers.

"Mr Narbrow went on to say how much he regretted the apparent lack of interest shown by the Ministry of Cultivation in this fresh attempt by urban industrialists to undermine the agriculture of the county.

"'I give due warning,' said Mr Narbrow, 'that unless the Law steps in to protect the agricultural interests of Oatshire the agricultural interests of Oatshire may be driven to take the Law into their own hands.'

"'What does that mean?' Mr Narbrow was asked by our reporter.

"'Wait and see,' Mr Narbrow replied.

"And if the temper of Oatshire is to be judged by the temper of that meeting held in the old cathedral city we shall not have to wait long."

"If the public are going to think that we were mixed up in this infernal stuff," said the Minister, "this fellow Narbrow must be made to leave our names out of it. Do you think it would be a good idea to send young Humphrey Mowart down to Oatcester and get him to tackle Narbrow? Suppose they break up this place where the milk is made? Narbrow is quite capable of suggesting that we put him up to it."

Sir Oliver considered Mr Upjohn's suggestion carefully.

"Yes, perhaps we should do our best to guard ourselves against unpleasant contingencies," he agreed. "Mr Narbrow rang us up to ask if we could divert our drain once more and lay it under Beechwood Farm where this Dandimilk is made."

"They must have other places about the country if they're hoping to distribute this Dandimilk in any quantity," Mr Upjohn suggested.

"I've been thinking, Minister, that Mowart might be told to notify Mr Narbrow that if names were mentioned again the Ministry would have to bear in mind the possibility of reverting to the original line envisaged for the main drain, passing under Mr Narbrow's farm."

"That's very canny, Huffam. That ought to keep his mouth shut. But don't you think Mowart should warn him that if there's any kind of violence the main drain will definitely be laid under his farm?"

"I don't like committing us to a positive future," said Sir Oliver. "I think Mowart will know how to suggest a contingent future on the lines I have just indicated."

"I'm sure he will," Mr Upjohn agreed.

Humphrey Mowart was naturally pleased when Sir Oliver told him that the Minister had suggested his going down to Oatcester.

"Shall I notify Mr Narbrow that I'll be calling on him to-morrow afternoon, sir?"

"I think Saturday afternoon will be better, Humphrey. You will have to stay the night at the Blue Bull and there will probably be at least one train back to London on Sunday."

"I was proposing to drive down, sir. Sunday trains are apt to be rather slow."

"Yes, well, but you'll make a point of being back at the Ministry by Monday morning. We shall have a heavy week, considering this circular the Ministry of Leisure will shortly be issuing to local authorities in England and Wales."

Presently Humphrey Mowart was to be even more

pleased when the Minister told him that he had been in touch with the Member of Oatshire and that Mr Ackroyd would be glad to put him up at Tailbush Manor on Saturday night.

When Sir Oliver turned his key in the Yale lock at 9 Chillingham Gardens a few minutes after six on that October evening his yodel in the hall was more like a real yodel than it had been for some time.

"Have you had a tiring day, Olly?" Lady Huffam asked at the head of the stairs.

"Not more than usual, Gertrude. I'm quite looking forward to our dinner with Nigel and Rosemary."

"Yes, I haven't seen dear little Noll for three days and he's growing so fast."

"We mustn't wake him up," said Sir Oliver quickly. "It wouldn't be fair on Rosemary."

"No, indeed. She rang me up just now to ask if we could possibly be with them by a quarter-past-seven. Apparently there's something important on the television which Nigel is anxious to look at?"

"Is there indeed?" Sir Oliver commented with an indulgent smile. "And that reminds me, Gertrude. I've been going into this question of television and I think it might be a good idea if we installed it upstairs. Apparently it has developed considerably and I may find it useful for keeping in touch with what is going on. I'm disinclined to read *The Times* when I get back. We have so much paper to deal with in the course of our work at the Ministry."

"The television has been a great success downstairs, Olly. They have something they call I.T.V. which they enjoy very much. It apparently gives all kind of useful household information. Ethel was telling me of a new washing-powder called Blanco which apparently washes whiter than white."

"White is white," said Sir Oliver. "If it were whiter than white it wouldn't be white."

"Well, that's what this I.T.V. claims. So I told Ethel

we would try it. The laundries are so bad nowadays.
They don't wash clothes any longer. They just tear them
to pieces."

Lady Huffam had expected that her husband would
want to walk along to Broomsgrove Mansions as it was
a fine evening, but to her surprise he called up just after
seven to say that the taxi was waiting. Poor Olly, he must
have had a more tiring day than usual at the Ministry,
she said to herself.

"I'm glad you're in splendid time," Rosemary told
her mother-in-law, when she was taking her to her room.
"Nigel's Western comes on at eight."

"Western Hospital?" Lady Huffam asked vaguely.

"No, no, he doesn't care for Emergency Ward 10
which I like much better than these Indians and cowboys
shooting at one another. Deadwood Gulch is a Western,
and it comes on to-night. Nigel hasn't stopped reminding
me since he got back from the Treasury."

"I hope they won't wake dear little Noll," said Lady
Huffam. "I had to go downstairs to see Cook about something the other evening and the noise was deafening in
the staff sitting-room."

When Rosemary brought her mother-in-law into the
sitting-room she announced that dinner would be ready
almost at once.

"Oh, that's splendid," Nigel said. "We won't have the
television on during dinner. There's nothing particularly interesting this evening till eight."

The future of Captain Quick remained continuously
in doubt until ten to nine, when the Sheriff arrived with a
posse just as the Carroway Chief had ordered the fire to
be kindled round the stake to which Captain Quick was
bound.

"I thought the Sheriff would arrive in time, Dad,"
said Nigel. "Do we want the News?"

"I think we should listen to the News," said Sir Oliver.

When the News had been given and the television was
silent Sir Oliver said to his son.

"I wanted to listen to the News because I am seriously thinking of installing the television upstairs at Number Nine, and I wanted to know if it was likely to be useful. I thought the presentation of the news was very adequate, and I think it *will* be useful to have the television. The only question now is whether we should instal it in the drawing-room or in the Den. I'm inclined to favour the Den. What do you think, Gertrude?"

"I think you should put it wherever you think it will be best, Olly. The only thing is that the television is sometimes rather noisy downstairs. I don't know if you would hear it in the Den."

"Well, that can be ascertained."

"You're evidently not expecting young Jeremy back just yet, Dad," said Nigel. "Have you heard from him again?"

"Not since he wrote from Greece. But he'll probably be writing soon again."

"Dear old Jeremy," said Rosemary with a twinkle in her dark eyes. "He's probably playing Indians and cowboys in earnest by now."

Chapter 10

Humphrey Mowart had made up his mind to drive down to Oatcester after he left the Ministry that Friday afternoon and he was rather taken aback when Sir Oliver asked him that morning if he thought he could arrange for the installation of a television set in the Den at 9 Chillingham Gardens before he went away on Saturday morning.

"The draft of a circular which the Ministry of Leisure is proposing to issue early in January has arrived and while you are studying it, sir, it might be as well if I dealt with the television matter right away so that if possible I could get it installed during the lunch hour to-day. Saturday morning is always rather a difficulty nowadays."

Sir Oliver reflected upon his Private Secretary's suggestion.

"How long do you think you'll be away, Humphrey?"

"I won't be more than half an hour, by which time you'll have carefully considered the circular. You may want to give me further instructions about my forthcoming contact with Mr Narbrow."

"Don't be longer than you can help, Humphrey."

"And may I suggest, sir, that after a snack lunch I drive you home to make sure you have a complete grasp of the knobs."

"The knobs?" Sir Oliver repeated.

"The knobs you turn to get B.B.C. or I.T.V. and increase or decrease the volume."

"This television sounds a more complicated operation than I had envisaged," said Sir Oliver. "But if an emergency arose I dare say our maids would be able to offer some advice based on their experience of the television downstairs."

Humphrey Mowart went off on his mission and left Sir Oliver reading the draft of the circular.

Circular No. 96/108
(Ministry of Leisure)

CIRCULAR FROM THE MINISTRY OF LEISURE
CHEYNE WALK, LONDON, S.W.3

Sir,

PROVISION OF FACILITIES FOR LEISURE

1. In recent debates of Parliament the Government has emphasised its concern for wider and more efficient provision of facilities for the enlargement for the continually increasing opportunities for leisure and the improved administration and organisation of such leisure. Although voluntary interests have played a large part in the development and administration of recreation, the main burden of capital investment in recreative facilities falls on local authorities acting under various statutory provisions. These include the duties of the local education authorities to secure that the facilities for primary, secondary and further education made adequate provision for recreation and social and physical training; and the powers of local authorities in general under the Recreation Acts and the provisions relating to parks, pleasure grounds and baths in the Public Health Acts.

2. The purpose of this circular, which is issued at the direction of the Minister of Leisure and the Minister of Accommodation and the Minister of Movement and the Minister of Sanitation, is to outline the measures which the Government is taking to encourage the further development of sport, hiking, camping, mountaineering, potholing, orienteering and all other forms of physical recreation and to suggest ways in which local authorities in co-operation with the voluntary bodies and other interests concerned may be able to improve and extend facilities in their areas for children and young people and for the community at large.

3. The Government has announced increases in the total of grants available towards the cost of recreation. Grants can now be given to Clubs catering for a single sport as well as to those with many sports activities provided that Club membership is open to the public in general in accordance with the principles of strict egalitarianism by which the Government is animated. Help can be given with the cost of provision and extension of recreational facilities such as:—playing fields, 9-hole golf-links, indoor and outdoor tennis courts, sports pavilions and halls from which the form of gambling known as bingo is excluded, swimming-baths, camping sites, boat houses, mountaineering and pot-hole rescue huts; up to half of the cost of an approved scheme can be met, provided that the Club can show that it needs the money. It will often save time if the Ministry of Leisure is consulted at an early stage about large or complicated projects. It will be advisable to consult the Ministry of Sanitation, Cork Street, London, W.1, when applying for grants towards the purchase of land for camping-sites. Applications for these grants are submitted through local authorities which are asked to add their observations and to forward applications to the Ministry of Leisure as quickly as possible.

4. It is estimated that capital expenditure on recreation-educational facilities provided as part of educational policy has escalated to about £13½ m. covering provision of playing fields, hard games areas, gymnasium and swimming baths. Capital expenditure by local authorities on recreational facilities outside educational establishments has escalated to about £11½ m. The total capital expenditure involved has thus escalated to about £25 m. and is likely to escalate steadily every year in the future.

5. Since the trend of expenditure seems likely to continue, it is all the more important to ensure that such escalation is paid out to the best advantage. It is important to see that the number, size and location of recreational facilities are planned over a sufficiently large

area with the needs of all sections of the community in mind.

6. It is therefore recommended that all local authorities should carry out reviews of their areas to avoid overlapping with the plans of an adjacent area. Collaboration between local authorities will be necessary because recreational facilities near the boundary may serve neighbouring areas. Furthermore, there will normally be more than one authority with power to provide them; in boroughs and urban and rural districts, the local authority for the area and the County Council have powers, and in rural districts there are also the parish councils.

7. When major recreational facilities and centres are in mind, it will be necessary to arrange for collaboration between the local authorities and other interested bodies over a wide area, and it is urged that early steps should be taken to bring this about. Where there is existing machinery there will be advantage in using it, but otherwise it will be necessary to make special arrangements for the purpose; the county and county borough councils within a convenient geographical area are probably in the best position to take the initiative in setting up the machinery and calling the necessary conferences.

8. Besides planning facilities for playing fields, 9-hole golf-links, swimming baths, running tracks, jumping-pits, hard courts and other sporting requisites local authorities in appropriate geographical areas are urged to afford every help to mountaineering, skiing, pot-holing and skating, by building hostels and huts, furnishing the latter with the necessary equipment to rescue mountaineers and pot-holers in difficulty. It will also be advantageous to purchase land on which camping sites can be established. Grants towards purchasing land for such sites will be made by the Ministry of Leisure where in co-operation with the Ministry of Sanitation the Ministry of Leisure shall be satisfied that such land is suitable for camping.

9. The recreational and hygienic value of hiking has been emphasised in recent debates in Parliament and the Minister of Leisure hopes that the influence of local authorities will be used to secure rights of way to enable hikers to proceed across country rather than make use of the roads which the Ministry of Movement is anxious to keep as clear as possible for lorries and motor-cars.

10. The Minister of Leisure trusts that local authorities in their various capacities will now consider the suggestions made in this circular and that they will take every opportunity to cater fully for the recreational needs of their areas. The Ministry for its part will give them every possible assistance.

I am, Sir,

Your obedient servant,

Thomas A. Robinson

The Clerk of the Authority
Local Authorities
England and Wales
M.L. 67556/4/202/3

"What is orienteering?" Sir Oliver asked when his Private Secretary came back only a minute or two after he had finished the careful mastication of the circular that the Ministry of Leisure was proposing to issue in January.

"I'm not absolutely certain, sir, but it seems to be some way of getting about the country by map. I know it has to do with using maps."

"And what is pot-holing?"

"That's something to do with exploring underground caves. One's always reading about pot-holers being lost in pot-holes and the whole neighbourhood turning out to extract them."

"That would account for this recommendation that local authorities should provide huts equipped with suitable rescue material. I was glad to see that this circular advises local authorities to consult the Ministry of

Sanitation before making grants to purchase land for camping sites."

"Have you any other observations to make, sir, before we return this draft to the Ministry of Leisure in the course of the next week?"

"Only one. In paragraph 4 it says that the capital expenditure is likely to escalate steadily every year. I have deleted 'escalate' and noted in the margin 'rise' with a note of interrogation, and in paragraph 5 I have deleted 'such escalation' and noted in the margin 'it' with a note of interrogation. I thought the notes of interrogation would be a tactful way of expressing my dislike of this American neologism which has already crept into a *Times* leader and which is now apparently creeping into official English."

"I've secured your television set, sir," said Humphrey Mowart to cheer up Sir Oliver's pessimism about the future of official English.

"You have?"

"And if you agree, sir, I'll drive you back to Chillingham Gardens in the lunch hour so that you can settle exactly where you want it."

"I'll telephone to Lady Huffam and ask her if she can manage to give us lunch."

"There's no need to bother Lady Huffam, sir. We could have a snack on the way at a little place I know in Brompton Road. The television people won't be at Chillingham Gardens till two."

"But I must let her know we shall be there for the installation of the television."

Presently Lady Huffam was on the telephone and her husband was speaking.

"No, Gertrude, nothing terrible has happened ... yes, yes, I know it's unusual for me to ring up home from the Ministry. What I am ringing for is to say that Humphrey Mowart and I will be at Number Nine about a quarter-past one. Humphrey suggested we should have what he calls a snack lunch on the way but I said I was sure you would prefer to give us lunch . . . yes, I thought you would . . . the reason for this unusual procedure on my part during the luncheon hour is that I have arranged for a television set to be installed and I was anxious for Humphrey Mowart to explain to me the operation of the various knobs and little etceteras of a television set so that I shall be in control of the machine when we are what they call viewing . . . yes, I know a television was satisfactorily installed downstairs but I do not want to find myself looking at and listening to advertisements for washing powders and chocolate. I should mistrust any advice they gave me about the knobs downstairs. There is, however, one important decision to make, and that is whether the television is to be installed in the drawing-room or in the Den. There is undoubtedly much to be said in favour of either alternative, but at the moment I am disposed to incline towards the Den as the more suitable location. If the Den can be decided upon I could retire there to view political or economic discussions in which you would not be interested. But before definitely deciding upon the Den I am anxious to ascertain whether the sound of the television they have downstairs is likely to penetrate the Den. I should not like to find that some political or economic discussion to which I was listening was being interrupted by advertisements. You could help me to decide between the drawing-room, where we know we are secure from being interrupted by the television downstairs, you could help me, I say, by ascertaining if, when you are in the Den, what I may call the sound-barrier of the Den is being broken by the television they have downstairs . . . yes, thank you, Gertrude, if you would ascertain this for me I should be grateful. Well, I have a hard morning's work before me and any further discussion between us as to the suitability of the location for the television must be postponed until Humphrey Mowart and I reach Number Nine."

Sir Oliver hung up the receiver and turned to his Private Secretary.

K

"I was sure Lady Huffam would want us to lunch with her, Humphrey. I must say I do rather hope that the Den will not be affected by the television. It's not fair to make a woman like my wife listen to political and economic discussions. Even in the old days, before I decided to give up the wireless after those deplorable broadcasts by Lord Braintree, my wife was apt to fall asleep during some of the items. I used to take in a paper they called the *Radio Times*. Does it still exist?"

"Indeed it does, sir," said Humphrey Mowart, managing to hide a smile. "You'll have to take it in again to find out what programmes the B.B.C. are giving out each week on television."

It is a tribute to the building and carpentry of once upon a time to be able to say that when Humphrey Mowart went down to the staff-room and turned the television on as loudly as if it were in a French or Italian restaurant the sound of it did not reach the Den.

"So I shall be thinking of you, sir, this week-end viewing Perry Mason in perfect peace."

"Perry Mason? What is that?"

"It's a serial about an American lawyer in California whose clients are all found not guilty week in week out. The principal witness against them always breaks down under Perry Mason's cross-examination and confesses to being in fact himself the murderer."

"That doesn't sound at all suitable for Lady Huffam. Her favourite writer is Charlotte Yonge, I hardly ever read a novel myself. By the time I've studied the various circulars and leaflets issued by other Government offices I'm ready for the land of Nod, and in the vacation I try to keep up with my classics. I devoted last summer to Lucretius and Plato."

That remark by his Chief recurred to Humphrey Mowart as he was nearing Oatcester on that Friday evening.

"Paper, paper, paper," he murmured to himself. "I wonder if I shall spend my evenings twenty years hence reading circulars and leaflets issued by Government offices. I wonder what the Civil Service would do if the country ran out of paper."

As he accelerated to escape from thoughts of a paper-wrapped future he said to himself that if to-morrow night at Tailbush Manor the Member for Oatshire gave him any encouragement to aim at a career in politics he really would resign from the Civil Service.

By coincidence, as Humphrey Mowart was accelerating from thoughts of a paper-wrapped future, Sir Mark Levett was saying to his old friend, Sir Oliver Huffam,

"Talking of paper, we really are getting rather seriously worried about the paper problem."

The Huffams and the Pettiwards were dining with the Levetts at the latters' house in Lord North Street, Westminster. For thirty years now Mark and Enid Levett, James and Mona Pettiward, and Oliver and Gertrude Huffam had been dining with one another, but only the Huffams had entertained in the same dining-room throughout that period. Sir Mark Levett, K.C.B., C.B.E., was now the Permanent Secretary of the Ministry of Production in Whitehall. Sir James Pettiward K.B.E., C.B., was now a Deputy Under Secretary of State at the Home Office.

The ladies had retired to the drawing-room; the men were sitting over their port at the dinner-table. Sir Oliver did not much care for port but he felt it was his duty to keep up the old way of life by pretending that he did. Indeed, he drank two glasses that evening because he had a slight feeling of guilt in betraying the old way of life by a surrender to television. Before they had left Chillingham Gardens in the Daimler Sir Oliver hired when they were dining any distance away from their own house, Sir Oliver had looked through the television programmes of the B.B.C. and had noted that a new serial called "The Sheriff of Bowie Knife City" was starting that very evening. He had sighed.

"Have you gone in for the television yet, Mark?" he asked.

"No, of course not. Enid can't stand it and I'm always too busy trying to keep up with the work."

Sir Oliver did not suppose that Mark Levett had gone in for television, but if by chance he had succumbed as he himself had succumbed he would have asked Mark Levett to switch it on in order to see how his set compared with his own; the Sheriff of Bowie Knife City was due to appear at this moment.

"I've just had a set installed in the Den," he told Mark Levett.

"You're as bad as Jim," said Sir Mark.

"Mona likes it and after a day at the Home Office," said Sir James Pettiward, "I find it a bit of a relaxation. I never told you, Oliver, because you were always so down on it. The old eyes are getting a bit troublesome, and with the amount of reading I have to do I find the print in these paper-back thrillers a bit of a bore."

It was then that Sir Mark Levett said,

"Talking of paper we are getting rather seriously worried about the paper problem. We're in touch with the Waste-Paper basket as Jim and I used to call it when you were Apsley Howe's Principal Private Secretary. Dear old Oliver, you used to manage a pained smile but you didn't think it a bit funny. I'm lunching with Hugh Havers at the Heraeum next Monday. They'll have to do something about waste paper at his Ministry. Why don't you join us at lunch, Oliver?"

"I don't think paper is our concern."

"It'll be very much the Ministry of Sanitation's concern if we have to ration toilet-paper."

"Mark must have his joke," James Pettiward laughed.

"All the same, Oliver, I think you should join us on Monday," Mark Levett told him. "But that's enough shop. Have you heard again from young Jeremy? Is he still in Greece?"

"Gertrude and I are hoping for a letter soon."

"You know, Oliver," said James Pettiward, "I'm still wondering how you and Gertrude ever produced that younger son of yours. You were very lucky."

"Lucky, Jim?"

"Oh, lucky Jim, how I envy him," Mark Levett laughed, "Not you, Jim Pettiward. But you're right about Oliver."

Sir Oliver looked puzzled. Were his two old friends trying to console him over Jeremy's escapade?

"Well, you know," James Pettiward said, "here are we three who have all got as far as we could hope in the Civil Service, and yet there are moments when I ask myself if in doing my best to make the life of the country run smoothly I may not somehow have missed making the most of my own life. That's why I said you are lucky, Oliver, to have a boy like Jeremy."

"I know what Jim means," said Mark Levett. "You'll be retiring soon, Oliver. You'll have the satisfaction of seeing Nigel rising upward at the Treasury with the possibility of one day being the head of the Civil Service. But suppose young Jeremy discovers for himself what he really wants to do and makes the grade, that will be just as much of a satisfaction. Don't we all at the back of our minds envy the people who are independent?"

"I think you and Jim and I can consider ourselves independent," said Sir Oliver.

"Except that we are all three tied to time and place," said Mark Levett. "I sometimes think that all Civil Servants should have to retire at thirty-five and earn their own living for the next twenty years when they could re-enter the Civil Service and stay in it until they wanted to retire."

"I'm afraid you will never persuade me, Mark, that the Civil Service of Utopia is a better Service than our own."

"However good it is, Oliver, you'll make a great mistake if you try to push Jeremy into it. However, Jim and I really have no rights to lecture you. Neither of us has a son. Our problems are sons-in-laws."

As they were going upstairs to join the ladies Sir Mark Levett reminded Sir Oliver.

"Do make a point of lunching with Hugh Havers and me on Monday. I think you ought to know what the position is about paper."

Chapter 11

As Sir Mark Levett was reminding Sir Oliver about lunch at the Heraeum on Monday Humphrey Mowart was entering the dining-room at the Blue Bull. There were no diners left and a waitress was laying the tables for breakfast. The waiter looked glumly at the late-comer.

"Dinner's over," he said.

"That's all right. I'll have something cold."

Humphrey was given a plate of lean ham with tomatoes whose faint flavour had been obliterated by vinegar. He asked for pickles; a pot of mixed pickles from which predecessors had removed all the onions and left nothing but snippets of gherkin and bits of cauliflower was put before him. The bread was white enough to compete with a washing powder and tasted of nothing. It was indeed a meal all too typical of a November evening's hospitality in the English countryside of to-day. Humphrey did not dally over his meal and to the obvious gratification of the waiter withdrew to the lounge where he ordered himself a whisky and soda and took a paper-back thriller out of his pocket. He had hardly read a couple of pages when he heard what sounded like nuts being cracked. He looked up and saw at the other end of the lounge the bright red hair of Miss Veale, who was indeed cracking walnuts. It occurred to him that she must have found out about the headquarters of Dandimilk. He got up and strolled across the lounge.

"Good evening, Miss Veale."

"It's you again, young man," she exclaimed. "Have you come to tell me that the Right Honourable Upjohn is going to be our patron after all?"

"No, I'm afraid that isn't possible; I am down here on some business for the Ministry and I was wondering what had brought you to Oatcester on a Friday evening in November."

"It was you who brought me down, young man."

"I?"

"Yes, didn't you advise me to ask Dr Emilius Scratchbury to be the patron of our Society? Oh, excuse me, will you take a walnut?"

"No, thank you, I've just had dinner. But won't you have a drink with me?"

The waiter had just come in with Humphrey Mowart's whisky.

"That's very polite of you, young man. I'll take a glass of cowslip wine."

Humphrey looked at the waiter who shook his head.

"They haven't got any cowslip wine."

"I always ask for cowslip wine. One of our members makes beautiful cowslip wine. We call ourselves the Cowslip League, you know."

"I'm sorry the Blue Bull doesn't run to cowslip wine."

"More shame to him. And him a Conservative bull. He ought to know better." She suddenly prodded Humphrey Mowart. "They may serve Dandimilk. This isn't Woolworth's. Ask him if they keep Dandimilk, young man."

"You ask him, Miss Veale."

"Have you got a nice glass of Dandimilk?"

"Dandy milk, mum? Oh yes, our milk is very dandy. Shall I bring you a glass?" the waiter asked.

"Is your milk cows' milk?" Miss Veale asked, suspicion gleaming in her greenish eyes.

"Oh yes, mum."

"Then I'll have a glass of whisky. But I don't want soda in it. Soda always makes me sneeze."

"Just as stupid as waiters always are," Miss Veale commented, when the waiter had gone. "He thought I was asking for Dandimilk with a 'y'. The sooner we get rid of 'y', the better for the English language. I told you about poor Mr Baillie with an 'e' getting mixed up with

Mr Bailey with a 'y'. Well, if we can't get rid of 'y' from the English language I shall suggest to Dr Emilius Scratchbury that he spells Dandimilk with a 'y'."

"Are you expecting to see Dr Scratchbury?" Humphrey asked.

"Yes, yes, I've got an appointment with him to-morrow at Beechwood Farm. I wrote to ask him to be patron of the Society for Prevention of Cruelty to Cows, and he wrote me such a nice letter." She picked up her bag. "Here it is."

Humphrey Mowart took the letter with the all too familiar address of 13 Gog and Magog Lane.

Dear Miss Veale,

I am deeply gratified by your enquiry. Yes, I accept with pleasure your suggestion that I should become the patron of the Society for the Prevention of Cruelty to Cows. I am confident that when the nation realises that cows' milk has great nutritional value for calves but none for human beings the demand for cows' milk will rapidly diminish, and the premature weaning of calves will soon become a survival of the ignorant and barbaric past.

Thanks to the growing achievements of technology we now have in Dandimilk a substitute for cows' milk. I shall be happy to welcome you next Saturday at Beechwood Farm where it will be my pleasure to offer you a brimming glass of Dandimilk with your lunch. I am a strict vegetarian as you have probably surmised but I think you will find our carrot cutlets made by a special process discovered by myself superior to any cutlets of which meat is the ingredient. But this is only one of the delicacies which by a new method of compression discovered by myself and with which I hope to convert our countrymen to that vegetarianism which will undoubtedly once again restore to Britain the leadership of the world. It was the roast beef of old England but the young England of to-morrow will despise it.

You will find the train which leaves for Oatcester on Friday afternoon at 3.15 somewhat overcrowded until it emerges from the Green Belt. This is due to the praiseworthy efforts of the Ministry of Leisure to make Saturday a day of rest according to the Mosaic precepts. I wish I could write with equal appreciation of the efforts of the Ministry of Sanitation and the Ministry of Hygiene.

When you reach Oatcester I recommend you to stay at the 'Blue Bull' which when the praises of Dandimilk resound everywhere may quite suitably call itself the 'Blue Bell'. I shall come for you in a car at eleven o'clock on Saturday morning and look forward to showing myself worthy of being the patron of your Society.

Yours sincerely
Emilius Scratchbury

"That is a noble letter, is it not, young man?" Miss Veale asked earnestly.

"Most interesting," Humphrey Mowart assured her.

"And you will notice that Dr Scratchbury expresses disappointment about the way the Ministry of Sanitation has ignored Dandimilk."

At this moment the waiter came in with Miss Veale's whisky.

"Say when," Humphrey asked her as he prepared to add the water.

"To-morrow. I shall meet that great man to-morrow."

"Say when I've added enough water to your whisky."

"You can never add enough water to any whisky for me," Miss Veale declared.

Humphrey filled up her glass which she raised to her lips with the ejaculation 'Yeeyeea!'

Humphrey raised his glass, a puzzled expression on his jolly face.

"Your very good health, Miss Veale."

She smiled at him with a kind of maternal fondness.

"I'm glad you understand Greek, young man."

"Greek?"

"Tut-tut-tut! I was misled. You evidently don't understand Greek. You don't know that 'Yeeyeea' means 'health'. Spelt H-Y-G-E-I-A but pronounced 'yeeyeea'.

I do not grudge the Greeks their 'y's. The French are more honest than we are. They do at least have the *comme il faut* as they say in Paris to call it 'y-grec'."

"I'm afraid I should have pronounced it like Hygiene," said Humphrey apologetically.

"A word which we stole from the poor Greeks."

"You have travelled in Greece?"

"Not yet, young man, but one of our members, a Mrs Jones, had a Greek grandfather and it was she who taught me to say 'yeeyeea' when I very occasionally partake of a glass of whisky. When I say 'yeeyeea' it reminds me that a very occasional glass of whisky is highly hygienic."

"You'll have to teach Dr Scratchbury to say 'yeeyeea' when he offers you a glass of Dandimilk to-morrow."

Humphrey was finding himself fascinated by Miss Veale's absurdity and was almost tempted to suggest accompanying her to-morrow to Beechwood Farm. He would have given much to be present at the meeting between her and Dr Scratchbury.

"Do you believe in the importance of numbers to our daily lives, young man?" she asked.

"In what way?"

"In every way. The first name of Dr Scratchbury is Emilius. My first name is Euphemia."

"Both beginning with E."

She shook her bright red head impatiently.

"That is of secondary importance. What *is* important is that both are names of four syllables. Added together they make eight. And you know what eight signifies? You evidently don't. Eight, young man, is the number of fate. There are eleven letters in Scratchbury and five letters in Veale. Eleven and five make?"

"Sixteen," said Humphrey.

Miss Veale nodded approvingly.

"Well, you may not understand Greek, young man, but you are certainly good at arithmetic. You are quite right. Eleven and five make sixteen. Sixteen is twice eight, and as I've just told you, eight is the number of fate. But that is not all. The letters of Beechwood Farm add up to thirteen."

"But isn't that supposed to be an unlucky number, Miss Veale?"

"Thirteen is not a whole number," she said, "Three and one make four. Four is half eight, the number of fate. But even that is not all. The letters in Oatcester and Blue Bull would add up to seventeen. Seven and one make eight. So perhaps you can understand now, young man, why I look forward to meeting Dr Emilius Scratchbury to-morrow almost with awe. Eleven o'clock. One and one make two. Four times two is eight. Fate again."

Involuntarily Humphrey was counting the letters in his own name.

"Fourteen letters in my name," he said.

"Four and one are five," said Miss Veale. "When were you born?"

"May 5th."

Miss Veale ran the fingers of a well-shaped hand along the table.

"The fifth day of the fifth month. Oh, there's no doubt of it. You are a five. I was born on the eighth day of the eighth month."

It was now Humphrey's turn to count with his fingers.

"August 8th."

"The Eighth of August I prefer to say. And why is it called August?"

"For Augustus Caesar, wasn't it?"

"Ah, I know what you're going to say, young man. You're going to say that, before we upset the Roman calendar by making the First of January New Year's Day instead of the First of March as it ought to be, August was the sixth month. But what was the name of Augustus before he became Augustus?"

"Octavius."

"Eight again," said Miss Veale triumphantly. "So even when we upset the calendar it made no difference to me. I am still eight. If only we hadn't upset the cal-

endar you would have been born on the fifth day of the
third month, and you would have been another eight,
and fourteen added to eight makes twenty-two, in which
case you would have been a four instead of a five. Never
mind, we can't all be two's and four's and eight's."

"But aren't odd numbers supposed to be luckier than
even numbers?" Humphrey asked.

"There is no such thing as luck. Luck is fate."

Humphrey was silent for a minute or two. He hoped
Miss Veale would think his silence a tribute to the solem-
nity with which she had impressed upon him that luck
was fate. What he was pondering was whether he should
ask Miss Veale to meet him after her visit to Beechwood
Farm so that he could learn more about it. The snag was
Dr Scratchbury. It would not do for somebody from the
Ministry of Sanitation to give him another opportunity
to mislead a newspaper reporter. He decided against
such precipitate action. After all he was *still* in the Civil
Service.

"I should be much interested to hear the result of your
meeting with Dr Scratchbury," he said, breaking the
silence of careful consideration. "I was wondering if I
might call on you at Gladstone Terrace; of course, it's
8 Gladstone Terrace, isn't it?"

"And Gladstone Terrace adds up to sixteen, young
man, which with your good arithmetic you'll know is
twice eight. Yes, you may come and have tea with me
one day as long as you don't expect me to offer you milk
with your tea."

"May I come next Tuesday? I'm afraid I shall not
manage to reach you till after five. So please don't bother
about tea. I'll have had my tea at the Ministry."

"*With* cows' milk, I suppose?"

"Yes, I must be frank and admit that I do take milk
with my tea."

Miss Veale shook her bright red hair.

"Ah, well, well, Rome wasn't built in a day, but if
Dr Scratchbury succeeds in turning people away from

cows' milk the building will get on much faster. And now I'll say 'good night', young man. I have a memorable day before me."

Humphrey Mowart thought it wiser to drive off to see Mr Narbrow before Dr Scratchbury arrived next morning to take Miss Veale to Beechwood Farm, much as he regretted not being a witness of their first meeting.

On his way to Ye Olde Farme he suddenly said "Steady on, my lad". He had been counting to himself— Oliver Huffam twelve, Henry Upjohn eleven, John Ackroyd eleven, William Narbrow fourteen. Humphrey smiled. He was picturing Huffy's expression if he told him that he was a three and that the Minister and the M.P. were both two's.

Presently he was sitting in the parlour of Ye Olde Farme with a mug of mead beside him.

"Sir Oliver Huffam was telling me about this wonderful mead of yours, Mr Narbrow. It's absolutely delicious."

"And all made from the fermented honey of my own bees. That's real honey. Not that stuff for which they have the imperence to charge you eight or nine shillings for what looks like a blooming pot of vaseline. But that Sir Oliver Huffam of yours made one big mistake. He wouldn't take a glass of Margery's punch. Mr Ackroyd made a rare good joke about her punch. He said it were better nor Punch and Judy and Dog Toby all in one."

"I'm staying with Mr Ackroyd to-night at Tailbush Manor."

"There's one of the old brigade. We're lucky to have a member like Mr Ackroyd to stand up for us in Parliament. And Mr Upjohn too. I'm always telling them in North Wessex how lucky they be. But mind you, Mr Mowart, I was in a proper frizz when I read in that blooming paper about him saying he advised everybody to drink this Dandimilk instead of cows' milk."

"You saw the Ministry of Sanitation's contradiction?"

"Oh yes, I saw that but the pity is that a dozen reads what was contradicted for one who reads the contradiction. You never see scare headlines over a contra-diction. But there you are, if the papers printed all the contradictions they ought to print there wouldn't be any room for the news."

"It's about that interview with the Minister which was contradicted that I've come to talk to you, Mr Narbrow. You asked us if we couldn't divert the main drain be-tween Oatcester and Hardingham to pass under Beech-wood Farm."

"I'm glad to hear you pronounce it Oaster, Mr Mowart."

"It was Sir Oliver Huffam who told me that was the old pronunciation."

"Then why did he keep on calling it Oat-cester when he came to Ye Olde Farme?"

"I expect he felt that as a Government official he ought not to suggest he was criticising the B.B.C."

"I daresay you be right. I asked Mr Ackroyd once why he didn't call it Oaster and he said right away he was afeard it might lose him votes because people nowadays take the B.B.C. for bible truth. Still, he's one of the old brigade all right, even though he didn't know till I told him that the Oatshire police were all in green until that blooming Great War broke up everything. I was only a nipper at the time but I can well remember those green constables of ours."

"To return to our drain, Mr Narbrow. If we were to divert it as you suggest to run under Beechwood Farm it would cost a great deal more, and we've already had difficulty over the diversion that takes it under Harding-ham Heath instead of under Ye Olde Farme, which is going to cost more than we anticipated."

"But something ought to be done about the way this blooming Scratchbury is letting a good farm of 150 acres go back to weeds to make what he has the nerve to call milk, and comes sneaking into my dairy with a tin of his unnatural stuff."

"I suggest you approach the Ministry of Cultivation,

Mr Narbrow. It is their business to intervene if they consider that good agricultural land is being neglected. We at our Ministry are concerned solely with the problems of sanitation, and believe me those problems are formidable enough."

"What do 'ee want me to do?"

"We hope you'll do nothing about Dr Scratchbury. Anything you do will only give him more opportunity to advertise his patent milk and if the public think he is being hindered in his experiments by dairymen, well, you know what the British public are, they're always on the side of somebody who they think is up against it. I am sure the best way to deal with Dr Scratchbury is to ignore him."

"There may be something in what you say, Mr Mowart."

"I'm sure there's a lot in what I say. You are in an impregnable position. We at the Ministry of Sanitation were so deeply impressed by your work here that we were able to justify the extra cost of laying the main drain between Oatcester and Hardingham under the Heath instead of through Ye Olde Farme. I know Mr Ackroyd would be glad to hear you have decided to ignore Dr Scratchbury and I should like to assure him when I arrive at Tailbush Manor this afternoon that such is your decision. He is as anxious as Mr Upjohn to keep North Wessex and Oatshire free of New Towns and if either of their constituencies become a centre of controversy the Ministry of Accommodation might think that was a good excuse to build a New Town in one or other of them. Or again the Ministry of Protection might decide that Oatshire was just the area they wanted for our jet planes to practise getting to America an hour faster than American jet planes can get to Europe. That would mean loud bangs at all hours with cows aborting and hens not laying and the peace of your countryside destroyed."

Humphrey Mowart took a pull at his mug of mead;

he almost felt as if he had sat down after making his maiden speech in the House of Commons.

"Don't worry, Mr Mowart," Mr Narbrow said as he filled up Humphrey's mug. "You can tell the Right Honourable Upjohn and Mr Ackroyd that I'm not going to bother my head any more about Dr Scratchbury."

"I felt sure you would understand why we cannot lay the main drain under Beechwood Farm, Mr Narbrow. It has been a great pleasure for me to make your acquaintance and I hope I may have the luck some day to be present at your Harvest Home."

The farmer pressed Humphrey to stay for the midday dinner but he said he thought he must drive on to Hardingham to see Mr Chuff the Mayor and after that get back to Oatcester to see Mr Gollop, the other Mayor.

"I want to explain how much our Ministry regretted that unfortunate interview in the *Daily Switch*. And there are one or two questions about the best date for us to start on the main drain."

By the time Humphrey Mowart reached Tailbush Manor he was able to feel that he had done all he could in Oatshire to allay the painful weals of the *Daily Switch*.

When he said good-bye to his host and hostess at eleven o'clock on Sunday evening to set out on his drive home the Member for Oatshire said,

"It's been great fun having you with us and if you *do* make up your mind to chuck the Civil Service and go into politics, Henry Upjohn and I will find a good hopeless constituency to try you out."

L

WHEN Sir Oliver returned to Cork Street from lunching at the Heraeum with the Permanent Secretaries of the Ministries of Production and Waste he was obviously worried.

"I'm sure we shan't have any more trouble from these Communists up in—" Humphrey Mowart mentioned a northern county—"who have been agitating to get all the Gentlemen and Ladies outside public lavatories changed to Men and Women."

"No, that's not what's worrying me, Humphrey. It's the paper position. Sir Mark Levett says that it may presently become very serious. We must see the effect of a circular which the Ministry of Waste will issue to all parish councils, rural district councils, borough councils, urban councils and county councils asking them to take all steps to encourage the collection of waste paper. The Ministry in turn will arrange to collect all the waste paper from them, which by some new process will then be pulped and allotted to the various paper-mills all over the country. One of the troubles is that this escalation . . ." Sir Oliver stopped abruptly. "I think you'll realise how worried I am, Humphrey, when I find myself a prey to that detestable American neologism."

"It certainly isn't like you, sir."

"Before I know where I am I shall be pronouncing it contróversy. I heard it twice yesterday on our television set, which as I told you this morning has otherwise been an unqualified success. But as I was saying, or alas, was not saying, one of the troubles is this competitive increase in the size of Sunday papers. None of them has yet reached the 946 pages of one of the New York Sunday papers last week but soon our Sunday papers will undoubtedly not be content until one of them achieves four figures and then of course the others will have to do the same. At the same time the daily newspapers are building up their circulations all the time, publishers keep publishing heavier and heavier books, paper-covers are taking the place of cloth bindings, and on top of that there is the amount of paper used by cigarette-smokers. You'll realise what a grave view Sir Mark Levett takes of the position when I tell you that the Ministry of Production are considering issuing a circular to all government offices, to urge the strictest consideration before they issue a circular or a leaflet. Sir Mark Levett is hopeful that the Ministry of Waste's circular to the various local authorities will succeed in rescuing a considerable amount of paper, and the Minister of Waste has consented to appear on television to explain the importance of saving paper. It is hoped that the Postmaster-General will appear on television and ask people to write fewer letters and have recourse instead to the telephones which the Post Office are supplying in larger numbers all the time."

"Well, sir, however much this threatened shortage of paper may worry other Ministries, we haven't got to worry."

"Have we not, Humphrey? Sir Mark Levett warned me that unless the Ministry of Waste succeed in reducing the amount of paper now being consumed there may be a shortage of toilet-paper; should such a disaster be imminent the Ministry of Sanitation will be indeed gravely involved. I am worried, seriously worried, very seriously worried indeed. Why are you smiling, Humphrey? There is surely nothing to smile about."

"I apologise, sir. I was thinking of a chapter in Rabelais."

"A chapter in Rabelais?" Sir Oliver repeated, an inflection of disapproval in his voice.

"But I'm afraid the substitute Pantagruel discovered for toilet paper would hardly be practical."

"I have never read Rabelais. What is called Rabelaisian humour has never appealed to me. Nor do I feel that a possible shortage of toilet-paper is a matter for mirth."

On his way back to Gloucester Road instead of finishing the crossword puzzle Sir Oliver turned over the pages of *The Times* with a critical eye on the contents. Much as he enjoyed his occasional games of golf at the week-end he felt that too much space was taken up by the performances of golfers with their rounds of 61 or 62 and pictures of their driving against a background of apparently vacuous spectators. As for the amount of space devoted to football, cricket, tennis, hockey, running, jumping and boxing it was surely exaggerated. And then the advertisements! Surely the Treasury should give a warning to the competitive advertising of electricity and gas. It was unfair to the public who had to pay for nationalised industries to brag about themselves in advertisements. *The Times* was a national institution. Was it right for a national institution to use all that paper for full page advertisements of computers? Computers were becoming a menace to the individual. No doubt Parliamentary elections would soon be conducted by computers and that might end in computers electing themselves to Parliament. Politicians were already enough of a problem to the Civil Service without computers trying to estimate what was the right way to run the country. However, if the worst apprehensions of the Ministry of Production were realised and the country were in the grip of a paper famine *The Times* would surely remember its duty as a national institution and set an example to the rest of the Press by reducing its size, even if it involved doubling its price. One had to remember with gratitude its impeccable attitude toward the Abdication, towards Appeasement, and not least gratefully its attitude toward the private morals of politicians.

When Sir Oliver reached Chillingham Gardens he told Ethel to be careful to preserve not only every day's *Times* but all the Sunday papers as well.

"And also, Ethel, keep every scrap of paper round every

parcel that comes to the house. And do not forget when you empty the waste-paper baskets that the contents are all to be carefully kept. No paper must be put into the dustbin. All paper must be stored in the old coal-cellar."

Sir Oliver had been loath to give up the kitchen range and rely on gas and electricity. For the first time he no longer regretted that surrender. No paper would any longer be required for lighting fires.

It was unfortunate that, when Sir Oliver retired to the Den in the hope of being transported by television to some western Erewhon in which he could forget for a while the paper situation, the first item to appear on the screen was mountainous flames rising from the largest paper-mill in Britain.

When Sir Oliver went up to join his wife in the drawing-room the sight of that burning paper-mill made him break for the first time his rule never to mention Ministry matters at home.

"You'll make a point of seeing that Ethel keeps every scrap of paper that comes to us, won't you, Gertrude?"

She knew better than to ask him why.

"I had some rather disquieting news at lunch," Sir Oliver went on.

"You were lunching with Mark, weren't you? Has that son-in-law of his been in trouble again by arguing with the traffic-wardens?"

"No, no. Mark was telling Hugh Havers and me that the Ministry of Production are worried about a possible paper shortage, and the Ministry of Waste will probably have to make an effort to induce the public to preserve all their waste-paper. I want you to be as economical as possible, Gertrude, with paper."

"Oh dear, and I was going to suggest we should have Jeremy's room papered while he was away."

"That's out of the question just now. Naturally one hopes that the worst will not come to the worst but one never knows and it would be wrong of us to indulge in wallpaper at such a moment. What was it Burke said?"

"I don't know what Mr Burke said, Olly. I don't think I've met Mr Burke, or have I? I'm so apt to forget whom we meet when we go to these official gatherings."

Sir Oliver sighed patiently.

"Edmund Burke has been dead long enough now not to be alluded to as 'Mr Burke'. Edmund Burke said 'Example is the school of mankind'. The general public is still at school in the Welfare State and we in the Civil Service are all assistant-masters. We have to set an example. So that is why I cannot sanction the re-papering of Jeremy's room at the present moment."

"I do wish we could have a letter from him, Olly. You don't think he's been captured by brigands?"

"I cannot bring myself to imagine that the most ferocious brigands would derive any satisfaction from capturing two schoolboys."

Lady Huffam's anxiety about her errant son was allayed next morning by the postman. Sir Oliver read aloud at the breakfast-table a letter from Jeremy with the address Poste Restante, Heraklion, Crete.

My dear Mum and Dad,

I am sorry to have been so long writing but Dick and I have been having a fabulous time. We did not manage to get to Cyprus but we got to Crete instead, and we were jolly glad when we did because Crete is a wow. Dad will be interested to know that there is a W.C. in the palace of Minos going back to about 1500 B.C. Dick said he wondered what they used for toilet-paper and I said 'papyrus of course'. Mum will be interested to hear what the women wore all those years ago. Well. I was staggered and so was Dick. They wore crinolines! One of them looked like Great-grandma Huffam when she was a girl in that photograph, well, not photograph but those glassy things that came before photographs. And they had puffed out sleeves like Grandma Huffam when she was young. And those topless dresses they're going in for now aren't nearly as topless as those dresses they were wearing about 1500 B.C.

But now comes my real good good news. A chap who is doing

excavations on the other side of Crete offered to put Dick and me up for as long as we could stay if we would help in the excavating. I think Dad will be pleased to hear this because I have now chosen what I am going to be. I am going to be an archeologist. That means I'll have to keep up with my Greek and that will certainly please Dad, but he will realise that I cannot now go back to school because I would have to be thinking about examinations all the time and anyway I do not want to go to Oxbridge or Camford because it would only mean swotting for more examinations, and as I have absolutely made up my mind not to go into the Civil Service there isn't any point in passing examinations. I am sick of paper, paper, paper all the time. I wonder what they'd do in the Civil Service if they ran out of paper.

Before we were lucky enough to get to Crete we went to Delphi and that was marvellous. Thebes was rather dull, but Mycenae! That really was smashing.

Dear Dad and Mum, don't be angry with me for not coming back. I have found out what I want to do with my life and you must try to understand what a difference it has made. Dick will go back in a month or two and says he will tell Mr Horner that he is willing to be what they call articled to become a solicitor. So you will be able to hear from him about some of our adventures.

> *With love from*
> *Your loving son*
> *Jeremy*

"Well," said Sir Oliver, "if he isn't going to enter the Civil Service I am not at all opposed to his devoting himself to archaeology. But I wish he wouldn't spell it with an 'e' instead of the more correct 'ae'."

"Oh, Olly, I am so glad you are in favour of Jeremy's becoming an arch . . . what he wants to become."

"Archaeologist, Gertrude. From the Greek words 'archaios' and 'logos', signifying one who devotes himself to systematic research into the relics and monuments of pre-history."

"I did know what archaeologist means, but I do sometimes get muddled over the pronunciation of very long words."

"Jeremy doesn't mention the name of this chap, as he calls him, who is excavating in Crete. I should be glad to hear. All the archaeologists I have known have been inclined to criticise other archaeologists. Jealousy is something to which we are not prone in the Civil Service."

"You'll ask Jeremy's friend Dick Horner to come and see us, won't you? I'm longing to hear about their adventures."

"Oh yes, but I have been considering another project, Gertrude. You will remember that Rosemary was urging Nigel to go on one of these cruises to the Aegean. I am tempted to suggest that we should accompany them, provided of course that the paper situation in so far as it affects us at the Ministry of Sanitation no longer threatens to deteriorate."

"That would be nice, Olly."

"I shall then be able to meet this chap, as Jeremy calls him, and ascertain from him whether in fact Jeremy does evince any unusual promise, in which case I shall be prepared to make him an allowance equivalent to any allowance I should have been prepared to make him at the University. I must confess I am very pleased to know that Jeremy intends to keep up his Greek. Yes, this letter has been a considerable relief to me." Sir Oliver turned to it again. " 'I wonder what they'd do in the Civil Service if they ran out of paper.' Pure coincidence of course that he should write that at this anxious moment. I could almost play with the fanciful notion that his visit to Delphi had inspired him with oracular powers."

When Sir Oliver opened his *Times* to glance at the headlines before folding it to a suitable size for the solution of the crossword puzzle he read with dismay of the millions of tons of paper consumed by yesterday's fire, and he told Humphrey Mowart to ring up the Ministry of Production.

"Is this deplorable fire going to make the paper situa-

tion worse, Mark? . . . what! Another large paper-mill
is now on fire? . . . indeed, I can understand how worried
you are . . . you are having a conference at noon . . . yes,
I shall be at the Heraeum. . . . Yes, I shall be anxious to
hear what has been decided."

Sir Oliver hung up and turned to his Private Secretary.

"Sir Mark Levett tells me that another large paper-
mill is on fire at this moment, Humphrey. Did you see
that appalling fire on television last night?"

"No, sir, but I read about it in last night's *Evening Post*.
I drove up from Little Hangover this morning and haven't
read a morning paper yet."

"Do you suppose this is another strategic move in the
cold war?"

"I don't see what the Communists would expect to
gain from a paper crisis."

"It would be very serious if the Civil Service were
deprived of paper. The whole fabric of the country
would collapse."

Humphrey Mowart decided to divert his Chief's mind
from such a prospect.

"We have just had the statistics for campers in the New
Forest, sir. Apparently there are five hundred times as
many campers as there were ten years ago. Nearly
300,000 this summer. You can certainly congratulate
yourself, sir, on that compromise with the Ministry of
Leisure. If there were nearly 300,000 campers in the New
Forest the number of campers all over Great Britain
can hardly be short of a million."

"But Great Britain includes Scotland and the Scottish
Office will have responsibility for the sanitary arrangements of campers. They will probably have trouble with
some of the Highland landowners. I recall from many
years ago a Highland landowner called Macdonald who
was known locally as Ben Nevis."

"What a marvellous nickname!"

"No, no, he really was called Ben Nevis up in the Highlands. He was Regional Controller of waste material in

the Highlands and Islands and was of some service to me personally in solving the problem of what to do with certain items of waste material. But what I was going to say was that this Highland landowner had a violent aversion not only to campers but even to hikers and I'm afraid the Ministry of Leisure may encounter strong opposition in their drive for camping and hiking. However, the solution of that problem will be a matter between the Ministry of Leisure and the Scottish Office. We shall not be involved."

"No, sir, quite, but at the rate that camping is esc . . . is rising, it looks as if our Inspectors and Assistant Inspectors will have to deal with at least 700,000 campers in England and Wales next summer."

"Ah well, Humphrey, it is not yet next summer and there is always a possibility that we may have a wet summer. At the moment the problem before us is the threat to the country's supply of paper. By a strange coincidence I had a letter from my boy Jeremy in Crete this morning in which he was wondering what the Civil Service would do if they ran out of paper. He is engaged in excavating under the direction of an archaeologist and told me that he wishes to make archaeology his profession. He was breaking to me the news that he could not enter the Civil Service because he was tired of examinations, and it was then that he made this remark about paper. Normally I should have dismissed such a remark as a piece of schoolboy folly, but coming as it did at this moment and after Jeremy had been to Delphi it made what I suppose I shall have to call a superstitious impression on me. Here is Jeremy's letter. You may care to read it."

Humphrey Mowart took the letter and when he had read it he made up his mind that this was the moment to break the news to Sir Oliver of his own intentions.

"You know, sir, *I* can understand what Jeremy feels and you've no idea what a relief it is to me that you understand too. I realise how deeply disappointed you

are that he does not want to enter the Civil Service but
after all for a boy not yet eighteen to know what he
intends to do as definitely as Jeremy is a pretty sure sign
that he will make a success of what he intends to do.
You made up your mind to go into the Civil Service
when you were much younger than Jeremy and here you
are to-day one of the top figures in the Civil Service.
Your other boy was like you and he may look forward to
being head of it one day."

"Yes, I understand Nigel is highly thought of at the
Treasury," Sir Oliver agreed.

"And now, sir, I'm going to ask you to be as understanding over me as you have been over Jeremy."

"Over you, Humphrey?"

"Yes, sir, because I have decided to leave the Civil
Service and go in for politics. But let me say at once that
I am not proposing to leave immediately. I appreciate
fully the privilege it has been to work directly under
you, and I shall not consider resigning until any problems created for our Ministry by the paper situation have
been satisfactorily settled."

"This comes as a shock to me, Humphrey. When did
you begin to entertain this strange idea of going into
politics?"

"Last year as you may remember I was left £10,000
by an uncle and it was then that I began to play with the
notion of going into politics."

"And perhaps crack what I remember calling a valuable nest egg."

"It was Mr Upjohn who made up my mind for
me."

"Wonders will never cease, Humphrey. This is the
first time I ever heard of a politician making up the mind
of a permanent official. We have been making up the
minds of politicans for what an old nurse of mine used to
call donkey's years."

"Mr Upjohn told me that he would find a hopeless
seat to contest and that if I lowered the majority by even a

thousand votes he would almost certainly be able to secure my adoption as candidate in a marginal constituency, after which it would be up to me. And then Mr Ackroyd was equally encouraging when I stayed with him at Tailbush Manor last Saturday. That letter from Jeremy you gave me to read was what prompted me to tell you now about my decision to leave the Civil Service, but do you know, sir, what it was that helped me to make up my mind?"

"No, I am at a loss, Humphrey."

"It was when you asked me to get you that television set."

Sir Oliver looked baffled.

"It was when I realised how much you were looking forward to that new serial, The Sheriff of Bowie Knife. I said to myself 'If Sir Oliver enjoys looking at Westerns he will understand my wanting to go into politics'."

"I may have been idly amused by some of the entertainment offered by television, Humphrey, but I have never been amused by the responsibilities I and my colleagues have to shoulder in order to extricate politicians from blunders of their own making, and if possible prevent their making too many."

"Oh, I agree, sir. Whitehall is the Maginot Line of Westminster. What I meant was that what you call your idle amusement was evidence of your ability to see beyond the paper lives which we in the Civil Service do our best to arrange for the common good."

"Paper lives are going to be difficult to arrange if there is a famine of paper. Perhaps it will be a lesson to people and help them to understand how much they owe to paper. And now bring me those papers we have about that presumably Communist-inspired agitation to change Ladies and Gentlemen to Men and Women. Not that Communists are the only trouble makers. These Empire Loyalists who are agitating to have Union Jacks flown over all public lavatories are also troublesome."

When Sir Oliver came back from the Heraeum after

lunch he told his Private Secretary that the paper situation was worsening.

"Sir Mark Levett is pessimistic. At the conference this morning the enquiries made by the various Ministries revealed a sad lack of co-operation. It was decided that the Minister of Waste should make an appeal to the nation to save paper but when he proposed to discourage the despatch of Christmas cards and Christmas greetings the Postmaster-General raised difficulties because he claimed that the whole of the arrangements the General Post Office had made to deal with the Christmas rush would be disorganised. He argued that owing to his recent broadcast about posting all Christmas greetings at least a week before Christmas many people had already bought their Christmas cards. The Minister of Waste, Mr Williamson, then suggested he should ask the public to send all their Christmas cards and greetings to him at the Ministry of Waste, but Sir Hugh Havers pointed out, rightly I think, that Wharton House was not equipped to receive all the millions of Christmas cards and greetings that would be arriving. No doubt Sir Hugh was recalling the difficulty we had at Wharton House once upon a time when old Lord Braintree in a reckless broadcast invited people to send him waste material they had collected. Mr Williamson appreciated the possible results of such an appeal on television and wisely deferred to the opinion of his Permanent Secretary. Sir Mark Levett was also pessimistic about the co-operation of the Press. Tentative approaches made to Fleet Street about reducing the size of newspapers had been unfruitful. The publishers of those enormously thick, heavy and expensive books, which people buy for table decorations to impress other people but never read, were equally unreceptive of the suggestion that they should abstain from publishing such books until the supply of paper was fully equal to the demand. The Forestry authorities rejected the idea of cutting down the huge areas of trees they have planted to turn them into paper.

They said such premature de-afforestation would destroy the economic plan that was the basis of their afforestation. The great tobacco firms protested that the success of the Ministry of Hygiene in banning the advertisement of cigarettes on television was enough. The Chancellor was sounded with a view to reducing the duty on cigars and pipe-tobacco, but like all Chancellors of the Exchequer his main hope of balancing his budget was to raise the duty on tobacco, beer and spirits."

"I suppose all Chancellors have been so used to balancing their budgets on paper that he couldn't believe paper could ever cease to exist."

"If ever you become Chancellor of the Exchequer, Humphrey, you will be less scornful of paper lives as you call them when I tell you that Sir Mark Levett, not in joke, suggested that if after Christmas the efforts to salvage waste paper have not been as successful as in his present pessimistic mood he fears they might not be, the Minister of Sanitation will be asked to make an appeal on television to—to——"

Sir Oliver stopped, evidently under considerable emotional strain.

"To be as economical as possible with toilet-paper," he said at last in a voice shaken by something like despair.

"But this will not be till after Christmas, at any rate, and Sir Mark Levett may be unduly pessimistic," Humphrey suggested.

Sir Oliver shook his head sadly.

"He is a lifelong friend of mine and I associate him with what I could almost call a light-hearted optimism. In the darkest moments of the last war I remember he was always convinced, as he used to put it with a confident smile, that we should take the hit out of Hitler and the nip out of Nippon. I fear that the paper situation is grave indeed."

Chapter 13

WHEN Humphrey Mowart left the Ministry that afternoon to visit Miss Veale he was in a very different mood from that of his Chief. The threat to the Civil Service from the possibility of a paper famine did not darken his future; his own future was no longer at the mercy of paper except in so far as he had promised Sir Oliver that he would not abandon him until the crisis had passed. He thought gratefully of young Jeremy whose letter had given him the opportunity to let poor old Huffy know about his own political aspirations. He tried to keep his dreams under control as he drove along Oxford Street, but before he reached the swirl of traffic round the Marble Arch Jeremy had dug up another Venus of Milo and he himself was Parliamentary Private Secretary to Mr Upjohn in whatever office he should then be holding. The die was cast; in Humphrey's present mood it was a double-six. The traffic-lights along the Bayswater Road shone green all the way to Notting Hill Gate, and a few minutes later after making the necessary financial arrangements with a parking-meter he was walking up the steps of 8 Gladstone Terrace.

The door was opened by Miss Veale herself.

"Come in, young man, come in. I've just flattened Miss Milligan while I was waiting to give you your tea."

Humphrey supposed that Miss Milligan was a female companion who had been arguing with Miss Veale. It was only when he saw a table spread with cards that he realised she was the game of patience.

"Yes," said Miss Veale. "I think I've taught Miss Milligan a lesson. I've always set my face against uppishness, and Miss Milligan was more than uppish yesterday when I came back from Oatcester. She needed flattening. Yes, I'm E sharp major now and poor old Miss Milligan is B flat minor. I'll send her to bed."

Miss Veale gathered up the cards and put them in a case.

"But she'll be as uppish again as ever when we meet again this evening. I see you looking at my pictures, young man. I used to be very good at poker-work."

There were half a dozen examples of Miss Veale's art on the walls of her room.

"But I gave up poker-work when in a careless moment I let the poker slip and singed poor Ching's hair. That was ten years ago and poor Ching has been in the dogs' paradise for over three years now. I haven't had the heart to adopt another Peke. I know Ching would be jealous and when he and I meet again I do not want to start with apologies."

While Miss Veale was talking her greenish eyes were watching the kettle.

"You're going to have a great treat with your tea, young man. And so am I."

Humphrey Mowart divined what the treat was going to be.

"Dandimilk?"

"Yes, I was right. You *are*."

"I am what, Miss Veale?"

"Psychic. When you offered me that glass of whisky last Friday evening I said to myself 'Euphemia' because when I am talking to myself I always call myself 'Euphemia' never 'Phemie' which other people are inclined to do. Well, of course I can't be held responsible for what other people call me but, as I was saying, 'Euphemia', I said, 'that young man is psychic'. And how right I was. Yes, Dr Scratchbury gave me a gallon tin of Dandimilk. Or to speak more accurately he gave me two gallon tins of Dandimilk, one of which I took to the headquarters of the S.P.C.C. at Highgate close to where Dick Whittington heard the bells say 'Turn again, Whittington, Lord Mayor of London'. And with that sensible cat of his to advise him he did turn back. Ah, the kettle's boiling. In a moment or two you'll have tasted Dandimilk for the first time. But don't be in too much of a hurry or you may burn your tongue."

Humphrey took a rather apprehensive sip from his tea-cup.

"It tastes very like tea with cows' milk," he admitted.

"But it isn't cows' milk, young man, and soon cows all over the country will be mooing gratefully to that heroic man, Dr Emilius Scratchbury."

"Did you enjoy your visit to Beechwood Farm, Miss Veale?"

"Enjoy is a poor word to express my feelings, young man. I was in the eighth heaven. Lots of people manage to get into the seventh heaven but the eighth heaven is my heaven. . . . Eight the number of fate!" Miss Veale exclaimed reverently.

"But did you gather from your visit to Beechwood Farm that Dr Scratchbury will be able to supply Dandimilk in sufficient quantity from there to threaten the future of cows' milk seriously? I forget the exact figure of the amount of cows' milk drunk annually in Britain but it runs into many millions of gallons."

"Dr Scratchbury is not yet in a position to make millions of gallons of Dandimilk. He explained to me that his laboratory at Beechwood Farm is experimental. He has promised to address a meeting of the S.P.C.C. next week when I shall have the honour of pinning to his coat the badge of the Cowslip League and announcing that he will be our patron for life. 'Dear me, dear me,' I say when I reflect what an opportunity the Right Honourable Upjohn was offered and what an opportunity he missed. But I have not yet told you my great news, young man. Dr Scratchbury has taken the vacant floor above and will very shortly be moving into 8 Gladstone Terrace. He finds that 13 Gog and Magog Lane provides him with inadequate sleeping accommodation, though it will be retained as an office."

M

"You will certainly be closely in touch with Dr Scratchbury."

"The number of Fate!"

"I'd like to make a suggestion, Miss Veale. You are evidently going to be very useful to Dr Scratchbury, and you will be even more useful if you persuade him not to give any more interviews to the Press, or if he does give an interview not to suggest that any Government office is associated with Dandimilk. During my visit to Oatshire I found that the local farmers were resenting his remarks about cows' milk."

"But not the poor cows, young man."

"Cows are hardly able to express resentment."

"Have you ever heard of being tossed by a cow? That seems to me a very eloquent expression of resentment. Dr Scratchbury is the cows' friend."

"That may be true, but the farmers consider him their enemy. I am told that the land of Beechwood Farm is being allowed to go wild. If Dr Scratchbury gives any more interviews to the Press like the one he gave to the *Daily Switch* the Ministry of Cultivation may use the powers granted to them by an Act of Parliament and compulsorily take over Beechwood Farm. I do not know the scope of Dr Scratchbury's laboratory but I imagine it would cause him some inconvenience if he were compelled to abandon it. I know how much you admire the work Dr Scratchbury is doing at Beechwood Farm and I am sure you will want to do all you can to prevent his work from being interrupted."

Humphrey Mowart, ever since the removal of that tin from Mr Upjohn's house in Hertford Street which had suggested to the Minister that he might have a career in politics, had felt well disposed toward Dr Scratchbury; he was aware as he gave that advice to Miss Veale that it was actuated less from a desire to spare embarrassment to the Ministry of Sanitation than from a genuine desire to let an eccentric escape from the ever growing centripetal power of modern conditions.

"Are you saying what you truly believe, young man?"
Miss Veale asked.

"I am," Humphrey could reply with sincerity.

"Then I shall pass on your advice to Dr Scratchbury.
And now will you please not say anything for eight
minutes from the moment you start not saying anything.
Before going to sleep I make my resolutions for the day
to come and then tapping my head on the pillow eight
times I turn over. At intervals of silence during the day I
check my resolutions."

Humphrey Mowart was silent while Miss Veale leant
back in an armchair and gazed at the ceiling, her lips
moving in a silent inquisition into the present state of her
resolutions.

"How stupid of me!" she suddenly ejaculated. "The
fifth of May! No wonder you were able to understand
how important it is that Dr Scratchbury's noble work
for cows should not be interrupted."

"I'm afraid I don't understand how my birthday
comes into it," said Humphrey.

"You are a Taurian."

"A Taurian?"

"Taurus ruled the zodiac when you were born. Taurus,
the heavenly Bull. No wonder you are able to see into the
heart of a cow. I, being born on the eighth day of the
eighth month at eight o'clock in the morning, am a
Leonian. I visit the lions at the zoo on the eighth of every
month and apologise to them for the way they are treated
in circuses."

"I agree with you, Miss Veale," said Humphrey.
"And if ever I get into Parliament I shall do my best to
make it illegal to exhibit any kind of performing animal
in the training of which cruelty was inevitable."

"Bravo, bravo, young man."

"And you will do all you can, won't you, to dissuade
Dr Scratchbury from giving any more interviews to the
Press? And now I'm afraid I must be getting along. I've
enjoyed my visit so much."

"But you must have a glass of cowslip wine before you go, young man," Miss Veale told him. "I shall not offer you a glass of parsnip wine because I think parsnip wine is apt to be a little potent if one is driving a motor-car."

She got up and bending down lifted a corner of the carpet to pick up a key.

"I have to keep my cordials locked up because Mrs Fludger downstairs, when she's feeling cordial and I'm not here, is apt to be too cordial to my cordials. So I hide the key of the cupboard under a different corner of the carpet whenever I go out."

"Why don't you keep the key in your bag?"

Miss Veale shook her bright red hair.

"Because I always lose any key I put in my bag. I started to lose keys when I was quite a tot. My pencil box had the dearest little key you ever saw and I lost it. That's why I told Mrs Fludger that if she put a Yale lock on the front door of 8 Gladstone Terrace I should have to leave. As it is I *am* just able to keep the big front-door key in my bag. But a Yale lock key. Pouff! It would just vanish without a tinkle."

By this time Miss Veale had taken from a corner-cupboard the bottle of cowslip and filled two small glasses.

"Moo," she said as she raised her glass.

"Your very good health, Miss Veale."

"No, no. What you say is 'Moo to you!'."

Humphrey with a smile obeyed her.

"Moo to you, Miss Veale," said Humphrey as he took a sip of what rather to his relief he found was a palatable enough drink.

"Can you taste the cowslips, young man?"

"I don't ever remember tasting cowslips," Humphrey replied cautiously. "But it tastes very nice."

"Oh dear, I'm tempted to offer you a glass of parsnip wine so that you'll know the difference between the taste of cowslips and parsnips, but I must remember that you'll be driving your motor-car and resist the temptation.

And so you're expecting to get into Parliament? I've met several M.P.'s as they call themselves for short, and though they were always quite polite I never took to them because they never seemed able to look anybody in the eyes. They were always looking either over the top of anybody's head or on one side or the other of anybody's head. I said to one of them 'You don't have to stand on a platform to look over the top of my head. I'm not so tall as all that.' And when an M.P. gets into this wonderful Cabinet of theirs he becomes as stuck up as if he were a piece of Dresden china. I suppose that's why they call it a Cabinet. Look at the Right Honourable Upjohn. He was too stuck up to see me."

"But Mr Upjohn isn't in the Cabinet. And I assure you, Miss Veale, he's not at all stuck up. He's just a very much overworked Minister."

"Oh well, I don't blame you for taking his part, young man. It's only what you ought to do."

A minute or two later Humphrey Mowart was saying 'good-bye' to Miss Veale. As he looked back from the pavement her bright red hair in the light of the hall-lamp, like a red sky at night to a shepherd, seemed of good omen.

"Well, I've done it, mother," he told her when he reached their cottage at Little Hangover.

"Done what, darling boy?"

"I've broken it to poor old Huffy that I'm going to chuck the Civil Service and go in for politics."

"Was he much upset?"

Humphrey told his mother about the fortunate arrival of that letter from Sir Oliver's younger son. She took his hand.

"I'm so glad you've made up your mind. Your dear father would have been so glad if he were still with us."

"You think he would?"

"I'm quite sure he would."

"He was awfully pleased when I got into the Civil Service."

"Of course he was. But he always worried a bit whether it was what you really wanted to do. Darling boy, he knew as well as I did that you were thinking about me. He knew then that for him it was only a matter of time. When four years after he died his dear old brother died and left you his money nobody would have been more glad than your beloved father to think that you could choose your own future."

"I feel I ought to take advantage of Mr Upjohn's suggestion. And Mr Ackroyd was encouraging also. However, I have promised Huffy I will play Casabianca while paper-mills are burning."

Humphrey went on to tell his mother about the paper crisis.

"Huffy could face the shortage of paper even for the Civil Service with courage, but when he was warned of a possible famine of toilet-paper he was almost in a state of despair."

"Well, darling boy, it would be rather awkward for all of us," Mrs Mowart commented, and then with a laugh added, "but it *will* be rather amusing to see how our various friends cope with such a famine."

Humphrey went on to tell his mother about Miss Veale.

"Quite dotty, of course, and yet while she was babbling away I couldn't help thinking to myself how much more she was getting out of life than so many other people who like their lives to be arranged for them by paper."

"You'll have to invite Miss Veale to come and see us. I really must meet her. Perhaps Dr Scratchbury will propose to her."

Humphrey shook his head.

"Bryant and May at it again," he said. "Darling mother, you're incorrigible."

Chapter 14

THE Ministry of Waste had pressed the Ministry of Production to let them hold over until after Christmas the issue of their circular to local authorities on the subject of waste paper. However, after Sir Mark Levett and Sir Hugh Havers had conferred together it was decided in view of the urgency to issue the circular before Christmas.

"Provided that Mr Williamson makes his appeal on television during the week before Christmas perhaps we can rush through our circular for issue on the following day. But that will hardly give us a fortnight in which to consider and prepare our circular. Have you considered the advisability of our issuing a joint circular, Levett?"

The Permanent Secretary of the Ministry of Production shook his head.

"It was considered very carefully, Havers, and we are still bearing it in mind. But Mr Camden thought that as we shall be issuing a circular to all Government offices urging the strictest economy in the use of paper it would be an inappropriate moment for us to issue even a joint circular. By the way, I've been in touch with the Post Office people and they have withdrawn their objection to your people at Wharton House adding to the volume of the Christmas post."

Before Sir Oliver left his house on the morning of the day when the Minister of Waste was to appear on television he asked Lady Huffam to be sure to tell them downstairs to tune in to Mr Williamson instead of looking at advertisements of washing-powders and chocolates.

"Oh, but Mr Williamson will be appearing on I.T.V. as well as the B.B.C. and he won't be interrupted by advertisements. What I will tell them, Olly, is not to cut off Mr Williamson as soon as he appears but to listen carefully to what he has to say."

The Rt. Hon. Ronald Williamson who was not in the Cabinet had been as unwilling as the Postmaster General to complicate the postal arrangements for Christmas. He had argued with the Rt. Hon. Walter Camden, who *was* in the Cabinet, that in as much as the responsibility for the country's paper rested with the Ministry of Production a television broadcast would come more appropriately from him.

"But the point of your broadcast, Ronnie, is to make people save and collect as much waste paper as possible."

"Yes, but I'm afraid they may resent being lectured about this at Christmas time. You've got a ten thousand majority, Walter. Since Eddy Pinkney started that confounded New Town, mine has become a marginal constituency. It's more important for me not to lose votes than for you. You can afford to lose them. I can't."

"The P.M. feels it would be a mistake for us to suggest at this moment that there are any grounds for criticising the country's productive capacity and Sir Mark Levett and I felt he was right. You'll be talking about paper that has already been produced and used. I know you'll put it across to the public, Ronnie, without creating a panic."

Mr Williamson, who was hoping like Mr Upjohn to find himself in the Cabinet at the next shuffle, ceased to argue. At any rate, he reflected gratefully, if the paper situation improved he would not be called upon to assuage the Press barons when they heard of a proposal to ease the paper situation by imposing a heavy tax on advertisements in the next Budget.

"We have never met Mr Williamson, Gertrude," said Sir Oliver as he and Lady Huffam settled down in the Den after dinner to watch the television broadcast. "Hugh Havers finds him always ready to listen to good advice. Not that I have anything to complain of in Mr Upjohn in that regard. I was a little taken aback of course when Humphrey Mowart told me that Mr Upjohn had suggested his leaving the Civil Service and entering politics but when I realised that, extraordinary as it may seem, Humphrey really was growing tired of the Civil Service I made no attempt to discourage this strange aspiration of his."

When the Minister of Waste had faded from the screen Sir Oliver led the way up to the drawing-room. He knew by the signature tune that Harry Lime was about to rush about the world in an aeroplane and normally he would certainly have sat back and followed him in comfort, but he felt that Gertrude might not appreciate the seriousness of the paper position if he followed Harry Lime to-night.

"No, I have nothing to criticise in Mr Williamson's television broadcast," Sir Oliver said. "His reminder to the public of the old fashion of taking down the Christmas decorations and Christmas cards on Twelfth Night was a tactful way of going on to ask them to keep their Christmas cards to be collected by the various local authorities all over Great Britain. No doubt many stupid people will suppose he is asking them to keep their Christmas decorations as well, and the local authorities will have to avoid being inundated with holly and mistletoe. But Mr Williamson cannot be blamed for that— unlike poor old Lord Braintree once upon a time. I liked too the way he wound up his talk."

"About people not forgetting to keep yesterday's paper until it became last week's paper to be collected every Monday morning by the—I don't think he called them dust-carts . . . yes, that was very good."

"No, no, Gertrude. Mr Williamson wound up by asking all his listeners to make their New Year's resolution a resolution to save paper."

"I don't think I remember that, Olly."

"I'm afraid you were asleep, Gertrude. Apparently television has that effect on some people."

"I didn't know I'd dozed off," Lady Huffam said.

"We none of us know we have dozed off. But I'm sorry

you missed the bit about New Year resolutions. Ah, well, Mr Williamson has done his best and we must hope that the best will come of it. We at our Ministry must just wait and hope that Mr Upjohn will not be called upon to give a television broadcast."

"But why should Mr Upjohn have to appear on television?"

"Sufficient unto the day is the evil thereof. We must just hope for the best. I think that the public will respond to Mr Williamson's appeal. I only hope the local authorities will respond. . . ."

He had been on the verge of mentioning the Ministry of Waste's circular to local authorities; that was not a matter for discussion in the home circle. It had not yet been issued; Sir Oliver had urged Sir Hugh Havers not to release it until after his Minister's broadcast. Sir Hugh Havers had told him that the draft of the broadcast had been very carefully read and that nothing in it would conflict with the directions of the circular, but Sir Oliver had reminded the Permanent Secretary of the way that old Lord Braintree had added an impromptu of his own and caused such trouble to the permanent officials in his Ministry.

"After that circular from the Ministry of Production stressing the importance of the utmost economy on paper in all Government offices you would be embarrassed, Hugh, if your Ministry was compelled to issue a supplementary leaflet modifying or even contradicting some of the directions in your circular to local authorities."

"Perhaps you're right, Oliver," Sir Hugh Havers had agreed.

"Caution is usually the wiser course, and as the local authorities will not be collecting paper during the Christmas season the delay in issuing your circular willl not matter."

So it was decided not to issue the circular until after Christmas in England and Wales and not until after January 1st in Scotland. It ran as follows:

Circular No. 102/96
(Minister of Waste)

Circular from the
Ministry of Waste
Wharton House, London, S.W.1.

Sir,

Provision of Facilities
For the Collection of Waste Paper

1. The importance of keeping all parks, pleasure grounds, public gardens and holiday resorts free from litter has already been stressed, and the failure of the public to co-operate with local authorities in making full use of the facilities afforded by local authorities for the disposal of litter has been noted by the Minister of Waste with regret.

2. For various reasons the consumption of paper has been steadily escalating from year to year and therefore the amount of waste paper has escalated accordingly. Such waste paper can be converted from waste into sophisticated paper and the Minister of Waste earnestly hopes that the local authorities in Great Britain and Northern Ireland will provide additional facilities to those already provided for the collection of waste paper.

3. The Minister desires to draw the attention of the education authorities in every area to impressing upon the youth of the country the paramount importance of paper to the community.

4. The Minister acknowledges with grateful appreciation that owing to the efforts of local authorities last year 125,000,000 lbs of waste paper were collected from October of last year to October of the present year and expresses his confidence that by October next year 250,000,000 lbs of waste paper will have been collected by an extension of the facilities which local authorities will provide for such collection.

5. The Minister is glad to be able to announce that the Government has agreed to allot grants to enable local

authorities to provide an extension of the facilities for the collection of waste paper by increasing the number of receptacles in which to deposit waste paper and by a similar increase in the number of vehicles allotted to empty such receptacles.

6. Applications for the grants announced in para. 5 of this circular should be submitted to the Ministry of Waste by the various local authorities, which are asked to add their observations and to forward such applications to the Ministry as quickly as possible.

7. The Minister trusts that local authorities in their various capacities will now consider the suggestions made in this circular and that they will take every opportunity to provide increasing facilities for the collection of waste paper in their respective areas. The Ministry for its part will give them every possible assistance.

I am, Sir,

Your obedient Servant

Hugh Havers

The Clerk of the Authority
Local Authorities
Great Britain and Northern Ireland
(M.W. 862111/1/97/1)

"I only hope Mr Williamson's optimism will be justified, Humphrey," said Sir Oliver when he had carefully considered this circular. "I only hope that we shall not be called upon to draft a similar circular on the subject of toilet-paper. I do not envy the Minister's task if he is called upon to make a broadcast appeal on television, asking the public to be economical in their use of toilet-paper. And this other word which is creeping into the language . . . I suppose 'sophisticated' paper means 'serviceable' paper," Sir Oliver sighed.

"There's one thing, sir. It will be a great deal easier for Mr Upjohn to give a television broadcast about toilet-paper now than it would have been not so long ago. I know you disapprove of the liberty writers have to-day to write as freely as they do, but it has cleared the air."

" 'Cleared the air' is hardly the phrase I should use for making the pages of a novel look as the walls of a public lavatory used to look. Nevertheless, I admit that such a broadcast by the Minister of Waste would have been unimaginable before the last war, even although his embarrassment would not have been visible in those days.

"We must hope Mr Upjohn will be spared. But if he does have to give a broadcast about toilet-paper, he'll certainly deserve to be in the Cabinet."

Humphrey Mowart gave "Cabinet" the French pronunciation.

"Cabineh?" Sir Oliver repeated, his eyebrows raised in interrogation.

"When the English went ahead of the French with water-closets in the last century the French called them *cabinets anglais*."

"Yes, well, but I'm afraid we shan't be able to make French jokes if we have to draft a circular to persuade the public to economise over toilet-paper. It will mean printing at least twenty million copies and no doubt the popular Press will delight in jeering at the amount of paper we used to persuade the public to be careful of paper."

"We shall be charging for the circular, of course. And it will be Crown copyright reserved by the Stationery Office. We charged fivepence for that circular we issued about the need for local authorities to build more public lavatories. We ought to be able to charge at least six-pence for a circular about toilet-paper."

"One might suppose, Humphrey, that you were almost looking forward to our circular about toilet-paper," said Sir Oliver. "You are quitting the Civil Service, alas, but if you adhere to your promise not to send in your resignation until the paper situation has been amelior-ated you will still be a Civil Servant when, or rather let me say with greater emphasis, *if* a circular on the subject of toilet-paper is required, and as a Civil Servant you will hardly be able to indulge in those strange Rabelaisian jokes of yours."

Humphrey Mowart laughed.

"I realise that, sir, and if you do call upon me to assist in the drafting of this circular I promise to behave. By the way, sir, while we're on the subject, have you considered the advisability of giving the official recommendation of the Ministry of Sanitation to the new pan that has just been submitted?"

"The variations of lavatory pans seem endless. I see a new name on every one. It has always been a puzzle to me. The same with motor-cars. I have always been puzzled to know why all motor-car doors seem to open differently. If we do give an official recommendation to this new lavatory pan, it must be given on the definite understanding that we shall expect the pans in public lavatories all over England and Wales to conform with the design of this new lavatory pan. We must also insist on the names being the same. We do not want to have the same pan called the Olympic in one public lavatory and Mont Blanc in the next. We are debarred from any superintendence of sanitation in Scotland and Northern Ireland. So if St Andrew's House calls a pan John Knox or Stormont calls a pan William of Orange that is not our responsibility. What is the proposed name for this new patent pan we are asked to recommend?"

"They have submitted three names, sir: Universal, Pull Easy, and Lodore."

"How does the water come down at Lodore, eh? One is tempted to encourage any sign of literary taste among sanitary engineers, but no, Humphrey, I think Universal will express better our recommendation if we decide to give such a recommendation."

"We ought to be getting the final draft of the Chief Sanitary Inspector early in the New Year, sir."

"Yes, we can postpone all decisions until after Christmas. Where are you going to spend the festive season, ironical as such an epithet is for *this* season?"

"I shall be with my mother at Little Hangover."

"We shall have our usual family gathering at Number Nine. Fortunately none of the party will have their Christmas clouded like mine by this threat to the country's supply of toilet-paper."

Sir Oliver's gloom was faintly lightened by a letter from Jeremy which arrived on Christmas morning:

My dear Mum and Dad,

I hope this letter will reach you in time to wish you both a Merry Christmas and a Happy New Year. Dick Horner will be back in England for Christmas and I have told him to come and see you and tell you about some of our adventures. The chap with whom I'm doing excavation is giving me free board and lodging in return for my work but if you could possibly let me have some cash for pocket money I should be awfully grateful. I cannot tell you the name of the chap with whom I am working because he may be on the verge of a terrific discovery. Nothing to do with Linear B so you must not expect me to be another Ventris. If you could send me a money order to Poste Restante, Heraklion, Crete, it will be a great help. I hope you will manage to take that cruise to Greece next April, especially if we have made this terrific discovery. Please tell Rosemary that if she and Nigel manage to come too I look forward to showing her this marvellous island, and tell Nigel he ought to find out how the Greeks pronounce Greek before he comes. Please don't ask Dick Horner to tell you the name of the chap with whom I am excavating because it must be a secret until we know whether this really is a terrific discovery.

Your loving

Jeremy

"I must say I am gratified by the boy's evident wish to see us in Crete," said Sir Oliver. "I wonder whether this discovery will turn out to be as terrific as Jeremy hopes. But I shall respect his desire to keep this chap, as he calls him, anonymous."

"We will go to Greece in April, won't we, Olly?" Lady Huffam seemed almost to plead.

"Provided that my work at the Ministry allows me to leave the country next April. All depends upon that."

"You sound worried, Olly."

"We have many little worries at the Ministry."

It says much for Sir Oliver's sense of public duty that he rejected a sudden temptation to ask his wife to order enough toilet-paper to last for three months. Instead, he announced his intention of sending a money order for £25 to Jeremy.

"Oh, how kind of you, Olly!" Lady Huffam exclaimed gratefully.

The family gathering on that Christmas day followed the course of such family gatherings all over the country. Only once was the subject of paper mentioned. This was when the men were alone for a few minutes in the afternoon after dinner.

"I wonder how these Production people think we can cut down on paper at Movement House," said George Micklewright. "Do they realise what it means for our Ministry to be responsible for Civil Aviation, Railways and Roads? If they'd do something to produce typing-ribbons that don't fade away almost as soon as the typists start on them we shouldn't have to use so much paper getting them re-typed legibly."

"And I wish they'd do something about these rubber sponges to-day." Nigel Huffam added. "After a fortnight one doesn't know which is the soap and which the sponge."

"Sticking plastics, eh?" George Micklewright said, laughing loudly at his joke.

"Talking of paper," said Nigel, "I hope Wharton House will be able to justify these grants they're asking the Treasury to sanction for additional facilities to collect waste paper."

"They will be more than justified," said Sir Oliver. "We all have to realise that the paper situation is grave."

"Before we know where we are," George Mickle-wright guffawed, "they'll be asking us to go slow with bumph."

"I think it's time we joined the ladies," said Sir Oliver quickly.

When the party was dispersing about six o'clock and Lady Huffam was expressing her grandmotherly love for little Noll in baby language, Rosemary took her father-in-law aside.

"I just want to say, Dad, how glad I am about Jeremy. I'm going to write and tell him that I'm determined to get to Greece in April and have him to show me round, and that Nigel shall get all his paroxygens or whatever they are right."

Sir Oliver was so much moved by the warmth of sincerity in her bright dark eyes that he did not tell her it was paroxytones not paroxygens. He reproached himself for having not so long ago feared she might have been encouraging Nigel to be flippant.

"Yes, well, Rosemary, I hope that Mum and I will be able to go to Greece in April. I am making arrangements to see young Dick Horner and hear more about what Jeremy is doing."

Sir Oliver rang up Mr Augustus Horner next day to ask if his son could come along to Chillingham Gardens.

"Do you mind if I come along with Dick, Sir Oliver? He's a bit shy of going to you alone. Apparently he promised Jeremy not to say the name of this fellow he's with in Crete and he's afraid you'll ask him."

"You can tell your son that I shall not ask him. Jeremy has explained in his last letter to me why the name is to be a secret at present."

"That's good of you, Sir Oliver. Will it suit you if Dick and I come round to your place this afternoon?"

"Would Mrs Horner care to come too? My wife would be most happy to meet her."

So at tea-time on Boxing Day Mr and Mrs Horner with their son arrived at 9 Chillingham Gardens.

N

Mrs Horner was a tall handsome woman and her eighteen-year-old son was as different from his father in appearance as Jeremy differed from Sir Oliver. He did, however, resemble his mother, whereas Jeremy was as unlike her as his father.

Dick Horner related in detail his and Jeremy's experience in France and Italy before they managed to reach Greece.

"We were absolutely thrilled by Greece, sir. But I felt a ghastly ignoramus beside Huff— beside Jeremy." A nudge from his father's elbow stopped Dick in time from saying "Huffy". "I was on the Modern side at James's and so of course I knew nothing at all about the history of Greece, but Jeremy had a story about every place we went to. In a place called Volo we found a bus which went half way up Mount Pelion. It was a hair-raising drive with precipices a thousand feet high on one side as we made hairpin bends on a rough road, but I was so interested in what Jeremy was telling me about a centaur called Chiron . . ." Dick Horner paused. "I think that was his name."

"Yes, indeed," said Sir Oliver, "that was the name of the centaur who taught the Argonauts."

"You'll have to excuse me if I get my names wrong, sir. Jeremy used to be down on me like a ton of bricks when I made a howler."

Sir Oliver was listening to Dick Horner with increasing wonder. Jeremy's Greek was associated in his mind with continual disappointment over his failure to appreciate the seriousness of his grammatical or prosodiacal howlers. "We tried our best to get to Cyprus but the people at our Embassy in Athens were very sticky and so we went to Crete instead. The Cretans had a frightful time with the Germans in the war and they were tremendously decent to Jeremy and me. We met an awfully nice chap who is doing excavations in a remote part of the island and he was so impressed by Jeremy's enthusiasm for the work that he has taken him on. There is some mystery about which I wasn't told, because I realised I would never become a professional archaeologist and had made up my mind to come back to England by Christmas. So I must leave it to Jeremy to tell you when the mystery is solved. But I think you'll be awfully pleased sir, when you see him. When he and I decided to leave school I knew he would be a good companion but I didn't realise quite *what* a good companion he would be. Sometimes he worried a bit whether he was upsetting, Lady Huffam and you, and he was awfully relieved when my father wrote to tell him that he had seen you and that you had been awfully decent about his going off like that."

"That was thoughtful of you, Mr Horner," said Sir Oliver.

"I did not tell you I had written to Jeremy, Sir Oliver, because I feared you might think it was an intrusion. But Dick has given us such a glowing account of Jeremy in Greece that I do not regret my intrusion."

"It was not an intrusion, Mr Horner," said Lady Huffam. "It was a kindness."

"And we are all devoted to Jeremy," Mrs Horner put in. "He and Dick between them have decided on their futures, and I need hardly say how pleased my husband is that Dick has decided to enter his firm."

"Do you ever look at television, Mr Horner?" Sir Oliver asked.

"Oh yes, occasionally."

"I was wondering whether you were interested in these representations of American legal procedure."

"To tell you the truth, Sir Oliver, I'm so tired of anything to do with the law by the time I get home that I always avoid the law in any shape on television."

"Yes," said Sir Oliver meditatively. "I suppose I should avoid watching a serial about the Civil Service, though no doubt both the B.B.C. and I.T.V. would hesitate before attempting to give the public a sensational aspect of the Civil Service."

"I listened to Mr Williamson last week on the subject of waste paper. I wonder if there is a serious threat to our supplies of paper."

Sir Oliver frowned. The skies of Greece were clouded over by toilet-paper when Mr and Mrs Horner and their son said good-bye.

Chapter 15

IT is good to remember the patriotic fervour with which the people of Great Britain and Northern Ireland responded to the appeal of the Minister of Waste to save paper. Nevertheless, by the end of January the paper situation was still critical; when one morning Humphrey Mowart came in to tell Sir Oliver that Sir Mark Levett had telephoned to say he proposed to reach the Ministry of Sanitation at eleven o'clock to discuss an important question with the Permanent Secretary, Sir Oliver said,

"I fear this is it, Humphrey."

"This is what, sir?"

"What I have been fearing all this month. I cannot suppose that Sir Mark Levett would be coming from Whitehall to Cork Street unless the future of the country's toilet-paper were in danger. Are there any pressing matters we have to dispose of before Sir Mark arrives?" Sir Oliver asked gloomily.

"No, sir, I don't think so. You'll be glad to hear that the Chief Quantity Surveyor is hopeful that work on the main drain between Oatcester and Hardingham can be started by the end of April."

"That should mean the work will almost certainly be commencing by July or August."

"Then that firm of sanitary engineers whose pan we accepted as the approved form for all public lavatories in future. The Universal it was to be called, if you remember—"Sir Oliver nodded—"apparently this firm of sanitary engineers with its subsidiary companies is now engaged in a merger with another firm of sanitary engineers and its subsidiaries, which may mean some delay in the production of the Universal pan."

"That is their loss. Whatever may be the situation of

toilet-paper, there is an abundance of lavatory pans in the country."

"Finally, sir, there is what you will probably think a rather exaggerated example of racialism from that place where the Empire Loyalists wanted to fly Union Jacks over the public lavatories. They did in fact hoist a Union Jack over one of them. This started up feeling among the immigrants, and a petition has now come in signed by over a hundred immigrants requesting that instead of the usual Ladies and Gentlemen we should put up Memsahibs and Sahibs outside the public lavatory which serves the district with the largest population of immigrants."

"We cannot consider that."

"I didn't suppose for a moment we would," Humphrey Mowart said with a smile.

When Sir Mark Levett came into Sir Oliver's room Humphrey was about to withdraw when his Chief said,

"You've no objection, Mark, to my Private Secretary's being present at our conference? I shall be losing his services soon and I want to make the most of them while they last."

"Not at all. Well, Oliver, you've probably guessed why I've invaded you like this."

"Toilet-paper?"

The printer's note of interrogation should be hung with crape to express the misery behind that brief question.

"Precisely. Mr Williamson did a great job with his television broadcast and the amount of waste paper saved this month has exceeded our most optimistc expectations. We can only hope that the amount of paper normally left about daily in the spring, summer and autumn will be rescued from waste by the additional facilities afforded by the local authorities. I may add that the Treasury has been unusually prompt in sanctioning the grants my Ministry is empowered to make to ease the burden of the ratepayers in providing such additional facilities."

"Is the Commonwealth doing nothing, Mark?"

"The Commonwealth is rallying splendidly. But ship-ments of paper take time and until our supplies are once again adequate to meet the growing demands of the Sunday Press, the multiplication of universities, the raising of the age limit in schools, the proliferation of new Ministries, the increase of cigarettes since the Ministry of Hygiene started their campaign against them, the increasing size of books in hard-backs to counteract the appeal of books in paper-backs, and the almost hourly increase of paper-backs to counteract the rising price of hard-back books, the production of enough paper will remain a problem for my Ministry. Indeed, we may have to persuade the Government to start a Ministry of Paper and relieve the Ministry of Production of any further responsibility for paper."

"You were objecting just now to what you called the proliferation of new Ministries, Mark."

"I was thinking about this new Ministry of Exceptions they talk of creating to deal with the problems which an Ombudsman is bound to create. But to come back to toilet-paper. We now hear that there is a danger of exhausting the supply of toilet-paper in the country before the Commonwealth can ease the situation. That's why we feel that a broadcast on television by Mr Upjohn might enable us to carry on until the supply of the country's toilet-paper is once again fully adequate. I don't have to tell you, Oliver, what a mess the sanitation of the country would be in if people started to use substi-tutes for toilet-paper."

At this point Humphrey Mowart turned his head to hide a smile. He was thinking of that chapter in Rabelais.

"You may feel that a broadcast on television by Mr Upjohn would be useful, Mark, but Mr Upjohn may not feel able to give such a broadcast, even on the radio, still less on television."

"He had quite a success with his broadcast last autumn."

"That was a political party broadcast. He was telling viewers what the Government had done for sanitation. It did not involve him in any embarrassment. Would you like to address an audience of millions about toilet-paper, Mark?"

"I'm not a politician, Oliver. You're not a politician. Our job is to save politicians from embarrassment. You'll have to draft a speech for him, and do your utmost to persuade him to give it. The B.B.C. are all set just now to *épater les bourgeois* as we used to say. I saw a programme of theirs the other day called 'This Was Not the Week As It Was' or some such name, and they were all talking smut like prep-school kids, and the women in the audience were all tittering like girls in the top form who wanted to show they knew more than the junior girls. I'm sure the B.B.C. will welcome a talk about toilet-paper. But I mustn't joke about it. The situation really *is* serious and the only Ministry to bring this before the public is your Ministry."

"I have to accept that, Mark," Sir Oliver said. "I have been haunted now for six weeks by the possibility of this dreadful famine. I hoped against hope that it might be averted."

"It may be averted if your Minister can persuade the public to exercise economy on their use of toilet-paper."

"I think you are making an excessive demand on Mr Upjohn's patriotism. Are you prepared to ask the Minister of Hygiene to make a broadcast appeal on television for the public to use fewer aperients? No, that would involve you with the Chemical industry because they would be expected to raise the price at which they were sold."

"There is no lack of aperients, Oliver. There *will* be a lack of toilet-paper. It is toilet-paper on which we must concentrate. Not on the preliminaries."

"What do you feel, Humphrey?" Sir Oliver turned to ask his Private Secretary. "Do you think *you* can persuade Mr Upjohn to give this broadcast?"

Sir Mark Levett looked surprised by this question.

"Mr Upjohn has been encouraging Humphrey Mowart to leave the Civil Service and go into politics."

"Well, sir, I shall do my best," Humphrey promised. "But it'll be you who will have to convince him that the situation is serious enough to make his broadcast imperative. May I suggest that you draft out a speech before you break it to him that it will be he who has to make it?"

"Mowart is right," said Sir Mark firmly. "It's now up to you, Oliver, to draft his speech in such a way as to give him no excuse to get out of facing the lights."

When the Permanent Secretary of the Ministry of Production left Cork Street to return to Whitehall the Permanent Secretary of the Ministry of Sanitation turned to his Private Secretary.

"Will you arrange to have some kind of lunch brought up to me, Humphrey? I shall not have my usual lunch at the Heraeum."

Whether or not the Minister of Sanitation could be persuaded to face the lights, Sir Oliver himself was not prepared to face the prospect of lunching at the Heraeum while he was in the throes of drafting the text for Mr Upjohn's broadcast. The sight of various other Permanent Secretaries eating their lunches with nothing to disturb their digestion, the sight of bishops eating their lunches without a pastoral care to spoil their appetites, the sight of university professors, famous scientists, ambitious technologists and elder statesmen all eating away happily was more than he could bear to contemplate.

"I understand that a broadcast lasting for a quarter of an hour means 1800 words of script. I do not see how it will be possible to produce 1800 words about toilet-paper, Humphrey."

"May I make a suggestion, sir?"

"Of course."

"If Mr Upjohn spent at least ten minutes in more or

less repeating what he said in his last broadcast about the work the Government is doing for sanitation, he could go on to remind viewers of Mr Williamson's appeal for waste paper and then almost as an afterthought get in what has to be said about toilet-paper."

It was four o'clock that afternoon when the combined efforts of Sir Oliver and Humphrey produced the draft for the broadcast by the Minister of Sanitation. Sir Oliver told Humphrey to time him while he read it aloud. This was how the broadcast ended:

"Most of you will have heard what Mr Williamson, the Minister of Waste, was saying about the need to preserve as much waste paper as possible on account of the continually increasing demand for paper . . ."

"May I interrupt for a moment, sir? Mine is a stop-watch," said Humphrey as it clicked. "I know you object to the use of 'escalation', but if Mr Upjohn were to say 'on account of the continuous escalation in the demand for paper', I think the viewers would be more impressed."

"I am not prepared to encourage this American neologism. Besides, half the people listening won't know what escalation means."

"That would start arguments and while they were arguing the Minister would be well away with toilet-paper."

"I will not surrender to escalation," Sir Oliver affirmed as he resumed his reading.

". . . on account of the continuously increasing demand for paper. It is my privilege this evening to let you know how much the Minister of Waste appreciates the magnificent response made by all and sundry to his appeal for the collection of all the waste paper that can be salvaged. And while I am on the subject of paper I should like to take the opportunity of asking you all to . . ."

Sir Oliver paused and Humphrey's watch clicked again.

"I spent over an hour and a half before I finally decided upon the next sentence, and I am still not satisfied. '. . . of asking you all to exercise the utmost economy in your resort to toilet-paper.' Frankly, Humphrey, I'm not satisfied with the expression 'resort'. At the same time I feel that 'use of' is a little crude. Can you suggest a better word than 'resort'?''

"What about 'the utmost economy over toilet-p̀aper?' Or perhaps better still just 'with'?''

"The utmost economy with toilet-paper," Sir Oliver repeated. "Yes, I think that will lead on to the next sentence."

"And while I am on the subject of paper may I take the opportunity . . ." Sir Oliver paused again to delete 'I should like to' and substitute 'may I'.

"I think, sir, it would be better to read this last part again for timing. You may want to keep stopping."

"Yes, and next time you can read it to me, Humphrey, after you've shown me how your stop-watch works."

Sir Oliver resumed his reading.

"I should like to take the opportunity of asking you . . . of being able to ask you all to exercise the utmost, no, 'strictest' is better . . . to exercise the strictest economy with . . . no 'over' is better . . . the strictest economy over toilet-paper. Do not for instance employ toilet-paper for the purpose of keeping your hair in curl . . ."

Humphrey Mowart cut in.

"I'm sorry to interrupt, sir, but do girls still put their hair into curling-papers?"

"Mr Upjohn will not be addressing an audience consisting entirely of girls, my dear Humphrey."

"But do any women still put their hair in curl-papers? I thought they used these metallic things."

Humphrey was thinking of his mother. Sir Oliver was thinking of his wife.

"I am not an authority on trichology, Humphrey, but I recall on one occasion coming out of my room earlier than usual one morning and seeing our housemaid with her hair covered in curl-papers."

"All right, sir, carry on, but I'm afraid Mr Upjohn may jib at curl-papers."

"For the purpose of keeping your hair in curl. Do not employ toilet-paper for correspondence abroad in order to save postage. As Minister of Sanitation it is my duty to say how much I should deplore during this nation-wide drive to save paper any waste of toilet-paper on extraneous uses for it. I am authorised to state on behalf of the Minister of Production, that the whole-hearted response of the public to the Minister of Waste's appeal to save waste paper and by saving waste paper to increase the amenities of our public parks and pleasure grounds, encourages him to believe that the shortage of paper will be of brief duration. At the same time as Minister of Sanitation I should be neglecting my responsibilities if I did not remind you during this brief duration of the time-honoured phrase 'Waste not Want not'."

"I think it is unnecessary to repeat that it is toilet-paper which the public are being urged not to waste. As Minister of Sanitation he would not be asking them to waste writing paper. Well, now will you read through the draft to me."

Humphrey read it through, but the timing was not a success because Sir Oliver, unfamiliar with stop-watches, stopped it after Humphrey had been reading for two minutes.

"Never mind. We'll have a copy made for Mr Upjohn, and you can time him. But if it's too short he must add something to the beginning not the end."

Mr Upjohn had gone to the House before Sir Oliver and Humphrey Mowart had prepared the final draft of his broadcast. In the tube on the way back to Gloucester Road Sir Oliver turned to the *Times* crossword which he had not started that morning, having been reading twice through carefully an interesting and well-written article about excavation in Greece. One across. Five letters. A gentle imitator. P-a-p-e-r. Was that broadcast to haunt him even through the *Times* crossword? Two across.

Two hyphenated words of six and four letters. The cultivation of needlework? Sir Oliver pondered for a few moments and then shook his head. Obviously the answer was 'sewage-farm'. Sir Oliver abandoned the crossword and opened *The Times* to read again that excellent article about excavation in Greece.

Next morning after Mr Upjohn had read through the draft of his proposed broadcast he asked the Permanent Secretary to come along to his room.

"You'd better come along too, Humphrey," Sir Oliver told him.

"What on earth will you be asking me to do next, Huffam?" Mr Upjohn asked jovially. "Did you think up this joke?"

"It is not a joke, Minister. Sir Mark Levett, the Permanent Secretary of the Ministry of Production, came along himself to Cork Street to stress the vital importance he and Mr Camden attach to your appealing to the public to exerise the strictest economy over toilet-paper in view of the paper position."

"But, damn it, I was lunching with Walter Camden yesterday at the Oxbridge and Camford, and he never said a word about toilet-paper."

"The Minister may have decided on second thoughts that his permanent officials should explore every avenue before committing you to what is undoubtedly an extremely delicate assignment."

"If I've got to get up and tell several millions of people to go slow on bumph, I don't call it a delicate assignment. I call it a damned indelicate assignment," Mr Upjohn bubbled.

"We appreciate that, Minister, and I have done my utmost to present the matter in a way that will cause you as little embarrassment as possible."

"I realise that, my dear Huffam, but do you and the Production people realise that, if I stand there in those confounded lights and say what you're asking me to say, there won't be a packet of Blinko or a roll of toilet-paper left for sale before the week's out. People will start hoarding."

"That might be avoided by your telling the public that any hoarding of toilet-paper will involve rationing."

"Yes, and then the Press will start a campaign to say that the amount of paper required for the forms to be filled up for the public to obtain their rations would make toilet-paper scarcer than Shakespeare folios."

"Could not the Ministry of Production warn the Press that any kind of irresponsible agitation against the rationing of toilet-paper might entail the rationing of newsprint?" Sir Oliver asked.

"What? And have the whole Press gunning for us at the next Election? We don't mind antagonising the odd newspaper, but we can't afford to antagonise the whole Press. You permanent officials stand by to help us politicians, whatever party is in power. But you are apt to forget that nowadays politics is a profession and our professional future depends on the favour of the public as much as an actor's. We take a risk with our future when we appear on television in any shape and I have already taken that risk. But, my dear Huffam, I must be frank. I am not prepared to risk my whole political future by getting up in front of those damned lights and telling a few millions of people that they may have to queue for their ration of bumph. You can imagine what fun those young men on the B.B.C. would have making cracks about privy councillors and cabinet ministers when they're indulging in what they call satire. No, I will not give this broadcast. I'm going to ring Walter Camden and tell him that if the Ministry of Production have made a mess of the country's paper supply he must damn well go down to Shepherds Bush himself and tell the public to go slow on bumph."

Mr Upjohn sat back, exhausted for a moment by his own indignant eloquence.

"Humphrey Mowart will tell you, Minister, that I feel as much upset as you do by this request from the Ministry of Production. I spent almost the whole of yesterday trying to draft your proposed broadcast in such a way as to spare your natural repugnance for this task as much as possible."

"Sir Oliver really was terribly upset, Minister," Humphrey Mowart assured him.

"I was so much upset, Minister," said Sir Oliver, "that I carefully considered whether it was not my duty to retire from the Civil Service immediately instead of waiting until the time arrives for me to retire in due course. I finally decided after a long and anxious debate with myself that it was my duty to remain in the Ministry to see if the compromise we effected with the Ministry of Leisure over the sanitary arrangements of hikers and campers was as successful as we had every reason to hope that it would be. I felt also that it was my duty not to retire until the diversion of the main drain between Oatcester and Hardingham justified the extra cost involved by our deferment to the pressure of local opinion. And indeed there are many projects in which our Ministry is actively concerned and of which you have always been of such valuable assistance in presenting to Parliament. Humphrey Mowart here, thanks to the kindly interest you have expressed in his political future, will feel himself free to resign from the Civil Service as soon as the present serious situation of paper has been lightened. I will leave him now with you so that he can let me know if there is any chance of re-drafting your proposed broadcast in such a way as for you to reconsider your refusal to give it."

Sir Oliver left his Private Secretary with the Minister of Sanitation and returned to his own room.

"I've never known poor old Sir Oliver so much upset, Minister," said Humphrey Mowart.

"Well, if it upset him to draft this blasted broadcast, what about me, Mowart? Sir Oliver isn't being asked to deliver it. Don't they call a loo in the States a john? That'll give the Yankee newspaper correspondents a grand opportunity. No, I'm going to ring Walter Camden and tell him that I will not give this broadcast. The Production people are all so busy with computers that they forget all about paper. It's a pity one of their confounded computers couldn't compute how much paper was wanted. No, I will not give the broadcast."

"How would it be, Minister, if you said you would only give it if the Minister of Production was prepared to take part in it with you?"

"That's a good idea, Mowart. That's a jolly good idea. I bet you the Production people will postpone the broadcast. Yes, you certainly ought to go into politics."

Humphrey went back to tell his Chief what the Minister had decided.

"I think the decision is a wise one," said Sir Oliver. "I will get in touch at once with Sir Mark Levett, and it will be his task to persuade Mr Camden to agree. I think we may feel reasonably sure that this ghastly broadcast will be postponed."

Several conferences were held during which the Minister of Sanitation remained firm in his refusal to broadcast an appeal about toilet-paper unless the Minister of Production took part in it also; the Minister of Production remained equally firm in his refusal to partake in such a broadcast.

Finally a compromise was reached by the terms of which the broadcast was to be postponed for a fortnight when the paper situation would be reviewed and according to its gravity another conference would be held at which the appropriate measures that must be taken to ease the situation would again be discussed.

"In other words, Humphrey, to decide which is more necessary to welfare existence, toilet-paper or more pages in the Sunday newspapers," Sir Oliver said to his Private Secretary.

"Meanwhile, sir, I'm afraid the problem of that sewage-farm in the South Riding of Yorkshire needs your attention."

"The cultivation of needlework," Sir Oliver muttered to himself.

"The cultivation of needlework, sir?" Humphrey Mowart exclaimed in surprise.

"It was a clue in the *Times* crossword and the solution of course was sewage-farm following upon a clue the solution of which was paper. I dislike the notion of being susceptible to omens, but the mental strain of these last three months has made me superstitious. Sewage-farm? Well?"

"I have read through Mr Butterwick's report on the situation of the sewage-farm that serves the borough of Dipford, the report of our Chief Sanitary Inspector, and the report of the River Dippy Purification Board. All agree, to quote, 'that the effluent from the sewage-farm is again unsatisfactory'. At a meeting of the South Riding Council the Borough Surveyor told the members that the blockages had been caused by men's trousers, vests and socks and by women's underclothing. Certain parts of the pipe-line were completely jammed with clothing, and some even arrived at the sewage-farm. On one occasion a plastic mackintosh had caused endless trouble."

"Discarded clothes in the pipe-line," Sir Oliver exclaimed. "But how on earth can discarded clothes pass a W.C.?"

"That's what the councillors of the South Riding wanted to know, and a resolution was passed to get one of these garments identified and trace its source. To quote from the *Dipford Journal*. 'This awful waste and trouble must cease,' said the Mayor."

"Imagine the effect of that proposed broadcast by Mr Upjohn, Humphrey," Sir Oliver said. "Before we knew where we were every pipe-line in the country would be blocked with mackintoshes. Should the worst happen and this proposed broadcast have to be made, we cannot add an appeal to the public to avoid putting mackintoshes down their W.C.'s. But quite apart from the question of this broadcast, Humphrey, we evidently have to bear in mind that various anti-social members of the Welfare State are prepared to pull the plug on a mackintosh. This affects our decision about the Universal lavatory pan. We must take advantage of the delay caused by the merger and reconsider the pan which we have recently approved. In future every pan must be guaranteed by the makers to be incapable of passing mackintoshes or any other article of clothing before we give it the Ministry's approval. Indeed, it may be necessary for Mr Upjohn to press for an Act of Parliament making it an offence for any firm of sanitary engineers to issue lavatory pans capable of passing articles of clothing into main drains and pipe-lines. It will be an inauspicious opening for the new main drain between Oatcester and Hardingham if soon afterwards it is blocked by mackintoshes."

"There is another minor question to be settled, sir. The Ministry of Leisure have notified us that they have had a complaint from the Rural District Council of Oxlade. . . ."

"Oxlade?"

"A small town in the Lake District beside Honeywater. They say that what they call a toilet we have erected in accordance with our assumption of responsibility for the sanitary arrangements of campers is, to quote, 'a blot on the landscape'. The Ministry of Leisure say that the banks of Honeywater are a favourite resort of campers but an even more favourite resort of hikers, and they feel that nothing should be done to discourage hikers. They point out further that the view from the Oxlade Arms, the local hotel, apparently much frequented by visitors during the season, will be so seriously affected by what they call our toilet that Harbours of Refuge Limited, the company which owns the Oxlade Arms, are afraid that the interference with the view caused by our toilet may affect the demand for accommodation next season."

"It will be a precedent, and you know how much I

dislike precedents, Humphrey, but I suppose we shall have to give way to the objections raised by the Leisure people. But it must be made clear to them that our agreement to remove this particular convenience must not be considered a precedent for the removal of future conveniences to which the owners of local hotels object. We will underline 'convenience' in our reply, Humphrey. Yes, and you can add 'toilet' with a note of interrogation in brackets. Before we know where we are we shall be expected to call our conveniences 'powder-rooms'. Do you remember that long argument we had with the Ministry of Movement when they wanted to call the lavatories in their planes powder-rooms?"

"Would it be a good idea, sir, if we instructed our quantity surveyors to sound local opinion on satisfactory sites for our conveniences before they are erected?"

"Once we start encouraging local opinion to express itself our files will look like the correspondence columns of the popular Press or a curious new feature on television where the opinions of viewers about various programmes are read out—very well read out, I may add, with a gratifying emphasis on their almost always idiotic remarks."

It was nearly six o'clock that afternoon when Humphrey Mowart was ready to leave the Ministry. He was always busy now in arranging the files of the Permanent Secretary so that when presently Humphrey should be handing over to another Private Secretary Sir Oliver should not be too much upset by the new Private Secretary's slowness in finding his way about the files.

"There's a lady wants to see you, Mr Mowart," said the janitor. "I put her in the waiting-room because I didn't think you'd want to be disturbed while you were with Sir Oliver."

"Thanks, Sergeant-major. Did she leave her name?"

"She's a Mrs Scratchbury."

"What?"

"Yes, Mr Mowart. That's why I didn't let you know she was here till Sir Oliver left."

Humphrey went along to the waiting-room; there was the bright red head of Miss Veale.

"I hope you've not been waiting too long, Miss Veale," he said.

"It's not Miss Veale, young man. Dr Emilius Scratchbury and Miss Euphemia Veale became Dr and Mrs Scratchbury last Wednesday. He's an Aquarian."

"He's interesting himself now in ichthyology, is he?"

"No, no, no. Don't you know the difference between an Aquarian and an aquarium, young man? Dr Scratchbury was born on the 8th of January, which means that he is ruled by the watery sign of Aquarius. Those born under earth signs should wed those born under watery signs. And eight! The number of Fate. Dr Scratchbury is most anxious to meet you again and I have come to invite you to 8 Gladstone Terrace."

"But I thought I had made it clear, Miss . . . Mrs Scratchbury, that I could not discuss Dandimilk with Dr Scratchbury."

"You have not been invited to discuss Dandimilk, young man. You have been invited to share our simple meal of nut tournedos in order that Dr Scratchbury may inform you about the steps he has taken to save the paper situation."

Humphrey hesitated. He felt that Sir Oliver would disapprove but he could not resist the temptation to accept the invitation.

"Well, I'll come along, Mrs Scratchbury, but I'm afraid I shan't be able to stay to dinner."

On the way to Notting Hill the newly wed Mrs Scratchbury talked away incessantly.

"Deeply learned, though he is, Dr Scratchbury to my great surprise was completely ignorant of the great science of astrology and it has been my privilege to obtain his horoscope from one of the members of the S.P.C.C. After examining his horoscope most carefully he realised that in order to confirm the prognostication of a conjunction between Jupiter and the Sun it was essential for him to marry a Leonian. It was equally essential for me to confirm the prognostication in my horoscope of a conjunction between Jupiter and the sun for me to marry an Aquarian. I think I am justified in calling it a case of love at first sight. The Blue Bull was indeed the Blue Bell . . . but there were no Blue Wedding Bells for Emilius Scratchbury and Euphemia Veale, because we were married in the registry office. But I must not talk too much about that happy event. And when you meet Dr Scratchbury and hear of his discovery you will be able to tell the Right Honourable Williamson that the more waste paper he collects the more good food the country will be able to enjoy."

Humphrey's car stopped outside 8 Gladstone Terrace and as they walked up the steps the erstwhile Miss Veale told Humphrey that a sure sign of her having been right in accepting Dr Scratchbury's hand was the way Mrs Fludger her landlady, had welcomed the news. " 'I took to him like a duck takes to water,' she said. And I must say I was very glad because it would have been very inconvenient if Mrs Fludger had given me notice to leave 8 Gladstone Terrace. Indeed, it would have been more than inconvenient, it would have been really awkward."

"I am glad Mrs Scratchbury has been able to persuade you to pay us this visit, Mr Mowart," said Dr Scratchbury when Humphrey had congratulated him on his marriage, "because you will now be able to convey the glad news to Mr Williamson that I have solved the problem of waste paper which was evidently distressing him so much. Thanks to the machine which I invented for converting various vegetable products into Dandimilk and thus averting the threat to health of cows' milk."

"Except to the poor litte calves," Mrs Scratchbury put in.

"Yes, yes, Euphemia. I am talking of human health. When I read in the papers what Mr Williamson had to say about waste paper I was suddenly seized with an idea.

'If' I said to myself, 'I have been able to make Dandimilk out of vegetable products, why should I not extract the protein from paper, itself a vegetable product, and thus give nutritional value to waste paper? And that is what I have succeeded in doing. My machine pulps and squeezes the paper and the protein appears as a whitish mess. When this whitish mess is freeze-dried it becomes a pure white powder with a faint taste of tea. One thousand pounds of paper will produce thirty pounds of pure protein, the equivalent of one hundred and eighty pounds of beef. We all know the expression about eating one's words. If you will ask Mr Williamson to accept this pound packet of newspaper protein and tell him to dust it lightly over the dish before him he will literally be able to eat his words."

"But mightn't the printer's ink give him indigestion?" Humphrey suggested.

"The printer's ink used for newspapers and books once upon a time might have induced indigestion but the printer's ink used to-day is so sparingly used that it will not upset the most vulnerable digestion."

"I'm afraid I cannot take a packet of—what do you call your new substance?" Humphrey asked.

"It is called Papavite."

"I cannot bring Papavite to the notice of Mr Williamson myself, Dr Scratchbury, because Mr Williamson is the Minister of Waste and I am attached to the Ministry of Sanitation. I suggest you should send a packet of Papavite to the Ministry of Waste, setting out the claims you make for it. The Ministry of Waste will probably send it to the Ministry of Hygiene. . . ."

"Eeyeea. Eeyeea, Eeyeea," Mrs Scratchbury chirped like a budgerigar joining in the conversation.

"I was not impressed by the scientific alacrity of the Ministry of Hygiene when I brought Dandimilk to their notice," said Dr Scratchbury, his dark eyes glowing resentfully.

"But you will not be in direct touch with the Ministry

of Hygiene," Humphrey pointed out. "The Ministry of Waste will receive their report and should their report on Papavite be favourable the Ministry of Waste will no doubt communicate with you in due course. But may I offer one word of advice as a Civil Servant?"

"And he is a civil servant. He has been most civil to me, Emilius. Most civil. And he was so civil to that rude man, Narbrow, that you've had no more trouble with the farmers round Beechwood."

"I fully appreciate what Mr Mowart has done. And I will accept his advice."

"Do not in any circumstances grant an interview to the Press about Papavite, Dr Scratchbury," Humphrey urged. "There is nothing the Civil Service dislikes so much as Press publicity for something which is being considered and borne in mind. I shall shortly be leaving the Civil Service myself; so you must accept my advice as completely disinterested. And now before I leave *you* may I once again wish you and Mrs Scratchbury a long and happy life together?"

"And you can't stay to partake of nut tournedos with us?" We *are* having nut tournedos, Emilius?

"Slightly dusted with Papavite to provide additional protein," said Dr Scratchbury. "I should have liked you to note how the faint taste of tea is counteracted by the flavoursome taste of the nuts."

Humphrey pleaded his dinner engagement.

"I shall always be grateful to you, Dr Scratchbury," were his parting words.

And when he was telling his mother about that absurd pair he said,

"And you know, mother, I really am grateful to Dr Scratchbury. If he hadn't invented Dandimilk I should still be in the Civil Service."

"But you still are, Humphrey."

"Only until the paper situation is no longer a threat to poor old Huffy's sleep."

Chapter 16

WHEN on that Fourteenth of February Sir Oliver turned in the tube to the *Times* crossword, the clue for one across was "Cupid's paper dart", 9 letters. "Very obvious" Sir Oliver muttered as he filled in v-a-l-e-n-t-i-n-e. Paper? Sir Oliver rapped the knuckles of his fancy. "I must not pay this absurd attention to omens." He concentrated upon the rest of the crossword, but in spite of all his concentration that valentine in one across still haunted his fancy.

Sir Oliver was greeted in his room at the Ministry by the smiling face of his Private Secretary.

"Good morning, sir, and there's a marvellous valentine for you from the Ministry of Production sent round by hand."

"Paper?"

"Yes, sir, the Commonwealth has rallied round the old country in her hour of need. The shortage of paper no longer exists. There is a letter from the Ministry marked Confidential. That's probably a valentine from Sir Mark Levett."

Sir Oliver took the letter and opened it.

> *Ministry of Production*
> *Whitehall, S.W.1.*
> *February 13.*

Dear Oliver,

All is well. You can tell your Minister that he will not be asked to give a political broadcast on television about toilet-paper. The paper ships have arrived. I felt like a Roman official when the news came that the corn ships from Alexandria had passed Minerva's cape into Parthenope's fair bay. Will you and Gertrude come and dine with us on Thursday?

> *Yours ever*
> *Mark*

"We must bring the good news to Ghent," said Sir Oliver, as he passed Sir Mark Levett's letter to Humphrey.

"I don't know if the Minister has arrived yet, sir." But even as he spoke the telephone buzzed to ask Sir Oliver to go up to Mr Upjohn's room.

"You'd better come with me, Humphrey. You'll be wanting to tell the Minister that you will be leaving me —leaving the Civil Service, that is—almost at once."

"Thank you, sir. But when I say 'thank you' it is not just for going along with you to tell the Minister about the paper situation. The 'thank you' is for all you've taught me since I was lucky enough to become your Private Secretary."

"About life on paper, eh?"

"Yes, if you put it that way, but I would like you to know, sir, that I do realise the life of the country would not be able to go on unless the Civil Service kept that life going on paper."

The Permanent Secretary and his Private Secretary found the Minister of Sanitation in a jubilant condition.

"I told you, Huffam, two or three months ago that I didn't feel fifty on my birthday, but I've been feeling more like a hundred and fifty since that bloody awful broadcast was hanging over me. And now all is well. Walter Camden rang me up at breakfast with the glad news. He's getting a question put down so that he may relieve the country's mind to-day. I think his own mind was a good deal relieved. I was being absolutely firm about refusing to give that broadcast unless he was prepared to join in it with me. And here's some good news for you, Mowart. Were you ever in Gassington?"

"No, Minister, I was never there."

"Well, the Party Headquarters want you to go up and be looked over with a view to your being adopted as candidate at the next Election. The majority against you is about 15,000, but if you can knock off a thousand you'll get a good chance for a marginal constituency somewhere. There'll be plenty of them at the rate Eddie Pinkney's going ahead with these New Towns of his. But what I want you to do now, Mowart, is to slip out and get a bottle of champagne. You'll drink a glass to celebrate D-day for toilet-paper, Huffam?"

"I don't recall ever drinking champagne in the morning, Minister, but I must admit that I am intensely relieved the weight of that proposed broadcast has been lifted from our shoulders. Yes, I will break the rule of a lifetime. I was worried yesterday to read of a new Association which has been formed to keep television pure and I was dreading the letters of protest which both the B.B.C. and the I.T.V. would have passed on to us."

While Humphrey Mowart was away to get that bottle of champagne Sir Oliver was rung up by Lady Huffam.

"Oh, Olly, do forgive me for disturbing you but I felt I must let you know that a wonderful letter from Jeremy arrived by the second post. Can you possibly come home for lunch? I'm longing for you to read it. I felt it really was Valentine Day when Jeremy's letter arrived."

"Yes, Gertrude. We are very busy of course at the Ministry but I will manage to come home for lunch. I mustn't stop now to hear any more about Jeremy's val—about Jeremy's letter. I have to see my Minister about something. Oh, Gertrude, just before I replace the receiver I shall bring Humphrey Mowart with me. You only have mince? Well, order the Daimler and go round to Harrods for some smoked salmon and a pot of *pâté de foie gras*. You will find a bottle of champagne in the cellar. One was left over from Christmas."

Sir Oliver hung up and returned to the Minister's room.

"I said just now we must drink to D-day for toilet-paper," Mr Upjohn bubbled. "But of course what we ought to drink to is the evacuation of Dunkirk."

On the way to Chillingham Gardens in Humphrey Mowart's car Sir Oliver appeared more serenely unaware of the traffic than Humphrey had ever known him; as they passed South Kensington station he said,

"I've been wondering, Humphrey, whether I might not reconsider my decision never to learn to drive a motor-car. Of course, I should not consider doing so until I retired from the Service, but when my mind was not preoccupied with the multitude of problems created by Sanitation I might enjoy learning to drive a motor-car."

"I'm quite sure you would, sir."

Lady Huffam made haste to give Sir Oliver his younger son's letter before she went downstairs to direct Ethel's presentation of the smoked salmon and *pâté de foie gras*. While Sir Oliver was reading Jeremy's letter Humphrey looked up Gassington in the A.B.C.

Poste Restante
Heraklion
Crete.

My dear Mum and Dad,
The discovery has happened but it is a more deadly secret than ever. When I wrote to you at Christmas Mr X had been approached by a Cretan to say that he knew where a statue was hidden somewhere on the south side of the island and how much would Mr X pay him to show where this statue was. Well, of course that meant an awful lot of bargaining but in the end Mr X and he agreed about a price for his information and over three weeks ago Mr X and I set out with this Cretan over the mountains to a small rocky bay miles from anywhere with a cave in the cliff on one side of it. At the end of this cave was a glorious statue of Artemis in a short tunic with her bow. The only pity was that when they lugged this statue to this cave her head was broken off. But her head was there lying beside her in the cave and it can be fixed on easily. The statue was dug up under a plane tree somewhere in the interior and in great secrecy they had lugged it down to this cave long before the war in the hope of selling it to some American who was going to smuggle it out of Crete in his yacht. Then when the war came Crete was overrun by the Germans and there was the evacuation of the New Zealanders and our troops from the south side of Crete, so that it was impossible to think of getting the statue

away. Then the American died and to cut a long story short the statue is still where they hid it before the war. Mr X explained that it was impossible to think of smuggling it out of Greece and told the chap who showed us where it was that he would have to notify the Greek archaeological people about the statue. And the chap was furious. Well, we set out back to Heraklion but in the mountains on our way we were captured and kept prisoner in another cave and it was not until two or three days ago that we persuaded the Cretans to let us go, after we had finally convinced them that there was no possibility of getting the statue away from the island and that they would have to be content with whatever reward they were given by the Greek Government. As soon as Mr X heard that the Cretans will be well rewarded he will announce his discovery and then I will be able to tell you his name. I have had the most exciting time I ever had in my life and my name will be mentioned with Mr X's name. It is really a glorious statue of the 4th century B.C. And now you must *come out to Greece in April and see this glorious statue.*

Your loving
Jeremy

"Well, sir," Humphrey said when he had read this letter. "Jeremy certainly has sent you *some* valentine. You must be terribly pleased about him."

"Yes, Humphrey, when I think what I have been feeling like all this last fortnight and what I feel like to-day, I am indeed humbly grateful. And I am glad to see that he has spelt 'archaeological' correctly."

Sir Oliver went to ring up Rosemary with his news.

"You were right about Jeremy," he told her. "Come along with Nigel to-night and dine with us and we'll talk over our cruise to Greece in April."